Season in the Cold

IAN RIDLEY

Season in the Cold

A Journey Through English Football

The Kingswood Press

First published in Great Britain in 1992
by The Kingswood Press
Michelin House, 81 Fulham Road, London SW3 6RB

Copyright © 1992 Ian Ridley
The author has asserted his moral rights

A CIP catalogue record for this book
is available from the British Library
ISBN 0 413 66250 0

Photoset by Rowland Phototypesetting Ltd
Bury St Edmunds, Suffolk
Printed in Great Britain by
Clays Ltd, St Ives plc

Contents

Introduction

After a leisurely lunch we hailed a taxi, Jimmy and I, but it could only take us to within 500 yards of Stamford Bridge; such was the traffic, such were the crowds of people spilling over on to the road. So we joined them.

There seemed to be a different atmosphere about the place. This was Chelsea v. Tottenham Hotspur, traditionally one of the meanest and most attritional of London derby matches, yet there felt an unusual lightness of being in the day, neither menace in the air nor threat on the ground. This from a fixture that was attended routinely by police helicopters, dogs, horses and plenty of police themselves. It could almost have been a throwback to the times you read about and see pictures of, when huge crowds shoehorned themselves into grounds with no fear for their safety.

The reason may have been England's performance at the World Cup in Italy several months earlier in the summer of 1990, when they reached the semi-finals on a wave of feeling from the whole nation. After that, there seemed a swagger back in the step of the English game, a mood of optimism. It seemed, too, that hooliganism was now out of fashion. Although it would probably ever occur, given the nature of some of the people attracted by the game's mass appeal, it was more frowned upon, less condoned by more people. They seemed tired of the garbage surrounding football and wanted to reclaim the game. The noisy minority of the great stonewashed who inhabited the Brutish Isles, as we were perhaps perceived, were now being outshouted by the silent majority. At least, it seemed that way at home.

Today, many were drawn to Stamford Bridge by the presence in the Tottenham side of Paul Gascoigne and Gary Lineker, two of the chief contributors to that England adventure in Italy. It was back to the days when it wasn't simply the supporters of the two clubs who attended a match, but neutrals wishing to see two outstanding footballers at their art. The superhero of the lager-and-video age, Gascoigne, duly scored from an outrageous free-kick, and the placid emblem of what we aspire to, Lineker, finally found the net after missing a few opportunities. Even if Tottenham lost 2–3, it had been the kind of match so refreshing after two decades in which the fixture always seemed to finish 0–0, 1–0 or 0–1. Gascoigne would score an even more astonishing free-kick later in the season, shooting, driving, curling, powering – and everything else you can do to and with a football when you kick it – into the Arsenal net after only four minutes of the first FA Cup semi-final Wembley had staged.

The thought occurred at the end of that season that it might be time to try to capture this mood within the game, a game that was letting go in the 1990s of its sense of shame after the sickening disasters of the 1980s, which had followed the rampant, blatant hooliganism of the 1970s. The Bradford City fire of May 1985 took fifty-two lives; the Heysel Stadium tragedy of the same month, when Liverpool fans charged a section of their Juventus counterparts, saw thirty-nine more die in the crush to escape; and the Hillsborough disaster of April 1989, when Liverpool lost ninety-five of their supporters at the FA Cup semi-final against Nottingham Forest – all of these had blighted football.

The latter incident spawned the Lord Justice Taylor Enquiry and Report, which recommended all-seater stadia for first- and second-division clubs by 1994, and for those of the third and fourth by the end of the century. Taylor's findings and recommendations inevitably contained flaws but they were a positive response coming out of all the negativity. Maybe the game was beginning to emerge from its grief, beginning to rediscover its self-esteem.

Thus was born *Season in the Cold*, an attempt to recreate the colours of the English game, the joy and sorrow it provokes. The time seemed ripe in another way. It would prove to be the last year of the Football League in its traditional shape. The Premier League was being conceived, then delivered. Our season would be a turning point.

Gascoigne's goal against Arsenal – coming before his five minutes of madness in the subsequent Cup final, when he tore ligaments that would keep him out of the following season – was one of football's more meaningful and significant ones. For a split second, as possibly the greatest free-kick the grand old stadium had ever seen entered the net, there was disbelief around the arena. Journalists in the press box looked at each other with stunned faces, until smiles of pleasure took over. Half the crowd then went berserk.

Suddenly, the frustrating, never-again hour it took to cover the last mile to the ground seemed irrelevant, Suddenly, the sizeable slice of the weekly income it had claimed was not important. The hours it would take to get home were banished from the thoughts. The grey day mattered nothing. All because of a moment that lasted a few seconds.

Such a moment may be rare, but the emotions it inspires are not. They can come in FA Cup finals or Sunday cup finals, in the first division of the Football League or in the thirst division of the Pubs' League. They make everything worthwhile for the fan: the time, the cost, the travel, the inconvenience of it all. They are what keep him or her coming back to draw at football's well.

Season in the Cold seeks to get to the bottom of that well. During its course, it met fans from East Cornwall who had risen from their beds in the middle of a Christmas night to drive in support of Plymouth Argyle; supporters from the Home Counties who travelled by train to watch Leeds regularly. It came across Irish fans who had ferried overnight to see Liverpool and Manchester United. In fact, there were more than 20 million fans – 20,487,273, to be exact – who watched 2064 League matches during that 1991–92 season. Although this clearly contained the same fans repeating the experience, and it scarcely compared with the heady post-war years, it was still a huge number, being almost a million up on the previous season.

The book is not intended to be a definitive diary of a season. More, it seeks to use matches and events as a basis to try to encapsulate the richness and variety of English football and its people – players, managers, administrators, supporters, observers. Neither is it a journey through time, although it attempts to capture the warmth and optimism of summer, the growing realism and realisations of autumn, the slog – albeit enjoyable – of winter, and the rites of spring. Rather, it is a journey through the game, from its finest stadia to its most windswept parks; from its biggest occasions to its humblest kick-abouts. And there, in the sheer width and depth of the English game, its variety and contrasts, lies its appeal.

Issues and controversy dogged the season, as they always do. The labour pains of the Premier League were high among them, as the greed of the big clubs emerged as the main motivation for their breakaway, rather than any desire to streamline the game as the FA, keen to extend their

influence above the Football League, had originally envisaged. The Premier League's appointments of Sir John
Quinton as a non-executive figurehead, and Rick Parry as
chief executive, also provoked criticism. A players' strike
was even threatened, when the Professional Footballers'
Association insisted on their right to the agreed percentage
– 10 rather than the knock-down 5 they had accepted to
facilitate the previous deal – of any income to the game
from television.

There were disputes at Arsenal and West Ham, where
the clubs sought to impose on their supporters the bond
schemes, expensive ways of raising money for implementing the Taylor Report. Fans would also protest at the
Taylorian insistence that grounds in the top two divisions
become all-seater, preferring instead their prized areas of
terracing.

There was the crass imposition on the FA Cup of replays
being held ten days after the first match; the FA insisted
that this was due to the police wanting adequate time to
organise their work rotas, although some police forces
denied it. Then, in the 100th year of the penalty first becoming a rule, there were the penalty competitions held to
decide ties drawn after extra-time of the first replay. Thus
were undermined the ethics of a competition rightly
revered for its tradition.

Important as all these issues were, however, one sensed
that they were transitory, that they would be resolved,
perhaps later rather than sooner, but resolved. No matter
the inconvenience and the arguments, the lure of the
game remained undiminished for its committed watchers
because it still evoked, provoked and invoked that gamut
of feelings from pain to joy, perhaps more spontaneously
than any other sport. Administrators and club directors
have relied on just that for years. It is why football can
attract the uncommitted; why 25 million people in Great

Britain, half of them women, half of the population, saw Gascoigne weep as England slipped out of that 1990 World Cup semi-final against West Germany. That alone illustrated how deeply ingrained is the game in English popular culture.

The film director, Alan Parker, was once discussing the future of the British movie industry on a television programme and turned to camera to shout: 'What's the matter with you? Don't you want to dream any more?' It is how this writer feels about football. There are in the game many dreams to be dreamt and many around it who still want to dream them. This book is for those people.

Its thanks go to all the football journalists – a more maligned breed than they deserve – who have helped. I am especially grateful to David Lacey of the *Guardian*, Paddy Barclay of the *Observer* and Brian Glanville of the *People*, though more readily associated with the *Sunday Times*, for their influence and inspiration; and to Joe Lovejoy of the *Independent* and Colin Gibson, Chris Davies and John Ley of the *Daily Telegraph* for their help. Thanks, too, are due to the people and their books from which I have borrowed: Phil Shaw and Peter Ball's *Book of Football Quotations*; Simon Inglis's *The Football Grounds of Great Britain*; and Eamon Dunphy's *Only a Game?*

My gratitude also extends to Neil Tunnicliffe, my editor at Kingswood Press; and to John Feinstein, whose excellent books on American college basketball, *A Season on the Brink* and *A Season Inside*, helped confirm this book's idea. Thanks are also due to my dad, Bob, for taking me to football in the first place and giving me the game. I thank, too, my immediate family – wife Jo, children Alex and Jack – for their support, patience and tolerance in allowing me to indulge myself by tackling this project. And I am grateful to friends who have offered encouragement and wisdom when spirits were flagging: Jimmy Mulville, who bought the tickets at Chelsea that day the book was born, Bob Mason and Rosemary Clough. I thank finally someone without whom it would certainly not have been possible: Bill W.

June 1992   Ian Ridley

The publishers would like to thank the following for their kind permission to reproduce photographs: Steve Yarnell (Bryan Robson, Philip Don, the English Schools Festival, Sunderland); Dave Shopland (Barry Fry, Ian McDonald); Gary Prior (Graham Taylor); Phil Brown (Kevin Keegan); Pacemaker (Belfast); Phil Shepherd-Lewis (Doncaster Belles); and Russell Cheyne (Leeds United).

Summer

One: Optimism

1 Barnet Fair

There are only two certainties in life: that the sun will shine on the opening day of the football season; and that it will be cold, and wet, on the opening day of the cricket season.

The opening day of the 1991–92 football season did, of course, dawn warm and bright and, as usual, the heart of the fan rose with the sun. The radio was playing your favourite songs. Everyone was treating you nicely. Evangelically, optimism coursing the veins, you wanted to grab the nearest person, those who were planning to go shopping – shopping? – and take them to the ground with you to show them what the fuss was about.

Nowhere was the sense of anticipation being more keenly felt than at the neat, modest Bedford home of Barry Fry, manager of the Football League's newcomers, Barnet, its ninety-third club. Today, they would play their first match as a fourth-division club, against Crewe Alexandra, following their promotion from the GM Vauxhall Conference. Today, an ambition, a dream even, would be fulfilled. Not that there had been much chance to dream in the Fry household the night before; three young children and Fry's nerves had seen to that. By 10am, when he opened the door to me having agreed to let me spend this special day with him, he was his usual fidgety self. He could barely keep still as the photographer from *Today* newspaper, which had had the bright idea of wiring him up to a stress monitor, asked

everyone to smile nicely for a family portrait of him, wife
Kirstine, and children Frank, Amber and Adam.

Fry himself is a 46-year-old workaholic who had suffered
a heart attack seven months previously: hence the newspaper's choice of him for a feature on the pressures endured
by a manager leading up to, during, and after a match. Diet
has helped him reduce his cholesterol level from 6.9 to 5.1,
or some figures like that, he tells you proudly – Kirstine
has prepared a lunch box of carrots, celery and grapes for
him today – but he has scarcely changed. The family's summer holiday consisted of a day at Center Parcs (without Fry
himself) and a weekend in Blackpool (with him, except
that he spent most of the time at nearby Lytham St Annes,
on a Football League management course).

Fry hates being around the house on a Saturday morning.
'I just get under her feet,' he says. Kirstine is pregnant. Eight
months and three weeks pregnant. She has decided to go to
the match only for the second half. 'She can't stand all that
"Fry out" stuff,' says Barry. 'And that's just her they're
shouting it at.' Fry, it may be gleaned, is a graduate of the
Laugh-a-Minute School of Management, one who likes to
give the impression of devil-may-care. As we drove to the
ground later, he would say, 'I have never managed in the
League,' adding, as the car braked to avoid a tractor, 'And
I still may not.' He would also say things later, however,
that revealed just how deeply he does care.

As a non-League manager in previous seasons, Fry's routine on a Saturday morning for a home game had usually
involved leaving the house at around 10:30am and driving
via Luton to pick up the club's programmes from the printing works of Kevin Millett, a former Barnet centre-half and,
for the first two months of this season at least, player-
manager of Dunstable Town in the Southern League's
Southern Division. That club had provided Fry with his
first managerial job after a playing career which began with

an England schoolboy cap and took him to Manchester United for a spell: he was perhaps one of the less celebrated Busby Babes, although he enjoys being referred to as one. From the printing works, Fry would drive to Watford to pick up his secretary and on to Barnet's Underhill Stadium, where he likes to check the kit and take telephone calls.

But today is not routine. He already has the historic copies of Barnet's first League programme, all 3570 of them, collected the previous night. He seeks help in getting them into the car on account of his heart condition; the thought occurs as you oblige that you have in your charge something which many people will soon be desperate to get their hands on. And the telephone calls are arriving well before he gets to the ground, his mobile phone constantly ringing as we speak in the car on the way. Among the calls wishing him and the club luck is one from Holland, from Lee Payne, a left winger whom Fry sold to Newcastle United for £125,000, now playing in the Dutch League. In selling the likes of Payne, Robert Codner to Brighton, Phil Gridelet to Barnsley, Andrew Clarke to Wimbledon and David Regis and Paul Harding to Notts County in recent seasons, Fry has raised around £1 million.

Such sales have underpinned Barnet's survival, from the time a decade ago when Fry had to take out a second mortgage of £12,500 to keep the club afloat. He even once forewent the proceeds from his own testimonial to pay the players. You might say that his dodgy heart is in the club. For that reason, a brief spell with Maidstone did not work out.

There is another reason why Barnet have survived, and its name is Stan Flashman, Fat Stan of popular nomenclature. He became chairman of Barnet in 1985 when it seemed that the club might fold, and his considerable presence has attracted considerable attention ever since. In the less euphemistic 1970s, Flashman was described as a ticket tout. An Arsenal fan, he used to stand outside such venues as Highbury selling his wares. He could even get tickets, at imaginative prices, of course, for a garden party at Buckingham Palace. In the more entrepreneurial 1980s, he described himself more as a ticket broker, working out of an office near King's Cross station. People naturally expected to pay inflated prices, and Stan was your man. He has been variously vilified for his business dealings, though not then at Barnet – even if there are stories of him coming into the dressing-room, dishing out tickets for pop concerts to grateful players and then announcing: 'That'll be £20 each, lads.'

For Fry, with whom Flashman forms one of football's most colourful double acts, it is very simple: 'There wouldn't be a Barnet Football Club without Stan,' he says, adding, 'I love him, but he's evil.' He goes on to explain that the adjective is really a term of endearment. 'He used to shout in the directors' box: "Clarke, you're rubbish. Barry, get him off." It's not so bad for me, I'm protected by the dug-out, but the players can hear him. It's funny afterwards, but not at the time. Ray Harford used to phone me up when he was manager of Wimbledon the morning after a match and ask me how much I wanted for Clarkey. I'd tell him £300,000, and he'd say: "But your chairman says he's rubbish."

'Last season, after we lost at Kidderminster and it looked like we might not get up from the Conference, he came into the dressing-room and picked out Harry Willis, who had missed a couple of chances. "You'll never play for this club again, Willis. Barry, rip up his contract," he said. He phoned me the next morning to ask what I'm doing about Willis. "Nothing," I said. "Don't pick him again," he said. I said: "I'm picking him for the Herts Senior Cup semi-final against Watford on Friday." "I'll be down the ground to stop him getting in," he said. But he bottled it, and Willis scored two goals. Next morning, he phones up Harry and tells him he was just kidding, just winding him up. That's Stan.

'He's sacked me at least twenty times and he's meant it. But I have just got up the next morning, gone to the ground and got on with my work, and he's phoned up two or three days later as if nothing has happened. There is going to be a time when he sacks me and really means it. When that time comes, I shall just walk out and get another job. There won't be any slagging off the chairman from me. He saved my club. He's my hero.

'He's as good as gold, really. He'll spend £1500 to £2000 of his own money on a Friday night at a hotel for the players. They all say they get treated right. Even old pros we've had like George Reilly and Wayne Turner, who've been in the first division, say they have never been treated better.'

We are by now coming off the A1, heading into Barnet past a road called Trotter's Bottom, past rape fields and South Herts Golf Club. There is a queue at the traffic lights into the High Street, but then there usually is. This one is not to do with football crowds, however, more Saturday shopping in a prosperous suburb. For Barnet is neither one thing nor another, really. Perhaps it is designated as being in Hertfordshire because it is in that space where North London becomes almost rural. It is, though, also designated the London Borough of Barnet, which takes in Margaret Thatcher's former constituency of Finchley. That fact alone describes well the area.

It is a curious place for a football club to thrive. Indeed, for many years, it did not. Its amateur team was a match for most but, once the FA ended shamateurism and deemed all football professional in 1974, the club languished in the Southern League supported by gates of just a few hundred. In the mid-1980s, though, came the astonishing upsurge in attendances that helped it into the League. Perhaps it was cost, perhaps disillusion; but, suddenly, football fans in an area which also supported Arsenal, Tottenham and Watford were proving that another League club could be accommodated. And that seemed a strange thought on a day like today, as the car first-geared its way round the snaking High Street and down past the end of the Northern Line underground station of High Barnet – an appropriate name for the state of the football club these days – down to Underhill Stadium.

It still seemed an unlikely place for League football. The views are predominantly of fields; where buildings intrude, they are semi-detached suburban in leafy streets, protected from the ball at the High Barnet end of the ground by netting. There had been much work on the stadium to complete during the summer. A new police control box and a first-aid room had been built. In the newly-segregated visiting supporters' section, turnstiles and toilets had been installed. Indeed, money matters had occupied the majority of Barnet's attention as they prepared for this day. To start with, there had been bonds to lodge with the Football League totalling £320,000. And then a new seating area where once was standing room only, and the rebuilding of the social club burnt down by fire a year previously, pushed up the cost to more than £1 million. The old green corrugated-iron roof remained on one stand, still bearing an advertisement for the now bankrupt Levitt Group: 'Expert Financial Consultants'. One could only hope for Barnet's sake that it meant nothing.

As Fry proudly takes me on a guided tour, showing it all off, a passing lorry driver toots his horn and shouts: 'Good luck, Baz.' By now, Fry is unloading all those programmes from the car. 'I can't see George Graham having to do this today,' he jokes. It is believed, though, that the Arsenal manager is a better delegator. Fry's inability to do the same is evident as he sits under the main stand in the tiny office – still crammed with non-League annuals – which he shares with the club's only other full-time employee, secretary Bryan Ayres. Fry insists on taking every call, dealing with every problem.

He sells tickets to a Leeds United fan taking in the match, his own team being without one. He resolves a dispute between another supporter and a programme-seller over whether the lad can buy twenty-five programmes or not. And he checks the kit, a new design in common with many other teams, although it retains the club's traditional black and gold without too much of the modern embellishment. 'We got a good deal from a new sportswear company,' Fry says. 'It was free.' He checks the visitors' dressing-room, with its advert on the wall for the Blue Finn fish bar in Barnet High Street. 'I get free fish and chips for putting that up,' he says. 'If the opposition want fish and chips, I give them a ring and, when the team coach pulls up at the lights outside, it's ready to be handed on to the bus for them.'

Finally, mercifully, it is time for Fry to devote himself to the team. He has been like a bear on heat. And it is clear that asking Fry to slow down, as his doctor has, is like asking that same bear not to perform its ablutions in the woods.

At 1:55pm, Fry's new signing, Paul Showler, a police constable who was with Altrincham the previous season, is introduced to his team-mates for the first time. Not ideal preparation. Showler is a rare bird at Barnet, a new player. With all the ground improvements, and the wage bill doubling due to eleven players going full-time – top salary is £250 a week – Fry has not dared ask Flashman for money for new players. Besides which, he wanted to give a chance to those players who took Barnet into the League.

'The good thing now that we are a League club is that players like Bully, Pooley and Bodley [Gary Bull, Gary

Poole and Mickey Bodley] won't be so keen to go. I can hang on to them.' They, especially striker Bull, cousin of Wolverhampton Wanderers and England's Steve, are the most marketable items. 'Bully, he's top man with us,' says Fry. 'It's no good him going to a team that smashes it over the top. He's not like his cousin, who'll chase anything and smash it in. Bully's a footballer.

'I have been told by knowledgeable people in the game that we have not got a cat in hell's chance of getting out of the fourth division the way my team play open, attacking football, but I want to prove them wrong. I'm sure people will want to see the way we play. We always give the opposition a chance. We never stop their star player and we score bags of goals. I think that's what Joe Public wants. Last year, we were the first team in the Conference to score 100 goals – 50 at home and 53 away. I am very proud of that. I just like to give players the freedom to express themselves if they are gifted. Most of all, I want to play entertaining football. It's not cheap to take the family to two games a week these days. Clubs, managers and chairmen owe it to fans to give them something they can be proud of.' It was to prove as Fry saw it. Because Crewe were also an attacking side, he added, 'It could be 6–5.' He was to get the number of goals right.

How green was the field of summer – at the insistence of the League, the Underhill slope had been levelled marginally at its top – as the players ran on to it, the sun now beaming down as if this was a television series, the *Darling Buds of August* perhaps, or a holiday of your youth. To a huge, historic cheer from 5090 people, Barnet were led out by Eddie Stein, a substitute today but the club's longest-serving player and now its coach. It contrasted with the sad silence observed a moment later, in a reminder that this was only football, as crucial to lives as that may be. Kevin Durham, a versatile player who had been instrumental in

Barnet's promotion to the League, had died on holiday in Spain from a heart attack six weeks earlier. For a minute, he was quietly remembered, although he would remain in many minds there that day for much longer.

Barnet began with their customary exuberance. Crewe's Greygoose, their goal-keeper Dean, was almost cooked in the third minute but he saved well from Nicky Evans's header. Then, another three minutes into the game, Barnet scored their first League goal. It was a splendid through-ball from the left-back, Geoff Cooper, which found Gary Bull, and he slipped it home to provoke Fry into his traditional, jubilant, air-punching run up and down the touchline.

There seemed a symbolism when Jimmy Greaves took his seat in the stand after that goal. The former England striker had had a spell with Barnet in the actively alcoholic twilight of his career, when the club attracted a mere few hundred and seemed to be going only downwards. Now, some thirteen years into recovery and a successful television career enveloping him, he was a celebrity rather than a has-been. So, today, were Barnet.

Unfortunately, Crewe were not informed of that resonance. Relegated to the fourth division but imbued with the excellent footballing principles of their manager, Dario Gradi, they proceeded to take Barnet apart. Barnet's defence did oblige, though, parting for them like a theatre curtain: 'We created their space,' Fry was to say later. After sixteen minutes, Tony Naylor levelled; after eighteen, he began a move that ended with Ron Futcher, the sort of ageing know-all of a centre-forward that Barnet could have done without facing, heading home the second. After twenty-six minutes, Rob Edwards made it 3.

Mark Carter pulled a goal back, making it 2–3, five minutes from the interval, at which occasion Greygoose grabbed by the throat his left-back, Rob Jones – who, a month later, was no doubt glad to escape the clutches when he signed for Liverpool – to explain more forcefully than words might that he had not been over-impressed with his defensive work. Barnet were back in it, it seemed. But, on the hour, Cooper brought down Craig Hignett, who got up to score the resulting penalty. In another ten minutes, Edwards had added a fifth with a twenty-yard shot; in another one, Hignett had seized on a bad back-pass by Stein – who had been brought on with Frank Murphy as attacking substitutes in place of two defenders – to score his second and make it 6.

Bull squeezed home Barnet's third after seventy-five minutes but, after seventy-six, Edwards completed his hat-trick. Carter's second goal for Barnet just before the final whistle made it a bizarre 4–7. 'Welcome to the Football League,' sang the Crewe supporters, before breaking into their adopted song of *Blue Moon*, which somebody suggested they had started using because they won once in one. One Barnet fan with a curious sense of era and geography suggested they return home to tend their ferrets.

'Yes, I enjoyed it,' said the main-stand steward, Hilda Raven, who has been coming for sixty-four years, 'since my dad first brought me.' Her presence, like the little girls carrying round the winning raffle-ticket numbers on a blackboard at half-time, demonstrated that there is still a place at clubs for the unprofessional. 'I'll have to get used to all these visitors, though,' she added. 'I've spoken to some of them, and they seem quite nice. Can I tell you my age? No I can't.'

'It was a carnival occasion, and Barnet were the clowns,' said Fry to the journalists, an occupation in which he would surely have a future should he ever want to cross the divide. 'My defenders must have thought tackle is what they went fishing with . . . This could be the quickest sacking on record: ninety minutes as a Football League manager.' Meanwhile, back under the stand, Eddie Stein was reflecting on his League debut at the age of 35 and its effect on the real Fry. 'This has bitten deep with Baz,' he said. 'The team is an extension of himself. We play with a smile on our faces because that's the way he goes through life.' And, with that, it was off to the Red Lion across the street from the ground to dissect the performance. It was one ritual that arrival in the Football League would probably not change.

Not yet, though, for Fry. He sat in the dug-out trying to make sense of it all. 'I feel drained,' he said. 'I was so excited, looking forward to this so much, and the whole thing has been such a let-down. I take it personally because that was my team out there. It hurt. It really hurt. Every goal was like a kick in the bollocks. So embarrassing. So humiliating . . .' He was blaming himself, for attending dinners in midweek when he should have been on the training ground. He was worrying about some of the squad still being part-time and living in the north. Will it all work? What does he do about the goal-keeper, Gary Phillips?

Flashman comes to join him. To add injury to insult, a window of the police box has fallen on to his back and he has had to receive treatment in the first-aid room. At least a club official has tested the new facilities. 'What were the other results?' Fry asks. 'Altrincham drew, Wycombe won,' says Flashman. 'No, I mean Blackpool, Burnley, all them,' says Fry. Old habits die hard.

Kirstine looks on with a worried face as Frank, Amber and Adam kick a ball around on the pitch before the now empty terraces. It will be a long week until the birth of the baby, at which Fry is planning to assist. 'The stress machine? I should imagine I blew the bloody thing up.'

He is ready to go home now, just about the last person left in the ground. The sun is still shining, but the heat is really on.

11 Hoddle's Doddle

The match was just three minutes old, and he had the ball at his feet some twenty yards inside his own half. He looked up then back down at the object at those feet and persuaded it forward some fifty yards. It arced perfectly, like a spiralling pass from the arm of the best American football quarterback, into the path of one of his strikers, who dutifully opened the scoring.

Glenn Hoddle was making his mark on the English game once again. The artistic skill of the through-ball was becoming blurred in these days of the artisan labour of the long ball, but here he was to redraw the distinction. It was good to have him back, even in the unfamiliar shirt of Swindon Town, of whom he was now player-manager. His side were currently pitted against Millwall in a League Cup tie, one they would win in a replay after drawing 2–2 at the Den. The attraction for this long-time admirer of seeing him again was irresistible.

Swindon were responding neatly to the prompting of the former Tottenham, Monaco and England midfield player, who was adding the cladding to the edifice fashioned by his predecessor and former Spurs colleague, Osvaldo Ardiles. Now Hoddle was playing as a sweeper, the pace – never blistering – somewhat diminished but the brain ensuring that it rarely mattered. So elegant, unusual even, were his early-season performances that the former England coach,

Don Howe, was suggesting that he might yet play again for his country, at the age of 34. It was far-fetched, but not too much so. So attractive, too, was some of the passing produced by his Swindon team that September night, with him at its hub, that even the notorious Millwall crowd was moved to applaud. The dog with the bad name became a positive pussycat, proving that quality knows no boundaries. So much for image.

But image was what had attracted Swindon Town's new board of directors to Hoddle in March of 1991. They had, after all, endured a financial scandal involving illegal payments to players in the last year and had been told by the Football Association that the place they had earned in the first division was to be withheld. It had led, eventually, to Ardiles decamping to Newcastle. The club needed fresh direction. It needed someone young, gifted and, above all, clean-cut. Someone nice.

It was thought that Hoddle might be too nice. The man was even called Glenn Goddle and the Magic Christian for the faith he adopted anew in 1987. 'Glenn Hoddle has found God,' said a comedian once. 'It must have been quite a pass.' The image grew up around Hoddle the player, predominantly among fans in the north, of the archetypal southern softie nicknamed Glenda. For a long while in the 1980s, he was not so much a player, more a debate. Should England build a team around him? Or should he apply himself more, especially in the more physical aspects of the game? One remembers, though, the face contorted with effort and the clenched fist urging on team-mates at particularly difficult moments in games. Hoddle himself believed he could do no more than he did, week in, week out, for Tottenham.

The questions were never adequately resolved. No England manager had the courage to take the former option. Under Ron Greenwood, for example, Hoddle was one month in, one month out. At the 1982 World Cup finals in Spain, the soon-to-depart Greenwood was to describe Hoddle, then 25, as 'one for the future'. Bobby Robson got no further with the problem, vacillating like Greenwood. It was an insult when Hoddle's international career ended, at the European Championship finals of 1988.

England had lost their opening match to the Republic of Ireland 0–1 and were criticised for their lack of creativity. They needed something from their second game against Holland. They also needed somebody. Hoddle was chosen, not for the first time, as the saviour, this time of Robson's skin and England's place in the tournament. First he hit a post with a free-kick; Bryan Robson alongside was providing a powerful foil. But, as England faded, so too did Hoddle. Or was it the other way round, as his detractors so often claimed. 'Hoddle only ever gives you forty-five minutes,' they complained. If only some of the players England used in midfield during his time could have given that much. The next game, also a 1–3 defeat against the Soviet Union, was his last. Of his fifty-three caps, ten had been as a substitute. He might have had at least twenty-five more. All that having announced himself with a brilliant side-footed goal from twenty-five yards in a 2–0 win against Bulgaria in 1980.

At Tottenham, there was never any debate. 'Born is the King of White Hart Lane,' the Shelf – that section of terracing along one side of the ground, now a shadow of its former self – would sing to the tune of *The First Noel*.

Everyone has their memory of him. This one comes from a match against Feyenoord of Rotterdam in the UEFA Cup on Wednesday 19 October 1983. By half-time – those forty-five minutes again – Tottenham led 4–0, each goal the result of a Hoddle through-pass. A seat at touchline level gave more insight into the pace and physical difficulty of just such a performance than could the high, television-camera view, whence the game looks so easy. The Dutchmen, Johan Cruyff and a young Ruud Gullit among them, were baffled and bemused by a man at the peak of his graceful, incisive game. The ball either stuck to his feet as he turned away from each ankle-snapping challenge, or it was seemingly charged with a homing device as it left his boot. He was naturally left-footed, although it was never blatant. His own favourite goal was a powerful right-footed volley against Manchester United.

Cruyff, then in the twilight of his career – a sort of *Rotterdammerung* – was full of admiration for the young prince. Years later, he would express surprise that Hoddle had never really acceded to the throne of English football.

When he felt it had achieved all it could in the domestic game, Hoddle took his talent to Monaco after those European Championships of 1988 and, although the crowds could never rival those at Tottenham, the money and standard of living were some compensation. Most important, however, his ability was recognised beyond its immediate habitat in the French League. It was a competition frequently lacking in passion and atmosphere but which valued sophistication above endeavour. Hoddle duly blossomed. He became the first English footballer to be voted overseas-player-of-the-year in France. And all the while he had been absorbing and digesting the coaching and approaches this cosmopolitan environment produced. Now Wiltshire was to benefit from it.

In the sunny days of this early season, Swindon were drawing attention for their results, which included a 4–1 win at Ipswich and a 5–3 home win over Sunderland. Once people had gone along to see how they were being achieved, they came away with even more admiration. Later in the season, before a League Cup tie against Swindon, the Crystal Palace manager, Steve Coppell, would say: 'He's the most innovative manager we have had for a long time. He can go as far as he wants in management. His team's style of football is commendable, and he has been a breath of fresh air.' For Hoddle was developing to new levels the pass-and-move approach adopted by Ardiles. After a slow start in April, when the club were undergoing a touch of the relegation jitters, Swindon had emerged as swift and entertaining. In the days of hump-and-grunt football, they were becoming a *cause célèbre* – a phrase Monsieur Hoddle might appreciate – in the English game.

We met two days after the game at Millwall, on the club's rented training ground near the bucolic Wiltshire village of Wanborough. A drive half a mile long and the manicured lawns that bordered on a *nouveau riche* glass building, all belonging to an insurance company, proved that there were some growth industries in the early 1990s. In a playing pavilion, Hoddle sipped tea and reflected on how it had gone so far, and how his own playing comeback was surprising him. He had, after all, not played for two years due to a knee injury, but such was Monaco's admiration for him that they kept him on, never pressuring him to leave.

'The game needs passing teams like us,' he said. 'My view is that it should be played the way Spurs have always played it. I was lucky when I took over here because I had players who were good on the ball.' Later in the season, he would be more forceful verbally as he came up against teams, notably Cambridge United, who were more forceful physically. 'We have to match them for effort and intimidate them with the ball,' he said. 'We all want success, but it has got to be achieved in the proper manner. You have to play to the strength of your resources but, if you aren't careful, there's a danger of raping the game.'

Hoddle may indeed have been fortunate when he assumed the appointment but he also made some of his own luck by hiring as his assistant John Gorman. The two first formed a friendship at Tottenham when Hoddle, then

19, used to pick up his near-neighbour, then a full-back of 28, and drive him to the Spurs training ground, then at Cheshunt. The one was an especially talented embryonic playmaker, the other a more mature journeyman; a good blend, perhaps, for a managerial team. They remained friends and spent holidays at each other's homes when Gorman was playing in the United States and Hoddle in France. Gorman's knowledge of English football with Gillingham and Leyton Orient immediately came to Hoddle's mind on his return from Monaco: he had the sense to admit that he was out of touch with the players and the pattern of the game in this country.

He had, though, noticed changes since his return. 'It was always quick,' he said, 'but it seems to be quick for longer these days. It used to slow down after twenty minutes. Now you can go into the second half before it settles.' Yet the changes he introduced himself were rather more enlightening. In training he uses drills involving keeping the ball off the ground, for example, to improve the first touch of players. He has also hired a masseur who, as we speak, is working in another corner of the pavilion with Steve White, who scored both the Swindon goals two nights ago against Millwall. 'Don't manipulate him too much,' says another player to the masseur. 'He's just got himself right.'

Hoddle also encourages the players to use a health club and has issued dietary guidelines about meat and carbohydrates, as well as taking sessions in stretching and breathing. 'I learnt to stretch and breathe properly in France and now I'm more supple than when I was when I was 19. The players need to teach themselves,' he adds. 'If you try and force things on them, they turn off. I know. I'm a player too.' Afternoon training, with so many matches to play in England – and the prospect of playing them on heavy grounds – is not on the agenda.

It is all conducted in a civilised manner and atmosphere.

'You don't have to rant and rave to let the players know that there is a discipline expected on and off the field, in a spirit of enjoyment. Decisions have to be made, and I won't shirk them. But you guide people, you don't dictate to them.'

It is perhaps this civilised, decent, dignified manner that attracted Swindon's image-conscious directors to him. His Christianity is a personal thing, he says; he talks about it when asked but does not force it on other people. It influences every area of his life, although he is not a weekly church-goer. 'This is my church,' he says, gesturing to the training pitches outside and the players coming and going as they change after training. The example in behaviour, rather than too many words, is what counts in promoting Christianity, he adds.

And, as for being too nice, he may be what is described as a muscular Christian. When you suggest it to him, a polite but firm look comes to his face in the manner of a good-natured policeman. Indeed, football managers do seem to be getting younger these days. He does not suffer fools gladly, however, and this questioner had just become one. 'They don't know or understand me,' he says of those who suggest it. 'There was this stigma about him being soft as a player but, if anything, he can be ruthless,' says one of his admiring players, the full-back, David Kerslake. 'It has come as a bit of a shock to the players, but they see it as a good quality. He comes down heavily on slack trainers and he knows exactly what he wants. But he mucks in with everything, such as the pre-season running. He's an absolute pleasure to train and play with, because there is so much quality about him.' Quality in an age of change, as the advertising slogan went.

Earlier, Hoddle had been taking training wearing a bright red tracksuit as all around him wore dark blue. He always did stand out, first as a player and now as a manager.

Two: Realism

1 'Arry's Game

If you crossed the road to get to the football manager directly opposite Glenn Hoddle, you would come to Dave Bassett, for whom there is no middle of the road. While Hoddle is sophisticated as a person and demands the same in his team's way of playing, Bassett is blunt and direct, the traits revealed by his team, Sheffield United. Which is better, which is worse? You pays at the turnstile and you takes your choice. They are certainly different types of Londoner.

Bassett's overwhelming qualities are his openness and honesty. He remains forever approachable, no matter the circumstances. Some say, however, that they are also his weaknesses, that the honesty can turn into brutal frankness. 'I'm my own worst enemy at times,' he says. 'I should be more unavailable at times, more . . . what's the word . . . taciturn, yeah. But if I feel something is wrong I have to say so. If I feel someone is a prat I have to tell him some time. I can't go around saying what a nice bloke he is.' What you see with Bassett is what you get. 'You know where you are with me,' is his badge of honour.

A national television audience saw it all and more when he agreed to BBC cameras filming, fly-on-the-wall style, the inner workings of the club as it sought promotion from the second division in 1989—90. Bassett, language colourful, remained the same chirpy cockney, it seemed, whether celebrating the reaching of the first division that the series *United* was on hand to capture or telling an apprentice that he had no future at the club. 'Appy 'Arry, as his nickname has it.

But Bassett's openness is something which, in football, few people are willing to show. Perhaps there is a fear common to many in the game, that to reveal your true feelings is to show weakness, especially to opposition. Bassett is aware, though, as are the enlightened, that it can be a source of strength. Along with the honesty, it is the aspect of his character for which you forgive him much, on a personal level, despite the perceived excesses of his teams – through Wimbledon, now Sheffield United – from time to time.

He is realistic in self-appraisal. 'I'm fairly stable but I do get moody,' he says. 'Some days I do get after the players or the staff. I can be a bit short and sharp with them. But there's no point in being miserable. People don't want a big long face around the place. I'm generally quite good at home but I do find my mind wandering back to problems at the club.'

In 1990–91, United's first season back in the first division, as a mark of both of his great qualities, he called in an expert in team dynamics to work with the squad as they sought to end a season-starting sequence of fifteen matches without a win, the worst of any team in first-division history. And he allowed this observer, who was keen to follow up that TV documentary, to sit in on it. 'Well, you can't just be open in the good times,' he said. It was a measure of his stature as a man that he was willing to enlist help – and be reported to be doing so – rather than demonstrate the misguided I-can-do-it-on-my-own pride of so many managers. 'I have to admit sometimes that I don't have all the answers,' said Bassett.

It was a remarkable experience, certainly for a cold Wednesday morning in Sheffield. And it provided an insight into a first-division club rarely granted to outsiders. The expert, Simon Meyerson, a team-effectiveness consultant at the Institute of Group Dynamics in London, positioned himself in the centre of the room, a sponsors' lounge at Bramall Lane emptied of furniture except for Meyerson's chair. The players sat on the floor around the room. Appropriately, their backs were to the wall.

Football is sceptical about matters of the sporting mind. Best to ignore thoughts and feelings, seems to be the maxim. That attitude has long gone in the United States, where team dynamics is much valued. 'I think you have to be careful with players' minds. I'm a firm believer in keeping them clear,' Brian Marwood, the chairman of the Professional Footballers' Association, who had been signed from Arsenal earlier in the season, was to say pointedly. 'What with diets and everything, we're in danger of getting paranoid.'

At the outset of the session, Meyerson swiftly realised that another recent signing, one Vincent Jones, one of football's 'characters', was the touchstone of this group, and that his open-mindedness was crucial to making progress. In his way, Jones is a playing debate as heated as Hoddle, because of his, er, raw approach to the game. 'What's the score, then,' Meyerson asked the new captain, who had arrived from Leeds in September having been with Bassett at Wimbledon. '2–0 against us, usually,' came Jones's quick, flash reply. 'That's good. A sense of humour means you haven't lost your way,' said Meyerson. The problem is that Jones was not joking.

'I always get the feeling after about seventy minutes that somebody is going to score against us,' Jones went on. 'At Leeds, the longer the game went on I knew we were going to score. I feel the team are looking to me to do it. If I don't, they think, "Right, I'm not going to do it." ' 'Do you know

what a maverick is?' Meyerson asked Jones, who was wearing a polo shirt and blouson compared to the others all in
United tracksuits. 'Yeah, a rebel,' Jones replied. 'Well,
you've got to get that back,' said Meyerson. 'You've got to
get back to being Vinnie Jones, whoever he is.'

Having got the degree of honesty he was looking for,
Meyerson moved round the room giving every first-team
squad member the chance to express an opinion. 'A lot of
things are geared to stopping other teams rather than letting
them worry about us,' said the defender, John Pemberton.
'When we get corners we are more worried about teams
breaking from them rather than what we are going to do.'
'Footballers are ruled by their top six inches,' said Marwood. 'One that is positive and confident and one that is
negative, even though they have the same ability, they are
two entirely different players.'

Meyerson asked Marwood what he thought the manager
wanted. 'I don't think he knows at the moment,' Marwood
replied with a smile, which Bassett was forced to mirror. 'I
think we accept things too easily. At Arsenal, all hell would
have broken loose if we had conceded a goal like we did at
Aston Villa last Saturday.' 'I think we have lost the thread
of what we were,' said the full-back, Wilf Rostron, later to
join Brentford as assistant manager. Jones was soon back.
'Our lads seem scared stiff to take people on. Gascoigne
will do it, and it's only front. Some think the only way to
lose the ball is kick it behind their defence. They are afraid
to get caught in possession.' Mention of Paul Gascoigne
provoked much talk of inferiority complexes, which
Meyerson summed up. 'You've got to move out from being
fans to being opposition,' he said.

Training methods, lack of organisation and uncertainty
about the system – that Bassett hallmark of long ball and
feed off the pickings – were discussed. Modifications, about
five at the back and three in midfield, had produced con-

fusion among some. Jones assumed the initiative again. Tactics counted for little, he believed, when set against the attitude of players. Or words to that effect. 'I think it's just that we're not proud enough of the way we play. Some lads would rather be at Leicester playing pretty football that's not going to get you out of the second division. There aren't many of us with the ability of Gary Lineker or Paul Gascoigne. We wouldn't be here if we had. But Wimbledon have been through what we are going through now. Now they are cocksure of themselves. I think we are listening too much to the people sniggering at us now we're not doing well. Let's do what we do well.'

Bassett cleared up the doubt by saying that they were still playing a direct style and moving the ball forward quickly, but adding that they were also looking to play more inventive football. He was then asked by Meyerson to place the players in categories ranging from international class to fourth division. Only six made it into the first; most took umbrage at being in the second. They were then asked to place themselves. All were internationals. 'What you, Toddy?' someone asked Mark Todd, the midfield player. 'Well, it is San Marino,' he replied.

The players were then asked to form two circles, one first team, one reserves – the aim being to form a bond – but it became one large circle in the confusion. 'That's the answer, then. We're all playing on Saturday,' said one wag. There was also another exercise where a group was asked to form a tightly knit circle, and individuals were asked to try to break in. Significantly, the new boy Jones had more trouble than most getting in. But then it was time for the training ground and more conventional physical activities.

'I've never seen a group with so much energy and morale when they are so far down,' said Meyerson, gazing out on training where fitness experts from a company in Huddersfield were working with the players. 'They're here to make the players' running more efficient and maybe improve their balance,' said Bassett's assistant, Geoff Taylor. 'Vinnie runs like a fractured penguin, for example.' Meyerson pointed out a noisy murder of crows hovering nearby. A bit like vultures, he remarked, clearly having been touched by some of the gallows humour prevalent in the game earlier that morning.

Two days later, as we sat in his spacious office at Bramall Lane, Bassett thought Meyerson might have had an effect, that the airing of grievances was positive. He also thought that two valid conclusions had emerged: that they were not as bad as they thought they were, nor the first division as good as they thought it was. Around him, the club was getting that Friday feeling, a distinct change of atmosphere from usual weekdays. From the lull-before-the-storm tranquillity of a midweek without a match, the mood became busy and taut. The gap between telephones ringing narrowed to about ten seconds. Office staff were walking this way and that with items of trivia taken for granted on a Saturday afternoon, such as painted boards announcing the match sponsors. The tension was all to be wasted, though, as the following day Sheffield United's home match against Derby County was postponed due to snow. And, the following week, they lost 0–2 against Liverpool at Anfield, a result that extended their run of matches without a win to sixteen, and equalled Hull City's worst ever start to a League season in any division.

The week after, however, all Bassett's effort started to pay off. United beat Nottingham Forest 3–2 at home for their first win. Suddenly, the inventive song of their remarkably resilient and resourceful supporters was redundant: 'We'll win again, don't know where, don't know when.' And, finally, they had a riposte to a joke doing the rounds among Sheffield Wednesday supporters and concerning the two Unitedites who were passing a chemist's shop when they saw a sign offering two free season tickets for Bramall Lane. One goes in, coming out five minutes later, clutching a packet of condoms. 'Did you get them, then?' asks his mate. 'No, I was too embarrassed. I bought these instead,' he replies. Embarrassment was no longer an issue, however: seven consecutive victories in January and February meant that United, astonishingly, escaped relegation and finished what had threatened to be a catastrophic season in a creditable thirteenth position.

Today, though, it was all coming back to haunt them, the white-knuckle roller-coaster ride of the first division plunging them back down to the depths. For, nine months after those turning-point days of team dynamism, the Blades were as blunt as they had been before them as they went down 2–5 to an Arsenal side itself struggling to recapture the intensity of its Championship-winning display just four months earlier. By half-time, United trailed 0–4 to goals by Alan Smith, Lee Dixon with a penalty, Perry Groves and David Rocastle, their disparate collection of seemingly world-weary professionals wilting in the heat of late summer. The roasting they received at the interval from their manager was even hotter.

They 'won' the second half 2–1, Tony Agana – the only United player to escape a blast from Bassett – pulling a goal back before Kevin Campbell scored Arsenal's fifth. Clive Mendonca scored United's second in the last minute. Bassett sat in Arsenal's refurbished, opulent press room – one of the few in the country to offer good working facilities to journalists – and contemplated it all for thirty seconds before lighting his own blue touch-paper. There was scarcely any need to ask him a question. For there followed a twenty-minute railing against his own players, surprising in its force even to those familiar with his rantings.

George Allison, a journalist who went on to manage Arsenal, might well have approved, even if another

Gunners manager, Herbert Chapman, would not. His dignified black bust was downstairs in the marble hall of Highbury, an evocative if less impressive foyer for the stadium
than legend has it. 'We went to see *Buddy* at the Victoria
Palace last night,' Bassett said, referring to the musical version of the career of the late rock-and-roll singer, Buddy
Holly. 'He's got more life in him now than we had out there
today.' The journalists were eyeing each other as smiles
came to their faces. This was promising material.

'We are a team of nobodies with no effort or commitment,' he went on. 'When I see a performance like that I
know I can't trust anyone. It was men v. boys in the first
half, and that's down to personality. You begin to realise
that players only think of themselves, not the club or the
manager.' Selfishness and greed, he was concluding, were
the distinguishing marks of a modern professional footballer.

'I don't want to be at the bottom of the table, even if my
players do. We were given the acid test today, and we
failed. They don't know it, though, because most of them
are pretty thick. The players have got to take the next step.
Most of them took a quick step forward to see me about a
new contract during the summer. People pay good money
to watch us, and I expect better than that. We've had some
poor performances in the time I have been here, but at least
we have had a go. I've got to make sure that doesn't hang
around too long or else I'll get the sack. Players get you the
sack, don't they? That's the bottom line.'

They were among the more considered statements, the
language as ever being ripe. Bassett would also talk a month
or two later about resigning. He would not stay where he
was not wanted, he always asserted. But then, thinking
again, never one to walk away from a difficult situation, he
stayed on, sensing public opinion in Sheffield remaining
with him, even if, while out on a rare shopping trip with

his wife, he did once overhear someone say: 'What's he doing here, he should be out buying players to keep them up.' At the time, Chris Bassett felt like asking the woman how many hours a week her husband worked. Besides which, he would buy if he could; United were some £2.5 million in debt.

For Dave Bassett, it all heralded the erosion of the early-season optimism. A cold season might be in prospect again. It was a feeling, as League tables took shape and as patterns of results began to emerge, which was growing at many clubs, from top to bottom of the English game.

11 Wembley Way

From the Ron Clarke Memorial Gates of Wembley Football Club to the twin towers of Wembley Stadium, the distance is two and a half miles. You turn left out of Vale Farm Sports Centre into the Watford Road, then left again into the Harrow Road. About a mile down Wembley High Road you take another left into Wembley Hill Road, past the London Borough of Brent's Mahatma Gandhi House, and a right down Royal Route takes you to the stadium.

It might just as well be two and a half million miles, though, for the club bearing probably the most famous name in football has little in common with the venue of legends. Wembley FC, in the first division of the Diadora League – Isthmian to the traditionalists – is more the venue of fag ends. It seemed an appropriate place at which to start our own journey through this season's FA Cup, which would also end at the celebrated stadium.

Wembley's ground, with the missing section of corrugated roofing on its solitary patch of covered terracing opposite the main stand, is actually in the suburb of Sudbury where, a few pitches away, Wasps Rugby Club attract bigger crowds. 'It can get a bit dispiriting looking across there some Saturday afternoons,' says the Wembley match secretary, Roy Calmels.

But the ground of a club formed only in 1946 does have its own, touching tradition. The club history relates how 'in these early days, and for some years to come, the club's social activities were centred on the Vale Farm Café, which was situated in the old swimming-pool. The club ran the facilities on match-days, and there was a mass exodus at half-time during games for cups of tea.' It goes on to tell how, in 1951, 'Wembley were asked to represent the south in a special match to be shown live on BBC television to mark the opening of the Sutton Coldfield transmitter . . . in front of a huge crowd, which is undoubtedly the club's record attendance, although the exact numbers are not known. Wembley completed this red-letter day by recording a 4–1 victory.' It speaks also of Ron Clarke, a player for the club in the 1950s whose accidental death as a result of injuries sustained in a match is commemorated by those gates.

The boardroom also tells of stirring days, even if not enough of them, and of the link with the stadium, tenuous though it may be. A signed photograph of England's World Cup-winning squad of 1966, 'presented by Mr Alf Ramsey', hangs there as thanks for allowing them to use the ground for training. It might have been here that the soon-to-be Sir Alf told Jimmy Greaves that he was dropped; that Geoff Hurst practised breaking crossbars and nets; that Alan Ball wore out the grass; that Nobby Stiles mislaid his dentures; and that Bobby Moore rehearsed wiping his hands before receiving the Jules Rimet Trophy from the Queen. These days, usually at least one visiting international team per season trains here still before a match at Wembley. 'Over the years the club has been justly proud of its pitch, being similar turf to that used at Wembley Stadium until a horse show ruined theirs a few years ago,' says the club history.

Another framed photograph shows the Wembley team that made its only appearance at the stadium that bears its name. It was in 1988, when the astrologer, Russell Grant, with his own odd-ball passion for the erstwhile county of

Middlesex, managed to persuade the stadium authorities to allow the Middlesex Senior Cup final to take place there. Wembley, having surprisingly beaten Brentford in the semi-final, lost 0−2 to Hendon in front of 4000 people.

There is also a framed newspaper cutting from 1962 that tells of Malcolm Allison, later to manage most of the Football League and spend a lot of its money, accepting his first job in management here after ending his playing days with West Ham. 'He wore big hats even then,' says Roy Calmels. 'But he didn't get any dough out of us.'

Wembley FC, despite its downbeat character, is a colourful experience in itself. For, like so many non-League clubs, it is peopled by those salt-of-the-earths so utterly eccentric in their passion for such low-key, low-profile entertainment, but otherwise with the game and life in perspective.

Take Roy Calmels. A striped blazer and half-rim spectacles testify to that eccentricity. The history of his involvement with the club testifies to the rest. It is to him that the task often falls to deal with telephone and postal inquiries meant for the stadium. In the mid-1980s, a caller from New Zealand seeking Cup final tickets was told of his mistake but so enjoyed the conversation that he popped in for a drink on his subsequent visit. Calmels was born in Wembley, moved away then back, in 1980, and began to get involved. 'They conned me into doing the programme because I had a photostat machine,' he says. Within a year, he and his company dealing in football memorabilia were sponsoring the team. He reintroduced the nickname and logo of the Lions and restored them to their old red-and-white quartered shirts; these are sadly now abandoned for something more glitzy, something which resembles a video on the blink, as is the fashion in the shiny, jazzy 1990s.

Under a young chairman and a new manager returning to his roots, the club 'has a renewed enthusiasm,' according to Calmels. The chairman is Brian Gumm, a mere 37. 'But I feel old sometimes,' he jokes. 'Last year, I went training with the lads . . .' Can this be the non-League equivalent of Michael Knighton, who briefly took control of Manchester United in 1989 seemingly because he wanted to fulfil a boyhood dream of playing for them? Clearly not. 'Never again,' Gumm goes on to say.

He is also unique among football chairmen in another way: 'I don't claim to know anything about football.' He took over in 1988 at the urging of his wife, Jean, now the secretary, who was closely involved with the club. 'I didn't even know the ground existed, and I have lived in Wembley for nine years. That's the attitude I am trying to overcome,' he says. There is a lot of competition near at hand, like Kingsbury and Edgware Town, he points out with charming parochialism. He might also mention Arsenal, Tottenham, Watford and Barnet in and around North London.

A builder by trade, Gumm bought out the club in 1990 and negotiated for it a thirty-year lease on the ground, turning it into a limited company in 1991. The stadium allowed them to retain the word Wembley in their title. 'I have taken the bullet between my teeth,' he says, admitting to having upset a few of the older supporters with his methods for modernising the club. 'This club has never earned a penny and won't do for another five or six years.'

Work done so far has included upgraded dressing-rooms and toilets, and plans are afoot for development of the Nursery End. Lest that should conjure up opulent visions of Lord's cricket ground, it should be pointed out that it refers to a derelict children's nursery just outside the ground. Little can be done at the other end; it backs on to a cycle track used to teach children road safety. But Gumm is equally pleased about building of another kind, the development of youth teams at the club, even if there is one big drawback. 'You bring on boys, and then the big clubs come along and snap them up after you have done the donkey work. But that's the way of the world, I suppose.'

How much is it all costing? Gumm's face contorts as he refuses to name a figure. 'But it's well worth it. Everyone from the tea ladies to the players is friends here. It's a family thing for us,' adds the Chelsea follower, who used to spend his Saturdays horse riding with his more immediate family.

Part of the extended family is Alan Dafforn, who may be the only football manager to live in Hampstead. 'It's in the posh part but it's a council flat,' he concedes. 'A nice one, though.' The 41-year-old, a solicitor's clerk at a King's Cross office, says he reads the *Daily Telegraph* to find out what is going on in the world and the *Sun* to find out what people are talking about. He has returned to the club – 'because I have a soft spot for it' – this season after a spell as assistant manager at Redbridge Forest, this year playing their first season in the GM Vauxhall Conference after promotion from the Diadora League.

'I always enjoyed it here as a player, and people have always been very good to me. I left because I felt people weren't looking to go places. Now that's changed. There is a nice feel about the club, and I like working with people I feel comfortable with. It was a tough decision to miss out on a season in the Conference, but this club has something a little special about it. When I tell people who I manage, some say: "Do you play at Wembley Stadium, then?"'

So far, Dafforn has had difficulty in rebuilding the club to take it near the team he created in his first spell of ten years with the club, when they missed out by 1 point on promotion to the top division of the Isthmian League for the first time in their history. Their defeats so far this season have come at places such as Molesey, where the local paper headlined their report, with a vividness of which the poet laureate, Ted Hughes, would have approved: 'Happy Moles Break Duck'.

In the preliminary round of the FA Cup, though, they had produced hitherto their best performance of the season in winning 1–0 at Egham. Dafforn, fed up with the mobile telephone of the substitute, Mark Witter, constantly going off in the dug-out – one call was from his mother, who was getting remarried later that day – sent him on. 'Any message if anyone calls?' was Dafforn's parting shot. Of course, Witter scored the winning goal, with five minutes left.

Today, on this sunny September day, with a cricket match taking place on the other side of its walls, Wembley are at home to Windsor and Eton in the first qualifying round of the FA Cup. It is just one of a plethora of ties: the previous round, the preliminary, had featured 154. The match will attract 173 people, 123 of them paying. The following May, 80,000 people would fill that stadium those two and a half miles away for the final of the world's most vibrant club cup competition after its compelling slog through winter.

Windsor and Eton, from a division above Wembley in the Diadora League, are a much tougher proposition than were Egham. They certainly look it, their size and unshaven chins giving them a fearsome appearance. Can they really be representing such a genteel part of the country, where schools are public, parks are Great and royalty resides? Amid much shouting and rushing, Wembley hold their own for half an hour but then concede 2 goals in two minutes. Windsor's Richard Evans begins the move for the first, sending the ball wide on the right to Jerry Williams, who elbows aside the delightfully named Gursel Gulfer before crossing for Evans to head home.

Then, with Wembley still in turmoil, the Windsor midfield player, Steve Bates, drives home a powerful twenty-yard shot. Wembley's goal, turned home by Steve Lawrence seven minutes from time, merely sets up a frantic, fruitless finish. The old 1–2 it ends. To demonstrate how much intensity the game can generate even at this level, the Windsor manager, Alf Coulton, has to be restrained from approaching the referee, believing Lawrence's goal to have been offside.

Wembley have, in the past, produced their share of players who went on to the Football League: Richard Cadette with Southend and Brentford; Gary Roberts – whose fee of £10,000 paid for a new set of floodlights – also to Brentford; and Keith Cassells with Watford, Peterborough and Mansfield, for example. Today, however, there does not appear to be another candidate. The club has reached the first round proper of the FA Cup only once in its history – in 1981, when they lost 0–3 to Enfield. The final itself is a dream. Then they get the wake-up call.

So what can Wembley realistically hope to achieve? 'Enjoyment, really. But that's what it's all about, isn't it?' says Gumm. And, on that touching note, it was time for the club to close down for the evening and earn some money by giving over its social club to a wedding reception. The guests were now arriving in the twilight. The nights were drawing in.

Autumn

Three: Country

1 England, Ah England

International occasions are unlike ordinary ninety-minute matches. With previews followed by analysis, in pub and papers, they last a week. Then there is the one that has gone on for twenty-five years. A September confrontation with the Germans two and a half miles from Wembley Football Club was in the offing.

England v. West Germany is a rivalry etched into the consciousness of every football fan. For those of a certain age, it was 1966 and all that. For the younger viewer, 1990 represented a similar collection of memories and emotions. Between times, there had been a range of matches intense and unrivalled in their drama, but usually frustration itself for frequently defeated Englishmen. It has been a long time since '66 and that glorious 4–2 victory after extra-time at Wembley to win the World Cup; the day Geoff Hurst scored a hat-trick and the manager, Alf Ramsey, became the only Englishman in the history of football to remain seated as the nation scored a goal.

Everyone remembers the day England won the World Cup, where they were, what they were doing. It is our JFK. An 11-year-old boy, I moved house on the very day, Saturday 30 July, with my parents. We sat on bare floorboards to watch the only item of furniture in the room. I wept as Helmut Haller put the Germans ahead but stopped when Kenneth Wolstenholme reassured me that the team scoring first never won a World Cup final. Then I danced with delight when they thought it was all over and it was now; when England's captain, Bobby Moore, wearily wended his way up the thirty-nine steps of Wembley to the Royal Box and wiped his hands on the velveteen drape before shaking hands with the Queen.

This year, twenty-five years on, that 11-year-old would sit with the self-same Bobby Moore, perhaps the world's most languid, most elegant defender, as he approached his 50th birthday, in a stand at Coventry City's Highfield Road ground before a League Cup match against Arsenal. Moore was now working in his capacity as a summariser for the London radio station, Capital Gold; modesty, the preserve of the truly talented, was overwhelmingly his bearing. We talked about that time in relation to the Rugby Union World Cup going on this autumn, in which England had – *déjà vu* – reached the final. They even had a B. Moore in the team.

Had he ever thought about how life might have been had England lost? A puzzled look came to his face. 'No. It didn't come into it. No. No. Never.' It was the statement of a man who had been at the peak of his powers, who seemed assured of his sporting destiny. What had he felt at the Haller goal? 'By that time, you believe in your game plan,' he replied. 'You have to stick to it and believe in your own ability and confidence.

'You have a lot of time to think and rest in the week leading to the final but then you need it to prepare yourself mentally and physically. You know everybody is willing you to win but you have to withdraw into your own cocoon collectively as a team. In fact, some individuals do – we're all different. But you want to feel the tension, you want a nervousness which makes you aware of the importance of the occasion, to bring you to the peak of your condition. On the day, you try to make it as near to a normal match as you can, but it's not really possible.'

Is it possible to enjoy it? 'Yes, it is possible, even though the day goes by so quickly. You think you're aware of everything going on but, eventually, you realise it has passed you by. You just have to make the most of what you can. I think you realise afterwards the importance of it all, how important it is to everyone else. When you have detached yourself from the tournament and you're back in your own environment you have time to think about it all. Then you get overwhelmed by all the invitations, requests and demands. When you are away from the hype, excitement and razzmatazz of it all, you suddenly realise what you have achieved.'

As one directly involved, responsible even, Moore is entitled to such euphoric recall. For the rest of English football, however, it has often been a problem. And the sense of cockiness it gave a generation was false. To his shame, when the 11-year-old was two years later on a school trip to Paris, he boastingly baited an unfriendly French youth with: 'Qui a gagne la Coupe du Monde, then?'

If followers have mistakenly basked in the reflected glory then, for the game itself, failure to live in the present, to adapt and adopt the ways of the Germans whom we probably most closely resemble in attitudes and ambitions, has led to an inability to contest the latter stages of major tournaments. In the six World Cups since '66, the Germans have won two and reached two other finals; the English have reached one semi-final. It seemed that the worm turned in 1970 when, in the heat and dust of the Mexican city of Leon, probably the best England team ever to leave its shores squandered a 2-goal lead in a quarter-final. Replaying in the mind's eye Gerd Muller volleying past Peter Bonetti, replacement for a stomach-upset Gordon Banks, can still inspire a cringe. Whereas the Germans had grown from the experience of '66, the English were about to enter a trough.

The influence as coach of Helmut Schoen, as he allied finesse to physique, was to take the Germans to a new plane. In the European Championship of 1972, they were inspired by Gunther Netzer to a 3–1 win at Wembley as England almost looked on in awe and admiration. A little national pride was restored in a 0–0 draw in the return in Berlin: 'Every English player autographed my legs with his studs,' said Netzer. West Germany went on to win the tournament, beating the USSR 3–0 in the final in Brussels.

There was an oasis, a respite to the suffering, in 1975 when Malcolm Macdonald scored both goals as England won 2–0 at Wembley – but it was a friendly. Still, it laid to rest the joke, the one which went: What is taken to Wembley every year and never used? Instead of the answer being the ribbons of the losers to tie on to the FA Cup, it was, for his frequent disappointing performances, Malcolm Macdonald.

England did not qualify for another World Cup finals until 1982, meeting – wouldn't you know it – the Germans in the second phase in Spain. 'I've never met a team which squeal like the Germans,' said the England midfield player, Bryan Robson, after a 0–0 draw in Madrid which sent the Germans through at England's expense. England lost two more after 1982 and won one, by 3–0 in Mexico City in 1985 in a World Cup warm-up tournament only hours after the Germans had stepped off an aeroplane.

Then came 1990. Into a World Cup semi-final in Turin England carried all this emotional baggage. Surprise, surprise, though, they matched the Germans, certainly for spirit, which was embodied in an outstanding performance by the precious and precocious Paul Gascoigne in midfield. His weeping face, the result of a booking which would have meant him missing the final had England reached it, was seen back home by 25 million viewers. As well as making him instantly an English icon, and turning the nickname

Gazza into a marketing slogan – to be patented, indeed – it ensured that the Anglo-Teuton rivalry lived on with a new generation. Surprise, surprise, though, England lost. Not morally, of course, since penalties had to decide after a 1–1 draw.

The 11-year-old was watching that game on a big screen in a Rome hotel, which was hosting an Independence Day toga party – Rome, geddit? – for some 300 Americans. Those who drifted into the TV room during normal play stayed only a few moments. Those who then drifted in to watch the penalty shoot-out were riveted. Those, sports fans, are the people who are hosting the 1994 event. Read it and weep.

But back to 1991 and Wembley, as England met what was now just Germany, as sporting unity mirrored political reunification. It was the twenty-fifth, or first, anniversary match, depending on your age.

On the Monday morning at the start of international week, the newish England manager, Graham Taylor, sat by the Thames on a beautiful Indian summer's day at the training camp, the Bisham Abbey sports complex on the Berkshire/Buckinghamshire border. It was idyllic and fittingly English. Behind him, as he conducted his press conference alfresco, pleasure cruisers plied their way from Marlow to Henley-on-Thames. On adjacent tennis courts, English hopefuls were looking hopeless. For Bisham is a multi-sports centre, with its halls, hockey pitches and golf course. It is home to English squads of various sporting persuasions. British Olympic squads meet here.

As Taylor spoke he seemed only too aware of the inferiority complex that haunts the English when the words Germany and football are used in the same sentence. 'I want a positive attitude,' he said. From his players, it transpired, rather than from a media more used to seeing the down-side of events. 'I don't want to put in their minds the fear of failure. I expect to win whatever team I select.' He wanted, under his different regime, players to be free of that emotional baggage, perhaps. Trevor Steven, however, was just free of baggage. His had got lost on the way over from his club, Marseille.

The following day, at the same place, Taylor announced an inexperienced team – including Tony Dorigo, Gary Pallister and John Salako, with Paul Stewart and Paul Merson to win their first caps from the bench – due to injuries. 'Although this is a friendly, it is a big occasion,' he said, getting in the mood. Elsewhere in Southern England, the German manager, Berti Vogts, veteran of Leon 1970, was saying: 'It is not a normal game; it is always special, a classic.' His left-back, Andreas Brehme, however, was more sanguine. 'The English game is always the same,' he said. 'There'll be nothing new. It will be about the long ball and physical commitment. Technically and individually, we are better. And, from a tactical point of view, we are superior.'

It is a balmy Wednesday night as the players emerge from the Wembley dressing-rooms leading on to a tunnel some fifty yards walk to the pitch. The thought occurs that, if the Germans lose tonight, it will mean that they have lost two in a row: in June, they were beaten 0–1 in Cardiff by Wales – the Fatherland falling to the Land of My Fathers – in a European Championship qualifying match. When did that last occur? 'It did not happen, I think,' smiles Paul Breitner, former German captain and World Cup-winner in 1974, now working as a journalist at the match.

Indeed, it did not. England have their moments, but the one that counts comes from the Germans, shortly before half-time. Moving swiftly, silently and stealthily forward to escape the English midfield, the German captain, Lothar Matthäus, instigates a passing movement by playing the ball cleverly out of the left-back position to central midfield and Andreas Moller. Within seconds, Matthäus is up to support, and his pass wide on the left, as English minds wander with the interval approaching, finds Thomas Doll, an East German, whose centre is headed home by Karl-Heinz Riedle, from the west.

It is a happier crossing from east to west than the world has been used to. Doll and Riedle are team-mates at Lazio of Rome, two of the large contingent in the German squad who now ply their trade in Italy, where they import only the best. David Platt of Bari, desperately trying through his typically hyperactive performance tonight to prove that all is well there, is the only Englishman playing in that country.

Riedle's goal proves enough to win the game. It is described later to journalists by Graham Taylor as 'one minute of madness. There's your headline,' adds the man whose introduction to football was sitting alongside his journalist father in the press box at the Old Show Ground of Scunthorpe United.

In the Long Bar underneath the twin towers at Wembley – all thoughtfully modern with TV sets to encourage people to come early – there is disgruntlement among the fancy at England's defeat. But it is not yet serious for Taylor. It is, after all, the first under him, his unlucky thirteenth match. It is also only September, and England are notoriously underprepared in September. During that month in the previous ten years, England had won only three contests and lost four; in the process, they scored only eight goals. Still, the Germans are now the only nation to have won three times at Wembley. Since 1966, the countries have played each other twelve times, England winning two, drawing three and losing seven.

The match reinforced the feeling that the Brazilians may blend occasionally, the Italians may strut now and then, but the Germans just go on and on being, well, the Germans.

They had demonstrated again the consistency of their game, a competence enhanced by moments of inspiration. For England, the impetus provided by Turin was but a memory.

In the newly-furnished press room next to the first-aid centre, Taylor described the German performance as 'controlled' but saw only the luck in front of goal, coupled with that momentary lapse of defensive concentration, as the difference between the teams. It was, however, to overlook the contribution of Matthäus, the man who moulded their tactical and technical awareness into a formidable unit. Together with his colleagues, he had displayed his native qualities of intelligence and hard work. The former England striker, Tony Woodcock, once said how surprised he was by that latter quality when he joined Cologne and was sent out to run through the woods. He had been used to a Forest in Nottingham, but this was ridiculous.

'The Germans are very strong mentally,' added Kevin Keegan, who himself had a prosperous, Bundesliga-winning, spell with Hamburg. 'They take their training more seriously, and that breeds a better professional. Their attitude is to earn money, be successful and have fun in that order. The Bundesliga reflects the national side. All the teams play pretty much the same way, with a sweeper. They each have two foreigners so, with twenty sides in the league this season, that means 180 German players are on view every week.'

Such a system, which the concept at least of the FA's Premier League envisaged, might well lead to a national team with greater potential for success. But, when applied to England, that theory ignores several points, including the presence of Scots, Welsh and Irish – as well as other nationalities – in the League, and the decision of several English-born players to play for the country of their ante-cedents. Then there is the question of whether every English side should play in a similar way. Football is a broad church and the more entertaining for it. The depth and richness of the English game, from Swindon to Sheffield United, demonstrates that.

Yet one thing to be envied among the Germans – indeed, among the European nations in general – is their football's appeal more to the white-collar class, making it fodder for the mind as well as the body. And, at Wembley, the European player-of-the-year and world sportsman-of-the-year for 1990, Matthäus the managing director, illustrated the ability of all great players to take control when sensing that the game is entering a crucial phase. Johan Cruyff, himself an excellent role model, often talked of this instinct that special players possess – such as Ruud Gullit, he said – for seizing the moment.

England were without such long-term injured parties as John Barnes, Mark Wright and, of course, Gascoigne; it is another mitigating factor for Taylor, one that public and press would take into account. Without Wright as sweeper, he is back to playing the 4–4–2 system rather than the 3–5–2 that suited England so well in the World Cup. But one still senses the seeds of discontent: one newspaper goes so far as to describe England as Taylor's Dummies.

The problem has been all in the imagination for England – or rather the lack of it. It is a theme that has been with us for many years, is with us now and will no doubt be again, both this season and for years to come: whether to dig in with the English way of commitment and athleticism or to adopt more the finesse of the foreigners.

Things are not what they were; perhaps they never were, and there was a time when nostalgia wasn't so popular. Those were the days.

II 'At A Turk

Back at Bisham on a Monday morning in October, Chris Waddle was performing his Greta Garbo impersonation. The gifted Marseille roving striker-cum-midfield player, of the round, drooping shoulders and sweet left foot, no longer wished to talk about a potential England comeback. He wished to retain his own counsel and let his game do the talking when Wednesday's match against Turkey, in the qualifying rounds for the European Championship, came around.

Usually, a wood-panelled room at the rear of the country house is allocated for the interviewing of players. It is a bit like the school disco, not in the way that the latter stages of those can often bring to mind the reactions of goal-scorers on professional football pitches; but in the way that the players sit around at the sides waiting to be asked to dance, or rather interviewed.

But Vaddle vanted to be alone. It was one of those hypocritical attitudes to which players, England players in particular, are prone. They will frequently use the press for their own purposes, granting interviews to talk themselves into the team or to make some image-enhancing point. There was the unsettled player, for example, who told a tabloid that My Boozing Days Are Over, so that any manager potentially frightened to sign him would have his fears allayed. A short time later, he was caught for drink-driving.

Waddle himself has taken tabloid money for a ghosted column, which involves talking for five or ten minutes to a journalist who then writes up the comments, or embellishes them, under the player's name. It is money for old rope. The problem for a player can be, as it was at the 1990 World Cup, that he is in an embarrassing position when his team-mates refuse to co-operate with the papers who pay him. Loyalties are torn; but the more lucrative option usually wins.

Still, Waddle's silence this day afforded a good opportunity for a correspondent seeking his views to take in as an alternative England's opponents, Turkey, the fowl to the slaughter at Wembley. Seeing Sepp Piontek enter the hotel at their head brought to mind images such as Carl Davis with the Sex Pistols in tow, or Giorgio Armani preparing that sartorial Just William of an Everton and Wales goalkeeper, Neville Southall, for the catwalk. For Piontek was the last overseas international manager to have won a qualifying match at Wembley, when his Danish team triumphed 1–0 to reach the European Championship finals of 1984. They went on to reach the last four.

Turkey, by contrast, had lost their two previous matches at Wembley by an aggregate of 0–13. England just do not lose home matches in qualifying competitions for major championships; just that one in the last thirty-two. Even when they have lost out they have drawn, as against Poland in 1973 – if anyone can bring themselves to remember that stunning, numbing night when Brian Clough deemed the opposition's goal-keeper, Jan Tomaszewski, a clown and urged the nation on television that all would soon be well, to go and make a cup of tea while we were waiting.

As we stood in the lobby of the hotel discussing the forthcoming match, the urbane Piontek permitted himself the trace of a smirk when reminded – as if he had ever forgotten – that Danish result. 'You have got to have good players and catch England on a bad day,' he said of the qualifications needed. 'Your own players must be clever and keep possession. And you must have luck, of course. All these things must come together.

'There is a difference between Denmark and my team now,' added the wily German coach with a talent for getting the opposition to underestimate his team. When it comes to talking Turkey, he seemed to be saying, we were talking turkeys. 'Not good,' was his analysis of what he had found when taking over the job in the spring of 1990. 'If you see the reality in Turkey . . .' he continued, his voice trailing off, his cheeks puffing out and his shoulders shrugging. 'I should have known it would be difficult, but it is more difficult than I thought. There is no problem with the players' technique. But they must have strong minds and make no mistakes. For that, they need to concentrate, and this they do not do sometimes.'

But club results in European competitions that autumn, of such as Galatasaray, had been promising, had they not? 'Yes, but there are foreign players in key positions in the club sides,' said Piontek. 'And all they think about is clubs, clubs, clubs, especially the big ones. There is no tradition for the national team.' Some people may have heard this argument somewhere before. For Piontek, more than any Englishman, though, it was all the more acute; in Denmark, the club football of the 1980s did not match his team while, as a German, he has always been aware of the overriding importance accorded the national XI.

With that, it was off with his team to Wembley Football Club – those two and a half miles away – to run out the tiredness of the journey from Istanbul and the even more tortuous journey in from Heathrow Airport. Piontek chose to begin the session by working intensively with his two goal-keepers. Perhaps he had heard that, back at Bisham Abbey, Graham Taylor had been calling on his England team to shoot more often, not to be frightened of making fools of themselves. Perhaps Piontek feared a Turkey shoot. In the end, neither need have bothered: England were to make fools of themselves, but for the reason of not getting in enough attempts on goal.

Again, because of injuries, Taylor was forced to field a side he had scarcely envisaged. This time, however, it was back to the future as it included five players over 30 in Chris Woods, Gary Mabbutt, Bryan Robson, Gary Lineker and Waddle. Collectively, they stumbled and bumbled their way to a 1–0 win thanks to a goal by Alan Smith after twenty-two minutes. Individually, the team had an illustrious past and an impressive present. There seemed to be little future for many of them, however.

It was worrying enough that England looked so ordinary. More worrying was how good a team Turkey were allowed to look as they passed the ball the better; with finishing to match, they would have drawn at least. And that from a nation with a track record worse than most of the greyhounds who have run round Wembley's perimeter.

It was a disturbing night for Taylor, and not only because a section of the crowd ignored his appeal in the programme and distastefully jeered the opposition's national anthem. 'It would be silly to say that either I or the players were happy with the performance, especially in the second half,' he said afterwards. 'We lost a sense of urgency, some shape and any smoothness in our play. We got trapped between a controlled and an aggressive manner.'

Why? He wished he had the answer. It was a response for which he was to be criticised in the press the following day. After all, the England team manager was expected to have the answers. That was why he was England team manager. One did not recall hearing Margaret Thatcher in Parliament saying that she did not know why. Then again, Mrs Thatcher never had Chris Waddle to deal with. Nor questions that successive England managers have had to address, such as why players manifestly fail to carry out simple instructions, and why exceptional club players become different, less effective beings once they pull on England shirts. These rank with the great whys in life: why is there only one Monopolies Commission? Why does the person who snores always fall asleep first? Why does the radio play your favourite song just as you are parking the car? Why do floorboards only creak at night? England could be that maddening.

Taylor's bemusement and lack of amusement had been apparent before. 'If I could tell you that . . .' had been his response to a question after England's feeble 1–1 draw against the Republic of Ireland at Wembley the previous March. He was briefly entertained in the interview room tonight, however. Piontek had promised to swim the Bosphorus should Turkey win. Would Mr Taylor now be swimming the River Thames, a Turkish journalist enquired?

That interview for the 'quotes men' of the national press et al over, Taylor made his way to the banqueting suite, opposite the walkway down Olympic Way from Wembley Park tube station and behind the terrace under the twin towers, where he would meet the football correspondents of the same papers; they had, by now, around 11pm, finished their match reports.

This Taylor did so that he did not have to meet them on the Thursday morning, a tradition that his predecessor, Bobby Robson, had followed but which Taylor was breaking because he wanted the day off. Besides which, he believed that the correspondents should write their own opinions rather than his. This was not good enough for some newspapers, however, and the 11pm conference was the compromise. In it, Taylor's anger spilled out, in his words if not in their delivery. 'There were people out there who were happy to play it safe. They were playing nothing football,' he said. 'In certain situations, players – and it would be totally wrong to name them – didn't accept the responsibility for the kind of passing and movement we wanted. In those situations I learn things about players.'

Although he refrained from naming names, the Waddle case was clearly especially annoying for Taylor. Gifted, elegant, frustrating Waddle, a wow in France, a wally at Wembley. He looked thinner than during his time in the English club game and was a shadow, disappointingly hugging the right touchline for an hour and seemingly spurning the run of the pitch for which Taylor had licensed him. Only in the last half-hour did he vary his game, and then just to move to the left wing. Even if, at times, he delivered some curling crosses and looked a quality player compared to the scurriers that England had had in midfield of late, rarely did he look like hurting Turkey in the areas that mattered. Rarely did he demand the ball with the desire he showed at Marseille.

Taylor had spoken before the match of a team with a nice, balanced look to it, but the reality was the English obsession with a back four to mark one forward player. Only occasionally, notably when Smith headed home the goal from Pearce's cross – an example of the one area in which England dominated – did the home full-backs get forward the way one expects them to in domestic football. The contribution of Bryan Robson also disappointed. It was, as usual, energetic, but uncharacteristically ineffectual, given that he had once scored a hat-trick in an 8–0 defeat of Turkey. 'If a player like Robson comes back, you perhaps expect more ideas to change things,' said Piontek. 'It was like a pattern we could always read.'

And Taylor's decision not to make a substitution when Beardsley and Merson were on the bench smacked of him telling the team to stew in its own juice, to the strains of 'what a load of rubbish' from a remarkable Wembley crowd of 50,896. He had, after all, once gone into the Aston Villa dressing-room at half-time of a cup tie they were losing 0–2 to Crewe and told them that they had inserted themselves in to the mess and would now have to extract themselves from it. There was nothing he could do about it. They won 3–2. But nothing so dramatic happened at Wembley.

The following month, when it began to emerge that Taylor was considering making sweeping changes for the last of England's qualification matches, against Poland in Poznan, Bryan Robson was to announce his retirement from international football. It was a clear case of jumping before he was pushed. The Turkey match had been a sad way to commemorate a player who, for much of the 1980s, had been England's stalwart.

For the purpose, he used the conference suite of a hotel around the corner from the FA's headquarters in Lancaster Gate, at the West London end of Hyde Park. He would undoubtedly have preferred to go out at Wembley, or in the finals of a major championship, with 100 caps. But life is rarely that perfect, or even neat. He finished, at the age of 34, with ninety caps and 26 goals. Career-punctuating injuries, often due to his bravery, not to say daredevilry, denied him central roles in the World Cup finals campaigns of 1986 and 1990, and the century. But it was still a remarkable record.

When fit, he had been the driving force of the England team, as valuable to it as Matthäus to Germany, if not more so. His 'engine', as professional football parlance has it, was second to none. His timing of the run into the penalty area was perhaps his greatest asset, seen beautifully in a goal he scored after twenty-seven seconds for England against France in the World Cup finals of 1982. Add to that a powerful left-footed shot and an even more powerful tackle, and it made up one of the best, if not quite the very best.

'He never pushed himself forward, he never wanted self-glory,' said the England coach who worked most with him, Don Howe. 'He was a model team player. He had a terrific inner drive and an inner desire to win. He always wanted to win more than anyone else. And he wanted to do that not to grab a headline, but for his team and country.' Howe's and Robson's boss, Bobby Robson, called him 'Captain Marvel'. But now it was over. When he came off that night against Turkey he realised that his time was up, Graham Taylor was to say later.

Another player was soon to announce his international retirement as well, as the transition from one England era to another continued; thankfully, however, Gary Lineker's would not be immediate. It would come after the European Championship finals in Sweden the following summer, for which England were to qualify with a skin-of-the-teeth draw in Poland later this autumn thanks to an outstanding piece of his opportunism. The subduing of Lineker by Turkey, against whom, like Robson, he had once scored a hat-trick on his way to what was then a total of 45 goals – 4 short of Bobby Charlton's England record – confirmed how the team struggled when he was not himself. All would now be forgiven, even if England's shortcomings were not quite forgotten.

Taylor, having perhaps felt pressured by the press into picking a side to face Turkey that reflected England's immediate past rather than his vision of its future, reacted by doing things his own way. For a match in which experience might have been seen as the key quality, he boldly – or foolishly – chose to give international debuts to Andy Sinton of Queen's Park Rangers and Andy Gray of Crystal Palace, discarding more seasoned-in-the-cold claimants. It barely worked. England fell behind after thirty-one undistinguished minutes when a shot by the sweeper, Szewczyk, was deflected off the heel of Gary Mabbutt and beyond

Chris Woods in goal. Fear crept into the England game as they now came under heavy pressure; it seemed that their *bête noir*, the Republic of Ireland, who were winning a simultaneous match in Turkey, would go to Sweden instead.

Regrouping after half-time, England looked more organised but might have been finally buried when Woods appeared to bring down the Polish striker, Furtok. The penalty was denied, however and, sixty seconds later, England scored the goal that earned the point that was enough to take them through. It proved that, where there is Lineker, there is hope. Rocastle's corner came over, was flicked on, and Lineker, alert and acrobatic at the far post, lost his marker and hooked home on the volley a memorable goal, his 46th for England. By so doing he deflected any criticism away from Taylor and made a nation hope that everything in the garden could still be rosy.

England had been thirteen minutes away from departing the competition, Taylor thirteen minutes away from the wrath of the newspapers and perhaps some popular opinion; thirteen minutes away from being, ridiculously, a bad manager. Instead, England were among the eight best nations in Europe, Taylor at their head. This time it was a lucky thirteen.

That would suffice for now. All was well that had ended well, even if its execution was not. And, of course, English club football, which also might console Bryan Robson as his Manchester United team chased a Championship, was as riveting and thrilling as ever . . .

Four: Club

1 United Front

Ken Merrett, the Manchester United secretary, is constantly surprised when he looks out of his office at Old Trafford to see so many people milling around. It seems that, no matter the time of day or night, someone is always there. But why, on this chilly Saturday morning in October, with three hours to go until kick-off, is this forecourt thronged with people just standing and talking, marking time – just being there?

To this forecourt on 6 February 1958 came thousands, helpless, powerless, some in disbelief, some in the early stages of grief. That night the Munich air crash took the lives of twenty-three people, mostly players, staff and journalists. Indirectly, it is a big reason why people still gather there. For, from that day on, United became a legend; nationwide support for them, in spirit if not in person, was handed down from mother and father to son and daughter. Even those who have nothing invested emotionally in United feel an affinity for them. That may rile uncharitable elements from rival northern cities but its truth nevertheless remains.

Once, aboard a train, a group of Leeds supporters replied 'Which one?' when I asked them how United had got on. For most people, though, there's only one United, as the title of a book by Geoffrey Green, venerable and venerated one-time football correspondent of *The Times* and Red

Devil sympathiser, had it. In the United States, they call the Dallas Cowboys America's team; Manchester United must then be England's team. They are The Club. The slogan they themselves have adopted in these days of serious marketing proclaims them The World's Greatest Football Club. No one has yet complained to the Advertising Standards Authority.

'Some people call following United a religion, and I can understand that,' says Merrett, who is a member of the organisation Christians in Sport. 'Fortunately, I think I have it in perspective with being a Christian but I know what people mean all the same.' The statistics bear him out. United have supporters registered from 119 countries. In the British Isles alone, there are branches of the Manchester United Supporters' Club in Torbay and Gateshead, Cumbria and Norfolk, Scotland and Ireland. Motorways on match-days and banners in grounds on which they are playing testify to the widest support in the English game. But statistics tell not of what moves in minds or beats in breasts.

Should Merrett ever wonder about the significance of his post, he can just turn round and look out of the window at the scene: perhaps the offices, completed only in December 1984, were designed that way. 'It is astonishing,' he says, gazing from it. 'We get coachloads from Ireland who take the overnight ferry, then are at the ground early in the morning just taking it all in. Even when the ground's closed, there are always people around, looking in the museum or the souvenir shop, taking photos. It's probably not true of any other English club. We had 25,000 people through the museum in the summer alone.'

Today the museum, opened in May 1986, and the souvenir shop are doing their best business of the year so far. United are playing the champions, Arsenal, and will host the League's best gate of the season to date, 46,594. In the souvenir shop, the accents and languages are as many and varied as the merchandise on display. Mugs, balls, videos, books, shirts, just for starters. Much money changes hands for such as pillow-cases bearing a picture of Lee Sharpe and the young winger's message wishing you goodnight; for a bogus pass to the first-team dressing-room.

In the museum, there is a reverential silence that will contrast later in the afternoon with the noisy passion that accompanies the match. Parents knowingly point out to offspring Brian Kidd's shirt from the European Cup final victory against Benifica in 1968, supposedly still bearing the stains of Wembley's white lines. It is difficult to discern who, young or old, is the more excited by it, more in awe of the League Championship medal won by Enoch 'Knocker' West in 1910–11; more touched by the telegram that the outrageously promising Duncan Edwards sent to his land-lady to tell her that the plane from Munich was delayed before he was cut down before his prime.

There is also more modern 'infotainment', with a video featuring players and the manager, Alex Ferguson, and his assistants offering minor insights into the running of the club. Watching people watching it all, though, is infinitely more entertaining and revealing about this football club. Sitting there in the coffee bar, every group tells a story. Men with sons, families of four and more all placing in its historical context today's event. The youngsters are out-wardly excited, the parents inwardly. There is chatter, but also periods of introspective silence unusual around a foot-ball ground.

Before entering the stadium itself, many will wander past the clock that bears the date of that crash at the Scoreboard End, to the bronze plaque that commemorates the club's dead as a result of Munich. There they will stand in silence on the forecourt, gazing up some thirty feet at the plate bearing the names of Walter Crickmer, Tom Curry, Bert Whalley, Roger Byrne, Geoff Bent, Eddie Colman, Duncan

Edwards, Mark Jones, David Pegg, Tommy Taylor and Billy Whelan. Today, a man is trying to explain to his young son what happened and what it meant. It seems intrusive to dwell.

It is all this and more that makes up the folklore of United, the great survivors. Before Munich, they had also to endure being bombed out, quite literally, of Old Trafford by the Luftwaffe in 1941. They returned from Manchester City's Maine Road ground after eight years. 'There's a daily excitement about working for United,' says Merrett. 'Most people going to work in certain industries aren't excited. Working for United, whatever job you do, is exciting.' He is himself celebrating twenty-five years with the club this season. He and the assistant secretary, Ken Ramsden, are the only two employees who can remember United's last League Championship – apart from Sir Matt Busby, that is, the architect, as manager, of it all, now a director.

Merrett came to the club, a Manchester City supporter no less, to help out with wages and accounts. He also kept the books. Now he keeps the club – 160 full-time employees, including the players, and a further 350 part-time on match days – ticking over. 'You're never away from United,' he adds. 'As soon as people know where you work, you get loads of questions asked of you – what are the players like, what's the manager like. Confidential questions you can't answer.' He does answer, though, that Mark Hughes has been a favourite player on the field, Steve Coppell a favourite off it. 'Even though I have seen George Best, Denis Law and Bobby Charlton, and Bryan Robson, some of my favourites would surprise you, though,' he says. 'Jimmy Greenhoff, for example.'

There have been many moments when the privilege and enormity of working for United has occurred to him. 'I was at the European Cup final of 1968 but I was only really a junior then, even though I realised what it meant to United after Munich,' he says. 'For me, Rotterdam and the European Cup-Winners' Cup [final] last year was the most remarkable experience, because I had been involved in administering it all from start to finish. I arrived at the ground with the players and, as I walked out, the atmosphere and noise was incredible.'

That night, United beat Barcelona 2–1 to claim the trophy. Indeed, Barcelona provide Merrett with his other favourite memory: one of those heady European nights at Old Trafford when, in 1984 in the same competition, United overturned a 0–2 deficit from the first leg and won 3–0 to reach the semi-finals, in which they lost 2–3 on aggregate to Juventus of Turin. Next month, United would fail as they sought to do something similar in defence of their trophy, against Atletico Madrid, drawing 1–1 at home having lost 0–3 in Spain.

The effect United have has also struck Merrett on tours to Scandinavia, where United have huge followings. As we speak, Bobby Charlton knocks, then enters the office with a query about today's behind-the-scenes arrangements. 'There's one reason why United is so special,' says Merrett when Charlton has left. Yes, it is true, he says, people do come up to him on the continent, their only two words of English being 'Bobb-ee Shal-ton'.

The burdens of being United – 'the media attention, constantly being in the public eye, with football tending to look for a reaction to everything from United' – are outweighed by the benefits, adds Merrett. Personal pressures, abuse, for example? 'People are surprised I am not ex-directory, but I don't want to do that,' he says. 'If you have a chance to speak to people, they usually see reason. Usually, the complaints are about ticket allocations, or travelling arrangements. If the team is doing well, there are fewer complaints, except perhaps about not getting in. If the team is not doing well, you would be surprised at what else is wrong –

programmes, refreshments, a leak from the roof over the seats, people standing in front of you. There will also be one or two complaints about people's behaviour. When the team is not doing well, people's behaviour deteriorates, not necessarily physically but verbally.'

By lunchtime, Merrett's work is mainly done, especially for an all-ticket game. He will, however, miss the kick-off and a part of the second half. Now the inquiries are such as Gary Pallister seeking tea tickets, Bryan Robson asking about car parking for guests. There are those who will miss more of the game than Merrett but nevertheless know exactly what is going on. Just before the kick-off of each home game, United hear from one telephone caller in Denmark and another in South Africa seeking the team lists. They will call again at half-time and full-time for scores.

United are currently top of the first division, unbeaten in eleven matches, 4 points clear. This is the year when they will surely be more than merely champions of autumn, as they have been too frequently – most notably in 1985, when they won their first ten matches, and only Liverpool seemed to stay with them. But United were to slump and finish fourth; it was the first time, unkind observers said, that a team has finished fourth in a two-horse race.

This year, though, is the one when the grail of the Championship really does come to the club. Isn't it? In this season of significant footballing twenty-fifth anniversaries, it will be that many years come April since United last won it. After 1967, they went on to realise so gloriously, so beautifully, the ambition that Munich cruelly interrupted: the winning of the European Cup. It remained quite an act to follow.

Today's team news is that the Arsenal manager, George Graham, has omitted his Swedish left winger, Anders Limpar, whose feud with the United full-back, Dennis Irwin, in the corresponding match last year – in the corresponding week, indeed – led to a brawl. Having been seen on nationwide television, it provoked the Football Association into deducting 2 points from Arsenal and 1 from United. Graham, deemed ultimately responsible for the behaviour of his players, was fined £10,000 by his own board of directors. 'Be careful, this is Old Trafford. There'll be two journalists deducted,' Graham was to joke later today, as reporters jostled to hear his verdict on the match in the tiny press interview room in the bowels of Old Trafford.

Nevertheless, Arsenal boldly play four in attack and only two in midfield, their strength clearly being the pace and invention up front of Paul Merson, Kevin Campbell and Ian Wright, with the lanky centre-forward, Alan Smith, scorer of that England goal against Turkey, linking and leading the line. By allocating only David Rocastle and Paul Davis to midfield, Graham also ensures that the game will be more open and fluent, thus averting the crowded feel of last year's match that led to frustration manifesting itself in violence.

That midfield will include United's captain, the player more than any other over the past decade who has embodied them, Bryan Robson. Today will seem almost a relief for him: it is only four days since his international career had been resurrected and then snuffed out once and for all in England's feeble showing against Turkey. Before today's kick-off, Robson presents a local boys' club with a new set of strip as a result of United being awarded performance-of-the-week by the League's sponsors, Barclays, for their recent 2–1 win at Tottenham. Given Robson's own performance on the previous Wednesday, the irony of the ceremony is not lost on some in the press box.

United enter the arena, the Theatre of Dreams as it has been called – by Geoffrey Green, or Bobby Charlton, nobody seems quite sure – with their name reverberating around it, first from the terraced supporters on the Stretford End, then from the whole ground. It is a sound equivalent in terms of decibels to a jet taking off. Before the game, walking a pitch which has been in poor condition in recent years due to the roof that covers all of Old Trafford, in front of an empty stadium, scarcely prepares you for it. Indeed, that can be a disappointing experience, the Stretford End looking less intimidating than imagined, the seating not as steep.

Nevertheless, Old Trafford is a thing of beauty, the cantilevered stands on three sides affording uninterrupted views. The ground has more executive boxes – 103 – than any other in the country; but to be inside one may be to miss the point of the experience, as a young boy felt in the film *Charlie Bubbles*, which used one to illustrate his alienation.

Amid all the noise and fury, and remembering the events of a year ago, it is not perhaps the most sensitive of ideas today that the teams should emerge to the accompaniment of the theme music from the boxing film, *Rocky*. A man with that nickname, David Rocastle, proves to be the first half's most significant contributor, even if United's young prodigy, Ryan Giggs, hits the post after only six minutes. Rocastle's one breathtaking example of skill under pressure for time and space is to be the lasting memory – thankfully more lasting than that of Wright's challenges on Irwin and Bruce, the latter an elbow in the face, or Hughes's on Rocastle and Tony Adams combined. The match clearly retained an edge of ill feeling, if not a cutting edge, from the previous year.

Five minutes before the interval, receiving the ball forty yards out, Rocastle steps inside Robson, shrugs off Ince and looks up. United's Danish goal-keeper, Peter Schmeichel, is about where he should be, eight yards off his line, as Rocastle is now some thirty yards out. The midfielder chips, powerfully, the 6ft 5in figure who is unfortunate in that, as he back-pedals and tries to save, the ball hits him on the back and drops into the net after it has bounced down from the crossbar. Rightly, though, Rocastle's talent rather than Schmeichel's bad luck receives the acclaim. 'A brilliant piece of improvisation, innovation and any other kind of -ation you care to mention,' Graham was later to say.

Four minutes later, however, United are level. Hughes begins a spell of pressure by turning and shooting splendidly on the half-volley, prompting Seaman into an equally splendid left-handed save. Then, shortly afterwards, Irwin takes a corner on the left short to Giggs, whose cross passes over Robson, but there to stoop and glance home a header is Steve Bruce, the United defender worth his weight in goals.

United's second-half march, with Robson now the dominant figure in the van, fails to yield them the winner they so covet. Giggs snatches at a shot when clear, screwing it across the face of the goal; Brian McClair – who, in 1987, became the first United player for twenty years, since George Best, to score 20 League goals in a season – shoots against a post. It has been a fascinating early skirmish, although United did not seem, one sensed, disappointed enough at having missed the chance to go 7 points clear at the top of the table. The 1–1 draw was already their third sharing of the points at home, having been held in important games against Leeds and Liverpool.

Ferguson refuses to castigate Giggs for a couple of misses. 'We shouldn't need to look to him to win us matches,' he says. Yet. There will probably come a time when they do. As yet, though, the club have the 17-year-old left winger in cotton wool off the field, refusing interviews with him. Clearly, the George Best experience still haunts Old Trafford. And one can understand why Giggs is so closeted. In the reception area at luncthime, how childlike he had looked in a baggy suit and a shirt collar with seemingly two inches of space between it and its occupant's Adam's apple. Ferguson, though, talks of the steel in his eyes.

United's inexperience in such a situation as being involved in a Championship competition is evident from Ferguson's other post-match comments. Having won three Scottish titles with Aberdeen, it will be five years ago next month since he came south to try his luck. Where would the danger come from? 'We are the danger,' he says. 'We have to worry about ourselves. If we lose the spirit and desire that we have shown then we will be in trouble.'

Ferguson is said to be a man quick to anger but unlikely to hold a grudge. Usually, it is only his nice side that is on public view. The former United player, Paddy Crerand, tells the story of his son, a United supporter, saying twelve months back that Ferguson should go since the Championship looked unlikely. 'I told him that Alex was a nice man,' said Crerand. 'He said: "Give me a bastard that will win the Championship."'

Surely this time, more than any other time – why was that line from an England World Cup song going through the mind? – United would get it right. After all, their nearest challengers, Leeds, were even more inexperienced novices, having been promoted only at the beginning of the previous season. And other, bigger clubs were struggling: Tottenham, resources stretched, finances thin, were built for Cup competition rather than League; and Everton were floundering if receiving little criticism due to the more surprising strife of their Merseyside neighbours.

The World's Greatest Club was enjoying being top of the first division, the pleasure heightened by the travails of England's Greatest Club.

II The Peeving of Liverpool

It was 2am, but Bruce Grobbelaar could still stand and joke with a group of taxi drivers waiting at Speke Airport in Liverpool for the last flight of the night – or rather the first flight of the morning. Liverpool had just arrived back from France having lost 0–2 to Auxerre and fortunate still to harbour hopes of reaching the third round of the UEFA Cup. It was thanks to the goal-keeping of Grobbelaar that they did.

Grobbelaar is usually the retort to those who talk of the game being devoid of characters these days. Indeed, he does seem to march to a different drum than many. Although frequently described as a clown, for one of the most successful decades in the history of Liverpool he retained his place not only for his acrobatics, but also for his resilience in recovering from his mistakes with neither fuss nor histrionics.

All the while, he has retained his good humour, as could be seen that morning as he stood chatting with people who probably paid good money to watch him of a Saturday, while all about were anxious just to put behind them the bad experiences of the previous evening and get home. For Liverpool, it had been demonstrated, were in a state of confusion the likes of which they had not known for twenty years. No longer did their very name intimidate. Now they looked more vulnerable than anyone could remember.

That much had been evident to us, the attendant press corps covering their return to Europe, some thirty-six hours earlier when they arrived at Speke for the journey to Auxerre. They hardly assembled; for footballers, the rigours of travel are bypassed as they are checked in by a club official, then herded to the departure area to be first on to the chartered aircraft. There have been stories of one player getting up in a departure lounge to go to the toilet and the ten others following him; of players not knowing how to book a holiday or apply for a passport after their playing days were over.

One of the problems for Liverpool this autumn was that they currently had too many whose playing days were just beginning. Who were these young men sporting multi-coloured shell-suits? So that was the young star, Steve McManaman; that was the centre-back, Nicky Tanner. Was Jamie Redknapp going to make his debut? Never can Liverpool have gone into Europe with such an inexperienced team.

How had it come to this? Liverpool had, after all, been famed for the seamless turnover of their teams; where one falls, another takes his place. People have often sought the Liverpool secret; continuity was always one element of it. But when Kenny Dalglish resigned the previous February, it had become clear that the team was growing old together and that several hasty purchases had not rectified the position. Injuries – notably to John Barnes and the £2.2 million signing, Mark Wright – at the beginning of the new season had hardly helped the cause of the new manager, Graeme Souness; but there had always in the past been adequate replacements from the depths of the Liverpool squad.

A ninety-minute flight later, as they sat and waited in a niche of the complex Charles de Gaulle airport in Paris for the rest of us to pick up our bags – theirs, of course, were being taken care of – they seemed without the presence that Liverpool teams of the past had given off. It was here, standing by the carousel, that Souness outlined for the press his thoughts on the forthcoming match. 'I can't go for experience because we haven't got a lot,' he said, pointing out also the limitations imposed by UEFA, the game's governing body in Europe; they had ruled that a team could field only four non-nationals, meaning seven Englishmen. For a club whose first-team roster included Grobbelaar, Nicol, Houghton, Molby, Whelan, Rosenthal, Rush and Saunders – notwithstanding that more than one of these were injured – it was a serious drawback.

Souness still expected his team to react positively to playing in Europe. 'If you can't perform in these circumstances then you shouldn't be in the business,' he added. It was a hint about his own feelings for the job and the attitudes of the squad. For, while Souness was not wishing to upset too much his squad so near to an important match, he had had no such fear in an interview for the French magazine *France Football*, which was published that very day. It was as well that his charges were unaware of its existence.

'Some have been here too long and have become part of the furniture,' he told the magazine. 'Perhaps they are not as professional as they used to be. They will stay for the moment, but I hope to replace them as soon as possible.

'Certain things must change,' he went on; he planned to get back to Liverpool's 'work methods and famous system' by changing some players, bringing new ones in. 'The spirit is not the same, that's for sure. It has been allowed to drop. They are still very good players, but their motivation is no longer the same as before. Their aims have also changed because they are so well installed at the club. They are not hungry any more. I am not going to name the guilty ones,' he said of responsibility for the club's plight. 'But there are a lot of things to do here that should have been done before. I knew that when I took over the job.'

It was Souness the Liverpool manager reflecting Souness the Liverpool player – getting in the early tackle so as to intimidate. 'If he was a chocolate drop he would eat himself,' said a former Scotland team-mate, Archie Gemmill, once. *France Football*, echoing the country's general sense of inferiority when it came to contesting matches against English teams – just like the one the English had against the Germans – did not know whether to believe him. 'Do Auxerre Have A Chance?' they wondered on their cover.

Neither had the town of Auxerre itself, population 60,000, digested Souness's comments, for there was an air of the city slickers hitting hicksville about it. The cobbled streets of the pretty farming town on the edge of Burgundy were a long way from Merseyside in more ways than one. When Liverpool arrived there, at the less-than-pretty Hotel Mercure on the edge of the town after the 100-mile, two-and-a-half-hour coach journey from Paris, their general anonymity took aback several of the local fans who had turned out to greet them. One or two of the accompanying journalists were even asked for their autographs as they stepped off the coach.

This was the point where reality mingled with reputation. It was not uncommon with Liverpool. They had worked for such a reputation for a lot of years. Bill Shankly became manager of second-division Liverpool in 1959, taking them in to the first division as champions in 1962. Two years later, they were League champions and, in the next twenty-seven years, twelve more titles followed to give them a total of eighteen, ten more than the next club, Arsenal. In Europe, though, something was missing. They did reach the final of the Cup-Winners' Cup, in 1966, losing to Borussia Dortmund 1–2 after extra-time at Hampden Park; and, in 1973, they won the UEFA Cup by defeating Borussia Moenchengladbach over two legs. That something, however, was the Champions' Cup, the grail that

Manchester United had claimed and that Liverpool, accordingly, must also have, and more often.

Shankly's road to Damascus turned out to be the 1973–74 competition, when his side were beaten 1–2 at Anfield by Red Star Belgrade, who thus emulated their first-leg score. Shankly was stunned and stung by Red Star's panache, their ability to pass the ball at speed. Thus, legend has it, the following morning in the boot room, the Anfield cubby-hole to which Liverpool's coaching staff traditionally escaped to drink tea and discuss such weighty matters as the state of Tommy Lawrence's waistline – their goalkeeper of the 1960s was nicknamed the Flying Pig – Red Star became the model as Shankly plotted Liverpool's renewed advance on Europe.

Another UEFA Cup came in 1976, and then, finally, the first Champions' Cup in 1977, on a glorious Roman night when Kevin Keegan led Berti Vogts around the Olympic Stadium as if a poodle on a leash, and Borussia Moenchengladbach were defeated 3–1. The following year, Keegan's successor, one Kenneth Dalglish, scored the goal at Wembley that defeated Bruges and brought the trophy once again to Anfield. Another 1–0 victory, over Real Madrid in Paris, earned the trophy in 1981, and the fourth arrived in 1984 when Grobbelaar's knees wobbled but his nerve didn't in a penalty competition against the club hosting the final, Roma.

Having been inspired by a Yugoslavian team, they came to inspire a Yugoslavian team. Said the national team manager in the 1970s, Miljan Miljanic, of Liverpool: 'The team of our time, the ideal model of the contemporary team in which collective qualities have risen above individual qualities, as outstanding as such famous clubs as Real Madrid and Ajax . . . They are admired from Buenos Aires to Belgrade and have given many clubs an inferiority complex.' Such was the baggage that Liverpool took with them around Europe. There was, too, baggage of a more onerous nature.

As the club sought their fifth Champions' Cup in 1985, on the day that Dalglish was named player-manager, a charge of their fans on a group of Juventus supporters at the decrepit Heysel Stadium in Brussels led to the collapse of a wall and the death of thirty-nine spectators, mostly Italian. For six years – serving an extra year beyond other English clubs – they were banned from Europe. They had returned quietly in late summer, in a first-round tie against Kuusysi Lahti of Finland. Auxerre represented their first trip to mainland Europe since that mad May day of 1985.

But, on a damp, chilly Tuesday night in Central France, all was quiet as we scoured the town for authentic French cuisine. The odd fan, in groups of no more than three or four, sat in café or bistro. Auxerre was like that. It was rumoured that most of the support had chosen Paris for the night. For all the rural charm hereabouts, one understood why.

Being a Liverpool supporter was the best and worst of occupations. For years, they trailed from success to success, basking in the reflected glow of their team's achievements. After Heysel, however, revulsion had spread through Europe. Within a sickened England, their stock reached rock-bottom. The folklore that they were charming rogues, or 'scallies', with a penchant for pinching (at Speke there had been the odd joke about the safety of one's car in the car park) was now a myth. Something more serious had replaced that.

France also had good reason to remember them. On a visit in 1977 to St Etienne, many 'supporters' had decided against attending the match, where the bulk of the local police force was deployed, and chose instead to visit un-defended retail establishments in the city centre. In consequence, the mayor of Auxerre had wanted this match transferred to Paris. In his town, however, the good-natured citizens dealt politely with the invaders – *toujours la politesse* – even the 'erewigo' brigade having had one glass of burgundy too much. Even on match-day afternoon, Auxerre supporters had offered to entertain the opposition with a display of flag-waving and singing.

On the Wednesday morning of the match, the Liverpool chief executive, Peter Robinson, pondered a worrying situation, the concern apparent on his face. Auxerre were selling tickets to Liverpool fans, despite having been asked not to. Authorised package tours, by which method the club could monitor their following, were thought to be the only way for supporters to get to see the match. Liverpool had requested 2000 tickets, but Auxerre provided only 700 for the terraces and 150 seats, despite a guarantee from Anfield that they would buy any of those tickets which they could not sell, a policy that had cost them £8000 for their first-round tie in Finland. Auxerre thought they could sell the rest locally; Liverpool were told that UEFA regulations would be followed, that no tickets would be available on the day of the match, and that police would prevent non-ticket holders approaching the stadium. Organised trips were the only way to travel.

Those supporters who toed the line, accompanied by twenty-two of Liverpool's stewards, drew the short straw. They arrived at the ground only an hour or so before kick-off and returned almost immediately after the match. So much for the pleasures and education of travel. Such a voyage numbed rather than broadened the mind.

The players missed all this. After training and lunch in a private dining-room, they retired to bed for the afternoon. A journalistic colleague told of how he had been sitting drinking tea on match-day with Alan Hansen, the former Liverpool defender now retired and working for television. At 5:15pm, his hands began shaking as he looked at his watch. 'This is the time when the players get up,' he explained, the nervousness a legacy of his playing days.

As we arrived at the Abbé Deschamps stadium complex, the extent of the problem was clear. Six companies of the French riot police were in position around the pleasant municipal grounds, whose practice pitches, tennis courts and sports centre put many English facilities to shame. On one pitch were playing two young English players, Kevin Sharpe and Jamie Forrester, who had interestingly chosen to accept the offer of an apprenticeship in Auxerre for the way it might develop their games technically. It was a pity that this scene should be scarred by these riot police, German shepherd dogs at their beck and call. Liverpool had also taken some of the police from back home along; so that's who the men in suits at the back of the press bus were.

Those supporters who had ignored the official channel and found tickets on sale in Auxerre had been more fortunate than their package-tour counterparts in being able to enjoy some time in France. Unwittingly, however, they also contributed to a potentially frightening situation. Auxerre had allocated to Liverpool fans only a small fenced-in pen in a corner of a stadium whose overall aspect resembled a renovated Luton Town, without the gas showrooms that serve as executive boxes at Kenilworth Road. By kick-off, it was estimated that some 1500 were squeezed in there.

'Unnerving' and 'sickening' were just two of the adjectives that Rogan Taylor, former chairman of the Football Supporters' Association and a witness to the Hillsborough disaster of 1989, used to describe what he saw. Thankfully, no one was injured or arrested in the confusion and clamour. But their discomfort was only increased by the Liverpool performance they were to endure. But for Grobbelaar, Liverpool's 0–2 defeat would have been doubled. At the other end, his counterpart, Martini, was neither shaken nor stirred.

Liverpool sought desperately to relearn the old European technique of quelling the crowd's ardour with possession football, thus hoping also to douse the home side's fire. For the purpose, Souness employed a five-man midfield in which the 18-year-old Redknapp, a £350,000 Dalglish signing from Bournemouth, made his debut. Due to the rule that only four non-English players could be fielded, the £2.9 million signing from Derby County, Dean Saunders, was omitted.

Redknapp and his not-so-famous five were ultimately swamped, however, as Auxerre revealed a swiftness, especially through their wingers, Cocard and Vahirua, that was to outstrip Liverpool. The inevitable goal came after forty-two minutes, when Ferreri's neat one-two with the Hungarian striker, Kovacs, led to the Frenchman driving home a low shot. With Liverpool's best defender, Steve Nicol, prevented from playing the second half due to a pulled hamstring, a second goal was equally inevitable: it came on the hour when Cocard's cross eluded the hesitant Ablett and Tanner in the heart of the Liverpool defence, and Kovacs stole in to slam past Grobbelaar.

Liverpool's plight recalled the guide-book description of Auxerre and its Gothic cathedral of St Etienne, where the bishop St Germain is buried. 'Every year, on 31 July, there is a procession when the saint's relics are exposed.' Another procession this October had also exposed some relics.

The journey by coach to Charles de Gaulle immediately after the match – neither time nor inclination, it seems, for players these days to linger and exhange notes and conversation with foreign opponents – and thence to Speke was marked by a silent fatigue and wounded pride. In Paris, young Redknapp smiled with the optimism of youth, supped a soft drink and said, yes, he had enjoyed his night and thought Liverpool could do it in the second leg. Back at Speke, Grobbelaar said the same things to his taxi drivers. We cynics kept our counsel and mutely disagreed.

But, wouldn't you know, Liverpool did win the second leg 3–0, thanks largely to Anfield being at its noisiest and most atmospheric, even if nowhere near full. After Molby's third-minute penalty, 'you could see the fear in their eyes,' said Liverpool's Mark Walters, whose goal was the clincher after Mark Wright had added a second. So the Auxerre manager, Guy Roux, was being prophetic when he said before the first leg that: 'The intensity of the English game frightens me.' He runs his own insurance business in the town; he should have taken out a policy.

The win gave Souness occasion to berate 'so-called experts' who had been questioning Liverpool's current condition. He was forgetting that he himself had done just such a thing in France a fortnight earlier. And he would do the same thing again a month later as Liverpool lost 0–1 to third-division Peterborough in a League Cup tie, a Grobbelaar eccentricity deciding the match.

For, deep down, Souness knew that England's most successful club was in turmoil, not only due to injuries. He would need to work hard if the sign over the players' tunnel at their home ground which reads 'This Is Anfield' was not to be changed to employ the past tense.

iii Gunners Goners

Manchester United may be revered and Liverpool admired, but Arsenal are usually begrudged any success they achieve – outside certain pockets of the Home Counties, that is. They are seen as the model of overprivileged metropolitan haughtiness. 'Arsenal – A Nation Mourns' was the ironic headline in the *Guardian* newspaper after a cup defeat in the early 1980s.

It has been thus for a long time, certainly since before the Second World War. Admirers point to dignity, quality and success; detractors to snootiness, luck or tedium, and also, in recent years, disciplinary infringements that have undermined the image. Of the admirers, it was probably the England cricketer, Brian Close, who best summed up the club after his spell with them in the early 1950s: 'The place was like a palace. You were immediately conscious of belonging to something really, really important. Everyone at Highbury lived, breathed, talked, ate and drank Arsenal. Everyone believed in the club; everyone was proud to be part of it. It was just like playing cricket for Yorkshire.'

Times change, both in London and, even if less quickly, in Yorkshire. But perhaps there is envy at the root of the distaste for Arsenal, although the distaste had grown this season owing nothing to envy; their new away shirts of green triangles (supposedly an A) on yellow were a cacophony of mawkishness. 'They look like kitchen curtains,' said the television commentator, Brian Moore, not usually noted for his outspoken or controversial views.

Envy, though, there was. Arsenal had, after all, been frustrating opponents for so long; now there were sidelong glances for them again from other clubs, as they were the first English team allowed back in the European Cup after the lifting of the ban post-Heysel. It was time to find out where our champions stood among the continent's best. European football is a bonus to the English game, producing an atmosphere on match nights rich in anticipation, richer than usual for an evening kick-off. So it was at Highbury, the bowl of a stadium in a valley of North London, as Arsenal prepared to take on Benfica of Portugal, a club redolent of European tradition, a name with which fans of a certain age grew up.

The crisp November night was filled with breath steaming into the air, as the residential streets thronged with even more people than usually followed the League champions. The sight of the floodlights quickens the step, as people hurry to be part of the atmosphere. In Highbury's case, it is just a pall of white against the black of the sky in the distance; their lights are lined up along the roof of each stand so as not to offend the skyline of the London Borough of Islington.

That the expectation was heightened was due to Arsenal having drawn 1–1 in Lisbon in the first leg and being on the threshold of the last eight which, for the first time, would be split into two leagues of four, the winners going into the final. It meant some £2 million in extra revenue with three home matches guaranteed. That, however, was to trivialise the glory, which the Arsenal manager, George Graham, did not. With pictures of past managers in his office, from the ground-breaking Herbert Chapman – who had London Transport name the nearby, claustrophobic, tube station after the club for publicity purposes – onwards,

Graham was aware of the gilded baton he was carrying. He could become perhaps the most famous of them all with a European Cup win.

Highbury's press room was crowded with Portuguese journalists, some wearing Arsenal scarves to keep out the cold of autumn – or perhaps as one-upmanship street fashion for their return to the white city. They chattered and smoked, bringing an unusual, vibrant air to the place. They even formed a wall in front of the television screen on which Liverpool were playing their second leg against Auxerre. You wanted Stuart Pearce to line up a free-kick in here to disperse them.

But, really, their presence was welcomed. They were representative of European soccer as a whole, a different approach, a different perspective. Europe had missed the English clubs, we were constantly told and, indeed, so we assumed. But England had missed the European clubs, too. Just how much was about to unfold.

Benfica bowed to the Arsenal crowd before the game, but not to its team during it. The Eagles from the Stadium of Light entered the stadium of might that is Highbury and gave, ultimately, a demonstration of why might is not always right. Arsenal sought, in the modern phrase made popular by Jack Charlton during his stewardship of the Republic of Ireland, to inflict their game on the opposition. Instead, it was Benfica who imposed their talent. Before the night was out, a variation on the theme of English steel v. Continental style, and which was the better, was blowing in the North London wind.

There was little hint of it to begin with, as Arsenal, all muscle and bustle, ran the early exchanges. Kevin Campbell hit a post; the effervescent Paul Merson won a corner, from which the defender, Colin Pates, bundled home his first goal for the club after a bout of the flaps from the Portuguese goal-keeper, Neno. Soon after, though, the striker, Yuran, flicked on Neno's long clearance and Isaias, Brazilian-born but Portuguese-qualified by marriage, volleyed home a splendid equaliser from thirty yards. The Arsenal-like move had taken two seconds. The sound was of a petard being hoisted. 'Goooooooooooooooool,' bellowed the Portuguese radio commentator into his microphone in the press box.

An absorbing second half failed to yield a goal, although it was the Portuguese who looked the stronger as Arsenal's demanding game took its toll on them. Even so, in extra-time, Smith should have scored, Merson might have and Campbell could have before Isaias crossed for Yuran to lay off to another Soviet, Kulkov, to shoot home low. Tony Adams then hit a post as his team again spurned easy chances, before Isaias tiptoed through the rooted, wilting flowers in Arsenal's defence to make it 3–1. Technique and tactics had overcome commitment and clamour; and the argument previously enacted between England and Germany had brought its salient points to bear at club level.

The two managers were illuminating, in their differing ways. 'Physically, they were stronger than us but, on the ground, we were the better team with the better technique,' said Benfica's coach, the well-respected Swede, Sven-Goran Eriksson. 'We did the right job tactically and technically. If we had been playing the way that we can we would have won,' Graham insisted. However, both men conceded the virtue of each other's approach. 'For twelve to fifteen years, I have been a great admirer of English football,' said Eriksson. 'I like the mentality of always attacking.' 'Lovely to watch,' was Graham's generous verdict on the Benfica forward line, particularly Yuran and Isaias.

To suggest, though, that either approach was mutually exclusive, or better, seemed simplistic. They seemed rather different products of culture and climate. 'We are among the strongest in Europe for technique,' said Mr Eriksson. 'It

is an old influence from Brazil.' Arsenal under Graham
meanwhile had sought to ally the long with the short ball,
pace with power, talent with attitude – and even in the
American sense of meanness, given their goals-against and
disciplinary records, of the previous season at least. Skill,
after all, does not alone win football matches. And, for the
first half-hour, Arsenal's approach had been vindicated. It
was the purple patch that turns green with envy the England manager, Graham Taylor, who would seek to recreate
it at international level, even if it might be questionable
in the inevitable hot conditions of an end-of-season finals
tournament. But then, Arsenal's first wind gone, Benfica
got hold of the ball and seized their chance. Strategically,
Arsenal were out-thought with the move of the Soviet full-
back, Kulkov, forward into midfield – a turning-point that
Arsenal did not adequately counter.

The undermining of Arsenal, however, went deeper than
just a matter of style. Graham's argument was that Benfica
can remain fresh for Europe because of the comparatively
undemanding opposition in their domestic league. But how
does a team gobble up gourmet food having been fed a
diet of domestic dross? What, then, of Rangers, currently
perennial European failures, but still unchallenged in Scotland? And what, then, of Italian clubs, constantly playing
top-quality opposition and still bringing home the European bacon? Graham did, however, have a point about the
volume of competition inflicted on English clubs: it is not
that a reduction in intensity would necessarily improve the
ability to compete in Europe of England's better clubs, but
rather the number of occasions on which they are expected
to reproduce that intensity.

Graham was also undoubtedly right when he said that a
fresher Arsenal would not have looked so outclassed by the
end of the match, that a suspect Benfica goal-keeper and
defence would have been more consistently tested. It does

not help his cause, however, when England's top clubs, those who opt out of the less significant competitions such as the Full Members' Cup, seek lucrative friendlies in far-flung places whenever free dates appear on their calendar.

Graham was convinced that his team's way of playing was true to the English psyche. He believes it is possible to sustain a challenge for the European Cup with such an exhaustive style over a long season, given fewer matches. Not for him the change that Bill Shankly imposed on Liverpool, which turned them into the phenomenally successful role-model hybrid of English approach and European sophistication. Nor for Graham the self-doubt that Graeme Souness voiced when at Rangers. 'No, because then you are saying you are going to try and copy the Continentals, and they have got a head start on us on the skill factor.'

Although Graham's other decisions have frequently been proved right in the face of criticism – of buying so many tall centre-backs, of buying too many strikers, of not buying – he might well have dwelt profitably on Benfica's virtues of patience and tactical flexibility, changing of pace and the need to rethink as well as rerun when avenues become blind. But, instead of looking to adopt and modify in the wake of lessons learnt, the Arsenal answer was merely to add to existing assets. That it was spluttering even domestically had been demonstrated by League Cup defeat at Coventry on the night we ran into Bobby Moore.

It was, after all, Benfica who joined the last eight to generate the millions, ranging from escudos to roubles, in the two mini-leagues. The list – Anderlecht of Belgium, Barcelona, Sampdoria of Italy, Dynamo Kiev, Sparta Prague, Red Star Belgrade, Panathinaikos of Greece and Benfica – did not unreservedly please the television schedulers, nor indeed viewers, since there were no representatives from the lucrative markets of England, France, Holland and Germany.

Arsenal and, indeed, English football and its followers would still have done well to follow it all closely.

There were, though, other matches to be viewed. For winter was drawing in, and it was time to retreat inside temporarily, to get back to the enduring excitement of the domestic game. Television, the new king – or rather dictator – of the game, may not have been best pleased with the outcome of European competitions concerning British clubs, but there was still the home service.

Winter

Five: TV Times

1 Backdrop

A football administrator was once musing on the most important figure in the game. He was not a player, nor a manager. He was a chairman but not of a club, the Football League or the Football Association. He was the chief executive of London Weekend Television. His name was Greg Dyke and, as chairman also of Independent Television Sport, he had given £44 million to the League for a four-year contract to broadcast live matches.

Such is the power wielded by television these days, mostly because of the money they are prepared to advance the sport. It is personified by the TV man who stands on the touchline at half-way when a live, televised match is taking place, and signals to the referee when he may begin the game. For TV can decide when matches will be played and at what time they will kick off. Not for nothing was a fan magazine written around oft-televised Liverpool known as *When Sunday Comes*, since the club was so frequently pulled out of the Saturday programme to make the Sunday schedule.

The attending fans, as opposed to the armchair breed, are football's biggest source of revenue but are accorded only a semblance of respect, simply because it is assumed they will continue to spend because they always have done. Corporate sponsors and especially television are more fickle, and therefore command more attention from the game's administrators.

The formation of the Premier League for the 1992–93 season had been outlined by the FA in their Blueprint for the Future of Football in a blaze of money. The new competition, they said, would generate £112 million a season for the clubs involved. And it emerged that £40 million of this was expected to come from the television companies. Given that the figure was more than double what football was currently receiving, it seemed somewhat fanciful. But then the game had constantly undervalued itself, many said, including Robert Maxwell when he first burst on to its scene. It was probably the only thing he ever got right about it.

In the 1991–92 season, football was receiving some £17 million for the year, with £11 million going to the Football League from ITV for League and League Cup matches, and £6 million to the FA from the BBC and the satellite station, BSkyB – a merger of Sky and British Satellite Broadcasting – for the FA Cup and England games. Those representing the new Premier League wanted to involve them all in a new deal, incorporating also the Sportscast network, who provided televised events for pubs and clubs paying subscriptions. That foundered, however, when the company went bust during the season.

Instead, the Premier League thought, why shouldn't they all share a package over the weekend, which would also take in Monday games, thus maximising income. The BBC could have highlights on a Saturday night; ITV the pick of the weekend's programme for live transmission on a Sunday afternoon; and BSkyB would get the live Monday night game. The theory was ignorant of the politics of television, however. ITV could never get into bed with BSkyB, who were competing for the the same advertising revenue. Exclusivity was their main aim.

The non-commercial BBC could, though; they wanted League football back on their schedules, for all their successful FA Cup coverage. With no film of the League, they were unable to provide a proper preview of a Saturday lunchtime, when all are tuning in while tuning up for their afternoon's entertainment. And football itself wanted *Match of the Day* back to alleviate a feeling of regret at the passing of Saturday night highlights in these days of live conquering all. As Brian Barwick, the BBC's football editor, put it: 'ITV throw away the best part of the product in six minutes at the end of their programme on a Sunday,' referring to their short sequence of goals scored in the first division the previous day.

There was also a problem for the proposed Premier League in fitting in its scenario. Who would play when? Which teams would play on Mondays, in advance of a new week of fixtures beginning on a Tuesday and a Wednesday – with European games now to be accommodated as well as more England qualifying matches for the World Cup? The Football League left behind by the Premier clubs would also want a piece of the action; it was quite likely that the second division, destined to become the first, would attract TV time, money and resources too. But when would their live match be played? On a Friday night?

It was all a mixed blessing for the fan. The committed travelling supporter would be further inconvenienced by rearranged kick-off days and times. The armchair fan might be overwhelmed by it all. And therein lay another problem. Although viewing figures were not yet reflecting it, there was a perception within the medium that snooker was going through overkill on TV, that viewers were bored by so much of it. The worry was that too much football would lead to a turn-off and, with it, a decrease in attendances. For the current view was that a limited amount of coverage enhanced the product – a word football administrators had taken to using about the game – and increased attendances, rather than leading to people staying away.

Clearly TV wanted, even needed, the Premier League in particular and football in general. It was a relatively cheap, if progressively more expensive way of achieving good ratings. The most momentous game in its four years, Liverpool v. Arsenal in 1989 when Michael Thomas stole the title for London, attracted 10.3 million viewers. The average was around 7 million. But it was a question of whether the Premier League needed TV more than TV needed the Premier League; that would be the crucial issue of brinkmanship in any negotiations at the end of the season.

In February, ITV would hint at an offer of £20 million a season, backed by the satellite station, Screensport – less a British competitor, more a European network. It was an interesting opening shot. The Premier League's founders, though, wanted more money, of course, and were also unsure whether ITV had sufficient broadcasting time available to show the spin-off programmes, such as coaching clinics and chat shows, which they wanted to enhance the game's image.

But they were already having trouble with that image. Such was football's feeling for commerce that it had announced its Premier League at the outset of the 1991–92 season without having anyone in place to negotiate with the television companies. Only in December was Sir John Quinton, chairman of Barclays Bank, appointed as non-executive figurehead of the League, and a chief executive, Rick Parry, followed only after a squabble with club chairmen over how much power he should have.

It was a tangled web that would not be untangled until season's end. But the debate that would be returned to several times during it indicated just how serious was the role that television could play. It was worth seeing what all the fuss was about . . .

11 Public Service

Desmond Lynam sits back, arms behind head, makes himself as comfortable as it is possible to be in standard office furniture, and eyes the entertainment on offer on the screens confronting him in the sports production office of the BBC. 'I call this Cliché Saturday,' he says with that familiar-to-the-nation smile which alters for the better the droop of his moustache.

Indeed, the first round proper of the FA Cup is one of the eight most enjoyable days in the domestic game's calendar, especially so the longer your team stays in it. It is the day when the butchers, bakers and candlestick-makers – or, these days, the computer engineers, the insurance agents and the leisure-centre managers – step out of the pages of their local papers into the national press, and even on to television.

It is the November day when journalists who ordinarily know a little better indulge their craft along the lines that Lynam is thinking: 'Livewire electrician Dave Smith sparked non-League minnows Rutland as the lights went out for third-division giants Anytown . . .' Later, Anytown will themselves become minnows, when they are drawn against first-division giants Anycity. Still, it could be worse; there was the man who began his report from the World Cup with 'Minnows United States of America . . .'

The smaller clubs publicly tolerate being patronised for

the thrill and exposure it can give them. Privately, though, they sometimes resent it for, although theirs may not be a big business, it is a serious one. But they love the television cameras. Today, the BBC's will be at Gretna v. Rochdale and Colchester v. Exeter; the matches were chosen by the editor, Brian Barwick, and his assistant, Niall Sloane, who sit here today in the office on the second floor of the Beeb's headquarters in Shepherd's Bush, West London. Together with Lynam and the producer, Vivien Kent, they are surveying the afternoon for editing into a one-hour slot for *Match of the Day* tonight.

It will be a long day for them. They are here before lunchtime riveted to the screens – 'you should see it on third-round day when all the big games are going on, it's even more wonderful,' says Barwick. He is a genial giant of a Merseysider and a football enthusiast, an attribute he shares with all here. The empty paper coffee cups testify to the time and effort put in to making a silk purse out of what can be a sow's ear on such a day of varying quality of football and coverage from small grounds all over the country. Or even another country.

Gretna of the Northern League, for example, will accommodate them today with a band of bagpipes, who will pipe out for use at the end of tonight's programme the *Match of the Day* theme – the one that goes da, da, da, da, da-da, da, da, da; da, da, da-da, da, da. Or did before those ill winds that nobody blows good got at it. The club were chosen for several reason. There is the potential for an upset, but also the televisual potential; Gretna Green is, of course, that town just over the border famous for eloping English couples seeking to take advantage of more relaxed Scottish marriage laws.

And it is the first time a Scottish team has reached the first round of the English FA Cup since Queen's Park of Glasgow more than a century ago. 'Oh no, it's not,' says

Barry Davies, the terrestrial TV football commentator with the best vocabulary, whose voice has come over the line from tiny Raydale Park and out via a speaker in this office. It quite takes aback the unwary. A spectator has informed him of another, he says. The historian and statistician, Albert Sewell, is then dispatched to check it out. He duly discovers that, in 1890–91, the 93rd Highlanders were beaten 0–2 by Sunderland Albion. Thus are the BBC denied a piece of the history they so enjoy being a part of. Accuracy, though, is crucial for their image as a reliable station of record. Ask anyone around the world.

It is possible to criticise the BBC's football coverage for a variety of reasons. There is loathe-him-or-hate-him Jimmy Hill (actually, whisper it, but some of us almost like him for taking the risk of honesty) and some staid production values, although the defence would call them traditional and quality. And there is the over-researched and over-earnest commentary of John Motson, or that over-clichéd by Tony Gubba, even if today, by Lynam's criterion, he might come into his own. But they do continually show a commitment to sport, and football is no exception. Their coverage of the FA Cup has won them many friends within the game and considerable sympathy from supporters, who are willing to forgive them much.

It was thought that, when ITV won their four-year, £44 million contract for League football, the impoverished Beeb would be left with little. They had, though, with the aid of satellite television, struck that five-year, £30 million deal with the Football Association for the Cup and England matches. Out of weakness had come strength. It was said within football that the BBC had got the better deal. And by showing the Cup from the first round – doing what Barwick calls a 'real BBC job' – they had earned that approval from the game. At this stage of the competition, the viewing figures may only be some 4 to 5 million compared to 15 million for the final; but they are building up the competition from the one figure so that it will lead to the other.

Today, they will be unlucky. Neither Gretna and Rochdale nor Colchester and Exeter produce a goal between them. 'Make a name for yourself,' pleads Barwick as he watches locally famous, nationally unknown strikers bearing down on goal. None does. At Layer Road they have McDonough – player-manager Roy – but need more Maradona.

Names do emerge, though. Craig Whittington has turned again to score twice for Crawley as they beat Northampton 4–2; Lynam can remember playing with his dad, Jack, in Sussex football. Whittington fils is an unemployed builder rejected by Torquay – by the club for his footballing skills, that is, not by the seaside town for his labouring skills. In addition, Paul Brush's goal for Enfield has swept aside Aldershot.

'I bet we'll have more than 50 goals on the programme,' says Barwick with that football follower's always-look-on-the-bright-side-of-life philosophy, the one that involves shovelling a huge pile of manure on the basis that there must be a pony in there somewhere. Barwick is right: there will be 51 goals in the hour. For they have cameras stationed at twenty other matches to capture relevant action and, most important, the goals. They also have a reporter with Lincoln United as they play in the first round for the first time, at Huddersfield where they will lose 0–6 but bank a packet from their share of a gate of 6763.

The chairman of Lincoln betrays his roots, insisting on calling this stage the first round proper, stressing the word proper: he is more used to first round qualifying. He will also tell the reporter, Ray Stubbs, how the directors had a whip-round amongst themselves to raise the entry fee for the FA Cup – £75, and they were one of 558 entries for the

1991–92 season – despite some dissent within the club that they might be wasting their money. It will need a few takes, though, so nervous is the chairman as he is interviewed on the team bus.

Now, at 5pm, Lynam, Barwick, Sloane and Kent sit down to work on the introduction to the programme – in effect, what Lynam will say. Then the laid-back Lynam will pop home to nearby Acton to lay back for an hour. 'Des always appears unflappable but he does get tense,' explains Sloane. Meanwhile, downstairs in the BBC's basement, at the coal-face of television, the videotape department is mining the rich seam. Their job is to gather in all the footage from around the country and cut it together as requested by the editorial team. Barwick has started by asking them to pro-duce packages of eighteen minutes from the two matches covered. In addition, tapes of the 51 goals – I counted them in and I counted them out – are being relayed from regional studios from Newcastle to Plymouth.

There is Slough v. Reading, for example, the non-League team scoring twice in the last five minutes to force a 3–3 draw. 'Serves Reading right for wearing table-cloths instead of shirts,' says a videotape operator of the third-division side's red-and-white chequered outfit. 'If anyone went home with ten minutes to go, well, sod 'em,' the Slough manager, Alan Davies, was to say. Davies's full-time job is working for a company who make ejector seats. He might thus be well qualified for League management, an occupa-tion in which they seem commonplace. And, instead of John Betjeman's friendly bombs falling on Slough, the cameraman has captured a spectacular sunset. 'Let's keep that in. I'm all for art in football,' says a tape editor.

It is now 9:30pm, time to grab a quick bite to eat in one of the BBC's much-lambasted canteens. Think twice before ordering the steak and kidney pie. The real fun is in observ-ing the various characters wandering in from filming around the building; extras from a Second World War comedy programme, men in dinner jackets next to cleaners. It is almost as weird and wonderful as the first round of the FA Cup.

Then it is time to go to the studio, if it can be found through the BBC's rabbit-warren network of corridors. People must surely have missed their cues on live programmes over the years. Once there, it has all the atmosphere of an aircraft hangar but it illustrates the magic of television: all the viewer will see is Lynam, the programme's guest, and a rather clever footballing mural that serves as a backdrop. With less than an hour to on-air time, though, there is as yet no sign of the guest. Perhaps he is negotiating that rabbit warren.

Then Gary Lineker bowls in, his problem having been outside rather than inside the Beeb. It is difficult to comprehend that England's captain – scorer in midweek against Poland of the goal that took his country to the European Championship finals – and Cup-winner the previous year with Tottenham, can get caught in traffic on the Westway flyover from Central out to West London like the rest of us. But then it is said that the Royal family goes to the toilet.

There is another reason why he is late. He had forgotten when he stepped out of his house near Lord's cricket ground the winners' medal that the programme has asked him to bring in, and he had to go back for it. Some of us would probably never let it out of our sight; but then such apparent casualness has served Lineker well in penalty areas around the world.

'Anything happened?' he enquires and is told of Crawley's exploits. 'Ah, creepy Crawley,' comes his reply. He tells of his side's narrow win over bottom-of-the-League Luton in the first division that afternoon, and of the million-pound transfer that tomorrow's Sunday papers will reveal, to the Japanese club, Grampus Eight. He will also talk about his Tottenham and England colleague, Paul Gascoigne's latest escapade in a Newcastle night-club – one that ended with his knee further damaged and his recovery put back. Gazza's penchant for flamboyant cocktails while wanting people not to notice him is somewhat at odds, Lineker opines.

Lynam stores all this up and will ask about it later on the programme. He does not ask about the anecdote that Lineker has in the past swapped with a smile when reminded of it; about the time Gascoigne and he are out for a quiet drink in London's West End late at night, when Gazza hails a bus and requests it to take them to Lineker's home, which is not on main road nor bus route. It does, with the passengers' consent, and Gascoigne sitting up front singing: 'We're all going on a summer holiday.'

Upstairs in the gallery, the control area for the pro-gramme, they are ready to roll. Vivien Kent checks with her vision mixers, the people who cue at her command the pictures she wishes you to see, as she looks over the bank of screens. 'Do you understand what's going on?' inquires the genial Barwick and, when he gets a nodded acknowl-edgement, replies: 'You couldn't tell me, could you?' For live, immediate television, it is all remarkably relaxed, even if there is serious concentration in the air.

Lynam's intro is sharp, simple and sounds very good. 'This is how the FA Cup's Road to Wembley ended last season,' he says over film of Spurs lifting the trophy. 'And England's hero for the week is with us to enjoy the action as we set out on the Road to Wembley again with round one. John Aldridge, like Gary Lineker, has the goal-scoring touch: 299 in first-class football before today. Aldridge played for Tranmere Rovers against Runcorn. Yes, Tran-mere are in division two but, like Grimsby, they had to take part in the first round to make the numbers right.'

Over film of Leeds United being on the end of an oft-quoted upset he continues: 'Colchester United once had some famous names on the receiving end in the Cup. Currently the top non-League team, Colchester were up against third-division Exeter. We follow City and United – Lincoln City and Lincoln United – involved together in round one for the first time. We'll see who of the non-Leaguers could emulate Hayes, who last night beat Fulham. Jimmy Hill is almost speechless – a first.'

Then it is Gretna's turn. 'Once upon a time, a Scottish team got to the final of the FA Cup, Queen's Park. Today, a Scottish team played in the competition proper for the first time this century – Gretna.' The programme does have some slant on history after all. 'There's a tradition in the town of Gretna for matches other than football' are the words above those pictures of the wedding that has been filmed in the town earlier today. 'Mr and Mrs Walker had an early morning result there,' says Lynam, who then departs from his first script. 'Good evening, and if they are watching – why?'

Perhaps his original 'That's one we can't bring you the latest score in,' was deemed too risqué.

Lineker, although he has a barely discernible tick in his right eye, proves himself as relaxed as Lynam appears, and articulate in front of the cameras. Tony Gubba's comment that Aldridge 'knows where the goals are' provokes him into remarking, that mischievous little grin playing on his lips: 'They never move, which helps.'

By midnight, it is all over, to relief that it has all gone so smoothly – apart from the merest glitch when a picture appears seconds after it should have, leaving just a short interval – but also a tinge of sadness that there is no more. Lineker attracts glances and requests for autographs as he moves through the BBC reception area with Lynam, Barwick, Sloane and Kent out into the cold night towards a now-clear Westway.

A life in the day of television, a life in the day of the FA Cup, has come and gone, the one mirroring the other: ever fraught, ever fascinating. The Hereford manager, John Sillett, a winner with Coventry in 1987, whose new team had survived a tricky tie at Atherstone, drawing 0–0, has summed it up quite well: 'Playing in the Cup is like making love to a hedgehog – prickly and pretty risky at the best of times.'

But then, the best things in life involve taking a few risks.

III Independent Day

The streets of Birmingham are Sunday-morning quiet as the drizzle smears the tarmac. However, at the city's premier football ground – these days, at least – there is already a bustle of activity four hours before kick-off.

When you have found Villa Park, that is, no easy task given the fiendish one-way systems and motorways with no exits. With Aston Villa now being managed by the man with the golden bracelets, Ron Atkinson, it is tempting to follow the city-centre signs for the Jewellery Quarter.

Villa Park is one of those grounds where the waifs lie in wait, even this early in the day. You look around as you step from your car having parked it in the streets surrounding the ground when, out of nowhere, come the dreaded words in high-pitched voice: 'Mind your car, mister?' It is actually more of a threat than a question. It is strange how a 12-year-old boy can have such power over a grown man. For you know that failure to agree to the lad 'looking after' your car is to risk it having a dent put in it. So, in exchange for their benevolence in not doing so, you lay out the going rate, which is usually 50p up front and 50p on your return; in London, naturally, the price is doubled. You hope that, by the time you do get back, they will have become bored or tired or both and given up waiting for you.

The club car park is, of course, off-limits to us plebeians. Not only is it reserved for the Mercedes of players' agents and the Vauxhall Novas of players' wives, today it is also host to the equipment of Independent Television, who are putting out live Aston Villa v. Leeds United.

The executive producer, Trevor East, is sitting in one of the pantechnicons that house the production facilities, called a scanner. He is contemplating an article in one of the Sunday papers which describes them as having been lucky in selecting a game which features the team in fourth place in the first division hosting the one in second. 'There is nothing lucky about it,' says East. 'It was good judgement.'

ITV have to choose three matches from which their live game will be drawn ten weeks in advance; the final choice is made a month before. Their contract with the Football League enables them to show seventeen a season, three of which they may pull out of the schedule and rearrange for when it suits them. Their most celebrated success in so doing was when they realised quite early on in the 1988–89 season that Liverpool and Arsenal would be the two dominant teams, and put on the game between the two in May as the last of the season. Liverpool could afford to lose by a goal and would still win the Championship; Arsenal had to win by 2. Michael Thomas's goal in injury-time in front of an open-mouthed television audience of more than 10 million gave Arsenal a 2–0 win and the title.

The job of East, a surprisingly insouciant man considering that he is a Derby County supporter – indeed, a former director, pre-Robert Maxwell's ownership of the club – as well as working in television, is to smooth the day's operation. And he is a smooth operator. He will liaise with both the club officials and ITV's production team to ensure that everyone is happy, or at least not unhappy.

At midday, his presence is requested by the Aston Villa chairman, Doug Ellis. Or rather, he is summoned. It does not really do to ignore Deadly Doug, as he is known by most people within the game, at least behind his back. He was, it is said, angry when he first heard it uttered on television by Jimmy Greaves, but mellowed when he realised that it was on the lips of many of the good folk of Birmingham, thus increasing his celebrity. For he is said to enjoy celebrity, notoriety even. Low-profile is not really his preferred style; outside in the car park is his blue Rolls Royce with a number plate declaring AV1. The question when Graham Taylor took on the Aston Villa job two seasons earlier had not been whether he could manage the team but whether he could manage Doug Ellis.

'He's a pussycat, really,' says East with a smile as he negotiates the reception desk – that most fearsome and impenetrable part of any football club, although the switchboard can run it close – in Villa's newish red-brick office buildings under the South Stand, all functional and club crest on the claret and blue carpet. A receptionist seeks briefly to stop him, but a special, exclusive pass and the magic word 'television' does the open-sesame trick. East stops off at the office of the club secretary, Steven Stride, to check whether there will be any personalities at the match, besides Doug Ellis, on whom perhaps to train a camera or even interview. 'Nigel Kennedy, maybe?' he asks. But Villa's best known supporter of these days, the violin player who has somehow acquired a cockney accent to go with his punk haircut, will not be here. 'He might turn up at 10 to 3 wanting four tickets,' says Stride. 'But he probably thought the match was yesterday.'

Then it is in to Ellis's office, spacious and dark-wood opulent. On the wall is a framed picture of him holding up for show a 27lb salmon. He sits behind his desk, pen poised, all largesse and monogrammed silk shirt: HDE – Harold Doug Ellis – it declares. 'Of course, I have always been in favour of live television. It enhances the game,' he says after offering a drink. Phew, it is a social visit. 'Someone is selling your ITV *Match* magazine on the streets next to our programmes,' he goes on to East. Ah, this is not a social visit. East replies that it has nothing to do with ITV; Ellis says that this is not his information. The Villa underling who told the chairman is summoned; the underling insists he said Villa would be selling them, and perhaps Mr Ellis misheard. Mr Ellis said he did not, he was told ITV were selling them. The underling is, of course, wrong and will not do it again.

East now takes in the rest of the ground, first eyeing the camera positions. There are fourteen cameras in all, ten full-sized ones trained on the pitch, two miniatures in the back of the goal-nets, and two in a studio set up in one of Villa's executive boxes. There sit today's guest summariser, Trevor Francis, the current manager of Sheffield Wednesday – where he replaced Ron Atkinson – and *The Match*'s host, the small but perfectly formed Elton Welsby. 'We have done a lot of work with him, helping him to relax,' says East.

Then it is back to the public relations business. East takes a quick drink in the sponsors' bar, where he is buttonholed by two Leeds United directors dictating to him the reasons why their match over the Christmas period with Manchester United should be televised live, rather than the Everton v. Liverpool game. With £175,000 payable by ITV to the host club as a 'facility' fee, the lobbying is worthwhile. East soon makes his excuses and leaves, politely, of course. ITV will indeed pick Leeds's match as their festive live game, although dull, mid-table Everton will receive coverage twice later in the season.

The arguments over which clubs are chosen for live broadcasts are tiresome to East. 'We sometimes feel we cannot win with our match selection,' he says. Before Christmas, they are concentrating on the developing League Championship conflict between Manchester United and Leeds; after it, they will broaden their coverage. Both

approaches are criticised, mostly by clubs such as, and supporters of, Wimbledon, Luton and Notts County. 'We are
offering what we believe is the best of English football, and
so it would be perverse if we ignored the teams that were
doing well,' says East.

They also, clearly, choose the grounds most able to house
their technical operation and offer them comfortable facilities. And they go where the people are 'media friendly'. At
Villa, Ron Atkinson and his assistant, the Sky Television
colour man, Andy Gray, give the cameras free access, even
in this dressing-room area. There, now, Atkinson is taking
aside the Villa striker, Ian Olney, to explain to him why he
is not playing – 'and I don't usually do that.' It is a chaotic
scene, with people milling all over, as Villa go through an
aerobic routine. 'I don't know what the game is coming to,'
says, observing the effort, Gary Lineker, that well-known
television personality who has now arrived to accompany
today's commentator, Alan Parry, on the gantry. Lineker is
known in the game as a conserver of energy anywhere other
than on the pitch.

Lineker now here, it is time for all the ITV team to con-
vene a meeting, held over coffee and sandwiches in the
players' bar, to go through the afternoon's running order. It
should all be straightforward enough, beginning with a
taped interview between Welsby and Francis wondering if
they might get some goals today after the two previous live
matches this season, Manchester United v. Liverpool and
West Ham v. Liverpool, have both finished goalless. It will
end with the six-minute package of goals from the previous
day's first-division matches.

In between, there will be some of Gary Newbon, perhaps
the most controversial figure in British sports television
now that Jimmy Hill is in the twilight of his popularity.
Newbon, head of sport at Central TV in Birmingham but
'merely' a reporter with the network, is seen by many as a

buffoon, intruding with his live interviews that ask banal questions and get banal answers. There was once a time when he was interviewing a manager whose team he thought had lost, but had in fact drawn with a late goal that Newbon missed in his scurry for the dressing-room. There are even those who are grateful for a 0–0 result since it can often mean that there is no one really for him to interview.

Newbon's work in boxing has drawn no less criticism. His ringside interview with Chris Eubank, who suggested that his opponent might be on some sort of drugs, the night this September that Michael Watson slumped to the canvas with a blood clot pressing on his brain, was the final straw for many. A subsequent British Boxing Board of Control ruling which banned the immediate interview at the end of future fights was clearly aimed at Newbon.

The editor of *The Match*, Jeff Farmer, a former newspaper journalist, defends him. 'I would hope Gary asks the two questions that people at home would ask,' he says. 'People criticise the instant interview but, if you go up to the press room twenty minutes later, they are asking the same questions.'

The thick-skinned Newbon does not flinch, either, when the flak is flying towards ITV. 'There was a time when we deserved all the criticism for missing goals, coming off the air before the finish of an event, but I don't think it applies any more. I think ITV are now ahead. We are like a popular newspaper, mostly the *Daily Mail*, sometimes the *Sun*. Probably the BBC is the *Daily Telegraph*.' And personal attacks? 'Well, it's inevitable when you are in my position. But all I'm trying to do is get people closer to the event. People say I am trying to make a name for myself, but I don't need to. I have a name already around Birmingham.'

What's in a name? There was once, the story goes, a Midlands speedway rider who was being interviewed by Newbon on a Central sports programme and announced that he had named his newly-born son after Newbon. 'What, Gary?' asked the interviewer. 'No, Wally,' said the speedway rider.

Back in one of the scanners, the producer/director, Ted Ayling, is marshalling his forces. In front of him in the surprisingly comfortably carpeted lorry is a bank of screens, thirty-two of them, some showing what is on the network currently, most bringing him different angles, different information from within the ground. It is his choice which of the pictures the nation will see.

The programme does not get off to a good start. A camera instructed to find Dwight Yorke, Villa's Trinidadian striker, finds instead Tony Daley, then Mark Blake, who are also black. 'We'll have the race relations board on to us,' says East angrily. Another cameraman picks out the linesman when he should have captured the referee. Twenty minutes of lifeless football pass. 'Crap, isn't it,' says East. 'Who picked this game?' Over the intercom Ayling berates another of his cameramen: 'Sam, you're not going to get in this game unless you tighten up.'

East is soon more fulsome as Lineker interjects into Alan Parry's commentary to make a tactical point. 'Good stuff, Links,' he says. It seems an appropriate nickname for someone working in television. Lineker's performance is somewhat better than that of Parry, who has seemingly appointed himself public relations officer for the League in talking about how many good games he has seen this year despite what the press may tell you. Later in the season, from the comfort of a studio a continent away, he will upbraid the teams in the African Nations' Cup, players and officials he does not have to face in person, for the paucity of their play.

Five minutes before half-time, ITV sport's supplications are answered as Leeds take the lead. Gordon Strachan creates space for Mel Sterland to cross from the right and, although the Aston Villa goal-keeper, Les Sealey, saves Lee Chapman's header, Rodney Wallace stabs home. A minute into the second half, Leeds are 2 up, Strachan again the provider, his corner being powerfully headed home by Sterland. ITV's videotape department are in equally impressive form; instantly, they have it ready for repetition, from two cameras as well as the miniature one in the net. Lineker remarks that if you keep on the move you have a chance of getting in front of your marker.

Leeds are now rampant and, after fifty-six minutes, comes an excellent goal. Another corner by Strachan is back-heeled back into his path by Gary McAllister, and the resulting low cross is tapped in by Lee Chapman. Immediately, the Villa defender, Paul McGrath, is booked. Ayling seeks to keep up with it all and prepare videotape to repeat all the incidents.

Yorke's fifth goal in five games for Villa will have delighted his home island of Trinidad, where they are riveted to BBC radio for news of how he is faring in the mother country, but it does not signal a revival. A minute from time, Chapman heads home another Sterland cross for a 4–1 victory. East quickly makes arrangements for an interview with Chapman, which Newbon drags on longer than they wish in the scanner. 'Cut, cut,' Ayling yells. Newbon would say later that he could not hear.

The final Leeds goal had again been instigated by Strachan, 34 and toes still twinkling. The previous season, he had been footballer-of-the-year. Today, Leeds had played what was becoming a game of leapfrog with Manchester United at the top of the table and taken a 1-point lead, although they had played seventeen matches to United's sixteen. Remarkably, Leeds and Manchester were pulling clear of the field, a travailing Liverpool, Arsenal, Everton and Tottenham among them. Villa's performance in failing to take the chance to go third above Manchester

City had confirmed Ron Atkinson's pre-match assessment that 'We are a million miles away from being a Championship side.'

Post-match, he was to be found underneath the stand, in a bar reserved for him and his guests; Big Ron's Bistro, it had been irreverently termed by Jimmy Greaves. The Bistro Kid shook his head and winced that wince of his to the assembled TV people, who were winding down after the day's exertions. Atkinson had been undone by the little man he had bought for Manchester United from Aberdeen but then failed to sign for Sheffield Wednesday, Strachan having chosen Leeds instead. As he left the Villa manager might have contemplated the dent in the front of his white Mercedes, sustained the day before on his way to watch another first-division match, and thought how it summed up his weekend.

Thankfully, there was no dent in the car parked in the street neighbouring Villa Park. And, with the crowd having walked and driven away, no waif about either. The driver hurriedly got in and revved the engine when there suddenly came a knock on the window and a face at it. 'Hey, mister, I minded your car. Where's the other 50p?' it demanded. Out of fear, he paid up.

IV Satellite Night

Into the cosy cartel that was BBC and ITV has come satellite television, with the effect that the couch potato of a football fan can become a bloater. With the air time denied the terrestrial stations, the three satellite stations in England – Screensport, Eurosport and BSkyB – can indulge the viewer in a way ITV and BBC never could. In their 'wall-to-wall' saturation coverage that can fill that time, there is Italian, Dutch, Spanish, German and South American football on a weekly, almost daily, basis. It was possible during the 1991–92 season even to get the African Nations' Cup finals live from Senegal; a treat, even if the tournament proved a disappointment.

It is, however, domestic football that, televisually, most excites. The overseas stuff may be cerebral and interesting, but the home fare is stimulating and stirring.

Sky Sport's coverage of the FA Cup is appropriately lively and entertaining, as is their innovative *Footballer's Football Show* which enables people from within the game to talk about its issues at greater length than the sound-bite interviews permitted by the terrestrial channels. They have, too, a preview called *Sky Soccer Weekend*, which has its faults – notably its title with the American name of the game, and the banality of the comments from some inarticulate guests; and it could do with some fan input. It does, however, provide background to the weekend and stoke the anticipation.

Unfortunately for Sky, with satellite dishes selling slowly in a recession, it is the nearest thing possible to keeping a secret in the media age. It is especially a shame when it comes to their live coverage of a match, as could be seen on a chilly Monday night in December in East London. Yet the evening was a neat summary of the appeal of the English game.

Sky's coverage of Leyton Orient v. West Bromwich Albion – the tie of the second round, they billed it – began with the strains of *Jerusalem*: 'And did those feet in ancient times walk upon England's mountains green?' The feet to which Sky were perhaps referring were those of Peter Kitchen, who had walked upon Brisbane Road's green in those ancient times of a decade or so earlier, having played up front for Orient when they reached the semi-final of the FA Cup in 1978. Sky had discovered him living in Epping – the suburb in Essex rather than the forest itself – and invited him to be their guest. Where do they find them, indeed.

Sky's presentation includes several neat little touches such as a 'factfile' on both clubs. It includes the fact that Albion are unaccustomed to this stage of the FA Cup: the founder members of the Football League were in the third division for the first time in their 113-year history. It had been a 2–4 home defeat by non-League Woking almost a year earlier that had seen the end of the then manager, Brian Talbot. Now Bobby Gould, who had won the competition with Wimbledon in 1988, was in charge.

We had spoken in Gould's office at the Hawthorns shortly before the first round, in which his side faced Marlow but came through easily enough – 6–0 – even if the echoes of the previous year hung in the air. 'It's a volatile game,' he had said before adding, after a moment's reflection on the statement, 'but then I am a volatile character.' Just so. When he took over he had had enlarged a picture of a girl supporter weeping at West Bromwich's relegation and hung it in the dressing-room so as to stress the importance of the club in people's lives. Later in the season, after a bad performance at Bournemouth, he would invite an irate Albion fan into the team's dressing-room to air his views.

Tonight, Albion are a goal down within thirty-five seconds, giving the Sky cameras ample opportunity to beam the pictures of Gould's expressive face. As Greg Berry, not so long ago playing in Essex junior football, hooks home for Orient, Gould looks daggers. Now, when anger creases his boyish face, he can be fearsome. Those who have seen, or rather heard, what he describes as 'my bark', will probably view his own description of 'volatile' as a euphemism. It is possible to indulge him, however, because it is done out of the love of football. 'I only ever wanted to be a footballer,' he says, and he is a little bemused that, as a manager, he has to find ways to stretch players lacking the same drive. 'I just don't see people loving the game as we used to. I don't see players with that same pleasure and desire. That upsets and disappoints me.'

It was probably his enthusiasm, as much as any technical ability, that persuaded the board of a depressed club to hire him. That and his gift of the gab, which is much sought after in the media. He has even opened up the Albion dressing-room to reporters twenty minutes after the end of the game, the way they do in the United States.

Another such figure has been Andy Gray, the assistant manager of Aston Villa, who was hired by Sky as the summariser, the expert to sit alongside the commentator. Expert is often a misnomer. Ex-players or managers hired to add insight can sometimes merely trot out clichés rather than the colour they might bring. On foreign games they will refer only to 'the big No. 9' or 'the little midfield player', having done little or no research and having just turned up on the night. Then they take the money and run.

Not so Gray. He conveys excellently a passion for the game with natural voice cadences that roll up and down like a match itself. After two minutes of tonight's match, an Orient player clatters the Albion goal-keeper, Stuart Naylor. 'I like to see a goal-keeper being challenged. I like to see strikers letting them know they are around. They get too much protection as it is,' says Gray. It is typical of his forthright opinions, which strike a chord with the public and are in contrast with more mealy-mouthed talkers on other channels.

Gray, once the bravest of strikers, will tell you that a centre-half likes to clatter a forward near to the touchline, by the half-way line, because it is worth giving away the free-kick in a not particularly dangerous area for the pleasure and hell of it. Such nuggets are irreverent, honest, and just what we want to hear.

Alongside Gray sits Martin Tyler, whose at times monotonous delivery early in his career probably kept him from becoming the big noise among commentators on the main channels. Since being with Sky, though, he has developed a more exciting style to go with his unsurpassed depth of knowledge and wide vocabulary. He has also developed a clever little relationship with Gray. 'It's a pity we can't get a shot up here,' says Gray when the talk gets round to Cup-winners' medals. 'We have had far too many mentions of your medals,' Tyler admonishes.

West Bromwich Albion equalise: five minutes into the second half, Paul Williams heads home Simeon Hodson's cross. 'Great stuff. A goal at the beginning of each half,' enthuses Gray, who is developing a rasp in his Scottish voice reminiscent of a young Bill Shankly. He may more probably hope one day to become an older Bill Shankly. Gould's face is now minus the daggers.

Orient steal a good Cup tie, however, two minutes from time when Berry touches in his second goal after Naylor has half-saved a shot. Albion might thus have been said to have caught a dose of Berry-Berry. It is not that pun, though, that is causing Gould's face to crease; the daggers are back. In the studio, where Peter Kitchen's large nose is being unflatteringly lit, we have the final thoughts. Probably wisely, Bobby Gould has not been asked for his.

There are some errors of quality made in Sky's football service. Tonight, for example, a reporter had been referring to a back four when five names were listed. In a later round, a caption would refer to the Crewe Alexandra v. Liverpool tie as 'Liverpool v. Crewe Alexander'. But, for their mere provision of quantity, which also takes in live Scottish football, they deserve praise. 'The best football service on TV,' they announce. 'Proudly sponsored by Carlsberg.' They might amend that the way the beer was once forced to. It is probably the best football service on TV.

Six: Outdoor Types

1 Oxford Blues

They held a carol service in the social club at Oxford United two weeks before Christmas for the players, their families and officials. It was appropriate that they should be singing for a saviour. For the club were at the bottom of the second division suffering from PMT: post-Maxwell trauma. In common with many areas of the late tycoon's business concerns, the pinch they had been feeling for some while was now a squeeze.

The man who had saved them, then handed them over to a branch of his family to run, had died six weeks earlier after falling from his luxury yacht, the *Lady Ghislaine* – which was the name of his daughter, who was listed as a director of Oxford United – into the sea off the Canary Islands. Now Oxford were all at sea, too, in danger of sinking. The £3 million they owed was perhaps as nothing compared to some of the sums being bandied about in connection with other institutions in which Maxwell was involved – indeed, to other football clubs – but, to them, it was frightening.

Maxwell's sons, Ian and Kevin, were under pressure to repair, or at least explain, their father's tangled business dealings and had said that their support for the club must end. In addition, they would require back the £2 million invested by the Maxwell family; the other £1 million of debt was owed to the club's bank.

I came to the Manor Ground on a cold and frosty Thursday morning the week before Christmas to see how the club was reacting. Thursday being that 'limbo' day between professional football matches, it seemed appropriate. It was business as usual, albeit with a weight of circumstance in the air now that the pomp of Maxwell was gone. Earlier in the week, four directors had resigned having learned the full extent of the financial position and unable to inject more capital. In addition, the entire professional playing staff of twenty-six had been put up for sale. One of them had already gone – the striker, Lee Nogan, to Watford for £275,000 – to ease the cash flow. It had thus been ironic to encounter that morning on the A40, on the outskirts of the city, a poster demanding the reinstatement of the Pergamon Twenty-Five, a group who had worked for, then been fired from a publishing company owned by the man. 'No closures, no redundancies at Maxwell companies,' the poster urged forlornly.

How different it had been some nine and a half years earlier when Maxwell breezed in. Or should it be hurricaned in. The corpulent publisher had decided to help out his local club – he rented nearby Headington Hall for a peppercorn sum – and declared his intent to make it the Manchester United of the south. It was only the first of many ridiculous utterances he was to make, culminating in the denunciation of the game's governing body as the 'Football League mismanagement committee'. Actually, the latter may not have been so ridiculous . . .

In his first season as chairman, in the September of 1982, there was a top-of-the-third-division match against Portsmouth, when the weather was of the World Cup in Spain a few months earlier. It should have made for a day of wine and roses. Instead, it became a bouquet of barbed wire. High spirits gave way to hooliganism at the Oxford end as Portsmouth took the lead, with fighting breaking out as a contingent of infiltrating visitors celebrated. Those were the days before closed-circuit television, when the risk of being caught by the police was less and when segregation was less rigidly enforced.

Into the fracas, giving the day's outstanding performance, strode Maxwell. Theatrically, he made his way from the directors' box around the touchline to the terracing. Those involved were taking it out on whoever was at hand, mainly the police. Into the no-man's land between the fans went Maxwell, pleading for order. Peace duly broke out, mainly because Oxford equalised; and Maxwell was amidst the fans, celebrating with them. His silver tongue had prevailed. He even went walkabout afterwards, like an electioneering politician. It was an astonishing incident to witness.

But his interest in the game was minimal, for all his reminiscences about having grown up in Czechoslovakia loving Arsenal after seeing them on a club tour there. Such a tour at the time he suggested was not well documented; this probably explains why no one else seems to remember it. Neither was he especially knowledgeable. He did, after all, rush into the dressing-room one night at the Manor Ground to congratulate the team on an especially good performance in their quest for promotion. The problem was that it was the visitors' dressing-room, which was left baffled by the monologue delivered by Maxwell, who departed as soon as he had given it.

More, Maxwell enjoyed the profile the game gave him, particularly when Oxford won the League (then the Milk) Cup in 1986. When Oxford were no longer big enough for his ambition, he moved on to Derby County. He also had interests in Reading and sought to acquire Watford, until the League acted with legislation to contain his spreading, fragmented footballing interests. Attempts to get his hands on a really big club, such as Manchester United or Tottenham, failed despite his use of the *Daily Mirror* newspaper he owned to promote his own case and denigrate those of others.

Now, in contrast to all the warm, heady days when, if money was an object, it was an object of beauty, was the Manor on this hoary morning. The entrance to it was surrounded by rubble, as a petrol station at the approach to the ground in the suburb of Headington was being rebuilt. There was an eerie quietness to the place, but soon evident was that refusal of football clubs to give in to unpromising circumstances. An optimistic secretary in the offices had even pinned to a noticeboard a magazine article which explained how to get a rise. If nothing else, it revealed that sense of humour was intact, pecker up.

The club had even received a little good news the previous day. The local council's planning sub-committee had agreed to their proposal to build a new ground and leisure complex on the edge of the city. The club believed that the scheme would secure their future, when the money from the sale of the current ground was gleaned. In the corner of the offices, on its side, was a map of the proposal.

In terms of irreverence, it hardly compared with the time when the wonderful, huge old shield awarded to the Southern League champions was to be found, also on its side, on the floor, leant up against a wall, behind the pool table in the social club of Welling United. But, when it came to planning matters, the sub-committee's decision was the equivalent of a goal-keeper throwing the ball to the full-back to initiate an attack on goal, so many more bureaucratic stages were there to negotiate. But then every journey starts with the first step.

The club was just about coming to terms with Robert Maxwell's death and its implications. Just about. After we had found a quiet corner of Oxford's social club, away from the busy cleaners, to talk about the football club, its managing director, Pat McGeough, told of his initial reaction to the news of Maxwell's demise. 'I was devastated, in a world of total blackness when I heard,' he said. 'But then I realised that it need not be the end. It could be the beginning, a rebirth, and we could make it work.'

There would probably be no second coming, something even Maxwell could not achieve. No wealthy sugar daddy was immediately in the wings even if, as McGeough pointed out, 'everyone would love a Jack Walker, wouldn't they,' referring to the multi-millionaire industrialist who had taken over Blackburn Rovers. Speculation surrounding the possible involvement of the head of the Virgin organisation, Richard Branson, a resident of nearby Kidlington, remained only that. McGeough was more concerned in doubling the average home gate of just under 5000 to bring in half a million more pounds a year. 'It's fashionable to say that football isn't attractive any more, but I believe it is,' he said. It was public relations, but essentially correct.

So the rebirth McGeough envisaged would have to be effected without the aid of a Maxwell midwife, but he would hear no evil of the empire that Maxwell had created. 'There aren't many clubs of our size who have been in the first division, even fewer who have won the League Cup. It wouldn't have happened without Robert Maxwell,' he said. McGeough was with Pergamon Press when Maxwell seconded him to the club as financial director. Five years ago, he joined full-time and relished the chance, having been a football fan from the day his dad first took him to watch Wolverhampton Wanderers. 'My blackness came because I thought Oxford was going to be taken from me,' said the man from the Black Country. 'But I'm no quitter, and neither is Brian.'

Brian Horton, the former Brighton and Luton midfield motivator, now the manager at Oxford, sat in his office on the other side of the ground, beneath the stand that had

supported Robert Maxwell and presided over all the ups
and downs. Horton exuded positive attitudes. He brushed
aside a feeble joke about our conversation being bugged –
it had been revealed that morning that Maxwell had eaves-
dropped on the meetings of his employees – and ordered
one of the milling apprentices to fetch tea. 'I'm sick of reading about it all,' he said.

His continuing smile in the adversity of it all brought to
mind those words of Dr Johnson on the subject of marriage:
a triumph of hope over experience. It is perhaps the most
common attitude in the game. Thankfully. 'I keep looking
in the papers and turning on the teletext and reading about
clubs in trouble. We're probably not much different to a lot
of clubs,' he said. 'There's Walsall, Aldershot, even Tottenham. It's just that it's suddenly become public.

'We're not resigned to having financial troubles and getting relegated. That's rubbish. We're going to make the best
of it. Sometimes, things like this can pull people together.
I've told the players that they might even benefit. Some
might get a move somewhere else and do better. Then it's
there for the younger ones to make names for themselves.'
Outside in the corridor, players' banter could be heard as
they prepared for training, discussing their fancy-dress
party of that week, seemingly unaffected by all the up-
heaval. They were, after all, just players with little or no
interest in anything above playing. And it would have been
easy to believe that, as long as they were getting paid, they
cared little for which club was doing it.

That is, at least, the view of some onlookers of football.
While some of that may be true, with some players and at
some clubs, the majority have a deeper set of feelings for
which they are rarely given credit. It can be a game less
cynical than its back-page image might sometimes project.
The previous April, a testimonial at Highbury had proved
that while football can bitch, bicker, back-stab and back-

bite, it can also be very generous. Contested by Arsenal and Liverpool, it raised from a crowd of more than 18,000 around £100,000 for Ray Kennedy, the midfield player who won a host of trophies with both clubs, now suffering from Parkinson's disease. Even Kenny Dalglish turned out for Liverpool, just a couple of months after resigning as their manager.

That was a high-profile occasion. There are many less so but worthy none the less happening every week. It showed that players did care about something other than themselves. But any kid with any talent in his feet only ever wants, at the outset, to play football and hang everything else. The release of just playing, sometimes playing without wages, as some players have and were doing at more than one troubled club, demonstrates a feel for the game beyond money.

'We're just getting on with it,' was the best that could be managed by the midfield player, Les Phillips, signed from Birmingham in 1985 on the same day as John Aldridge – who had gone on to score and earn well with Liverpool and Real Sociedad in Spain – and had seen the fat and the lean. 'We've got to knuckle down and get off the bottom. It's just a financial thing. The players' morale is good.' It was standard sincere stuff.

Some of them would have to go, of course. Horton was not resigned to relegation but he was to selling the main assets, such as Andy Melville, John Durnin, Jim Magilton and Paul Simpson, the possession of whom explained why the bank had been indulging the club. 'The worry would be if we didn't have any good players to sell,' Horton said. Already he had had plenty of enquiries from other managers. 'People think managers are always fighting, but that's not the case,' he added. Today, he is not taking training as he has to meet with McGeough on financial matters and spend his time on the telephone.

Outside, the players are clambering into a set of very modest cars to drive to training on the iron-hard playing fields of Brasenose College, where they will forget the club's troubles and attempt to keep their balance for an hour and a half. They at least had a point to their week – the local derby with Swindon Town away from home on the Saturday. But, when that match was postponed, they knew how the rest of the club was feeling: carrying on despite the sense of loss, if not of Maxwell personally, then of the good times he had brought.

Football is the focal point of a football club – obvious but true. Without it, it drifts, no matter how high spirits are kept. Oxford United that morning, that week, with no game in sight, were drifting. Horton and McGeough would need to fight with the steering wheel to get the club back on course.

Back in the social club, meanwhile, the waitresses were laying the tables for a money-raising sportsman's dinner. The main guest was to be the former boxer, Alan Minter. Now he was quite a fighter . . .

11 Boxing Awayday

Time was when Boxing Day football meant a ten-mile trip to the match – if you were unlucky enough to be away – a meat pie, a cup of Oxo, ten Woodbines and change out of a halfpenny. Oh, and an orgy of goals, and home in time for the results.

Actually, it was never really like that. It only felt like it. But it certainly never felt like it did for Plymouth Argyle this Boxing Day. From Oxford to Cambridge may be a short, even logical, enough hop across country from dark to light for this book's journey but, for the Devon club today, it was some hike. They were the ones with the blues.

It was bad enough for the Plymouth players, leaving home shortly after *Only Fools and Horses* at 5pm on Christmas Day. They would arrive more than five hours later at the Cambridge hotel where they were to be billeted for three nights for their second-division matches against the local United today and Millwall in London the following Saturday, two days later. But take the group of Argyle supporters now gathered at the gates of the Abbey Stadium on a windswept Newmarket Road an hour and a half before kick-off. They were waiting for possibly the only perk of being a long-distance away supporter, one of the brave few, the happy band of brothers: a ticket from a player who had no one else to whom to give it, since no relative in his or her right mind would attempt the trip.

There was Robert Hellings, who was up from his bed in Redruth, West Cornwall, at 3:45am in order to pick up his friend, Ian Self, in nearby Camborne at 5am. They arrived at the Abbey just after 1pm. 'I'm certified,' Ian offered by way of explanation. 'I've brought my doctor's certificate with me.' The round trip from Plymouth was 610 miles; his and Robert's 750. Another fan, Noddy as he insists he is well known at grounds, mostly second-division, all over the country, could not afford to stay overnight ready for the Millwall game. Besides which, he had to be at work tomorrow. But he would be back up from south-west to south-east on Saturday on the supporters' club coach.

So too would Tony and Helen Hilton, who had driven up themselves. 'The worst thing was all the service stations being closed till 8am,' said Helen. They drive to every away match and had even reached fog-bound Derby ten days previously to find the match postponed. In following the Argyle, they estimate their travelling costs alone – thirty trips at an average of £20 – to be £600. Then, of course, comes ground admission, programme, eating. It is all a long way from that halfpenny of yore.

On the other side of the car park stood the club chairman 'since May, when we started improving'. Dan McCauley could also count himself among the superfans. He had driven up in the morning but was unwilling to make public his journey time; it was clearly wind-assisted, though, judging by the figure he mentioned off the record.

He was not too concerned about the cost of three days' accommodation for the team. 'We can get a discount at this time of year,' he said, in true chairmanly fashion. 'And, anyway, we want to get off the bottom of the League. We'll worry about the money later.' It could have been worse, he added. He had noticed Bournemouth being sent to Hull, if not to Hull and back: on the following Saturday, they were at Darlington.

The Plymouth manager, David Kemp, was being very professional about it all. 'It's not too bad for the players, because we normally train on Christmas Day anyway. But I feel sorry for the fans,' he said. 'I don't think there would be many of them waking up this morning and thinking, "Let's poodle up to Cambridge." And I don't suppose Cambridge United fans really want to watch Plymouth. I complained to the League when I saw the fixture list before the season but I was told that the police don't want derby games any more.'

He had hit on another way in which football tradition was being eroded: the game's authorities, having run scared after a riot by Leeds United fans on the Saturday of a Spring Bank Holiday at Bournemouth in 1990, had handed over power to the police. Now kick-off times were at the whim of the constabulary, and FA Cup replays, already being scheduled for ten days after the original tie in order to accommodate police work rotas, were being decided on penalties because it was not possible to wait another ten days for a second replay.

Kemp, like the Hiltons, remembered the postponed date at Derby. 'All these people in Derby were waving at the team bus as we were passing. I thought, "They must be a nice crowd up here." Then we got to the ground, and I realised why.' It meant that, temporarily, there was no Derby game, as well as no derby games for Plymouth; but they and their supporters might feasibly have been given one match at home over the holiday period. As Kemp pointed out: 'They could have at least sent us to Bristol. It was better in the days before the computer, when a bloke with a pencil used to work it out on a piece of paper.' In 1960, for example, in a couple of matches that so evoked those unrealistic Boxing Day memories, Argyle lost 4–6 at Charlton over Christmas, only to win the second set against the same opposition by the same score a day later.

In the end, about 200 Plymouth supporters did make the trip to Cambridge and were allocated seating in the stand – the empty visitors' end being opened up to home support. The number up from Devon was boosted by a sizeable contingent from the London branch, which boasts several hundred members and a fanzine called *Pasty News*. Perhaps Plymouth's best known metropolitan supporter was the former Labour Prime Minister, Michael Foot.

Such a number was a feat of endurance and loyalty, given the football served up by Cambridge United: the route-one, long-ball bump and grunt. It had been pioneered with a little charm at least by Watford but without the physical excesses of an in-their-pomp Wimbledon who had subsequently adopted, and probably perfected, the system. It was an acquired taste – acquired, and justified, only by their own supporters. It all began at Cambridge almost exactly two years previously, when John Beck took over from Chris Turner as manager. The team were in the doldrums, mid-table in the fourth division. Suddenly, Beck, impressed by the rise of Watford and Wimbledon from the bowels of the League on resources similar to those he now found himself stewarding, decided that theirs was the way up.

Two weeks after Beck had assumed the reins, he had allowed this loiterer on the wing of the game to spend an afternoon with the team at Millwall, then a first-division team, for an FA Cup fourth-round tie. The purpose was to see how a small team coped with going into the Lions' Den, a home stronghold where the dressing-rooms are, unusually, under one terraced end, the home Cold Blow Lane end. The inspiration had been a passage in the excellent book *Only a Game?*, the diary of a professional footballer, by the former Millwall player, Eamon Dunphy.

'We always expect to win at home. Teams hate coming

to the Den,' he had written. 'Which is partly why we beat the Football League record for being undefeated at home [fifty-nine matches, between 1964 and January 1967]. When I first went there I used to hate it. I remember going there with York City for my first visit. It took us half an hour to find the place. Eventually, we went up this dingy back street. I remember thinking, "Where is this?" Then you go and have a look at the pitch, which is bumpy, terrible. And you think, "Oh, Jesus, what are we doing here?" The dressing-rooms are terrible. Small, poky places. The away-team dressing-room is a dungeon, no light, no window. The bathrooms are horrible. Then you get out there to face them – the Lions. And they come storming at you, and most sides jack it in.'

But not only did Cambridge enter the Den and emerge unscathed, they were to demonstrate a tamer's flourish. It revealed much about their remarkable rise through the divisions over the next two years, which took them through the fourth and the third and now to the top of the second, the brink of the Premier League. It illustrated the them-and-us mentality, the out of adversity comes strength. Being around them that afternoon was an uplifting experience, a joy to be part of. It was how the style of football survives amid so much criticism from outsiders. The spirit was truly life-enhancing, even if some of the tactics were misguided and misplaced.

The visitors' dressing-room at Millwall had been tarted up with wood panelling and ceramic tiles but it remained that airless cell one-third the size of the home equivalent. An hour before kick-off, Cambridge revealed the ritual that was to characterise them: each member of the team was forced into taking a cold shower. He stayed under the jet while ten seconds were counted out, then had a bucketful of cold water thrown over him by one of the substitutes, who seemed to be trying to pretend he was not enjoying it while thanking his good fortune that he had not been selected in the XI.

A year previously, the then assistant manager, Gary Johnson, had noticed as the players stepped down from the team coach for a midweek match at Scarborough that there was a sluggishness about them. He suggested the cold shower as a solution. They won and had retained faith in it.

The team was a motley crew, a mixture of youngsters on the way up and rejects from bigger clubs. Their sense of humour was typical of a group of men united in a common pursuit: childish but enjoyable none the less to those who are a part of it, even if not to those who are not. Dion 'Dizzy' Dublin, the talented striker, was the butt of much of it for his new athletic-support shorts that day. 'They'll see you on TV tonight and think you must be a good player 'cos you're wearing those,' said one. 'They make you look like that runner, Tony Christie,' said another, winking. I duly fell for it: 'You mean Linford,' I said. Eleven players laughing compounded my embarrassment.

Gallows humour was also prevalent, especially about the reputation of the Millwall crowd. 'Any volunteers to take corners?' Beck asked. The volume increased when the local police chief came in to reassure them that it is a 'nice, friendly ground'.

The captain, Liam Daish, led the team in a session of pushing and shoving amongst themselves, of a sort for which American male bonding weekends charge a fortune. Then they ran on the spot, building up the speed and intensity until it reached a climax with a collective shout. 'Let's go to war,' shouted Daish. 'I have been telling people we have got arsehole,' said Beck. 'Now prove me right.'

At half-time, they were a goal down but had surprised themselves by the quality of their play under the new system – getting the ball forward quickly and early to

Dublin and his partner, John Taylor, then winning the knock-downs and 'doing a bit around the penalty box'. 'Chris Turner told me never to say "well done" at half-time,' Beck said after the bickering about conceding the goal had died down. 'But you have been magnificent. Now slap some thighs, and some chests. Do what you have to do so that you do the same again. Kick quickly, squeeze tightly.'

They equalised within three minutes of the restart, the gifted left-sided players, Chris Leadbitter and Lee Philpott, combining for Taylor to score. They might have won the game after that. After directing some abuse towards their own team, the Millwall supporters – as appreciative of good football of this sort as they were to be of Hoddle's – generously applauded them. Beck, too, was lavish in his praise. 'And they tell me we are not good enough to get out of this division,' he said. 'The bad news is you are in at 11 tomorrow.' Such was the physical regimen of Beck. In two years time, he would have them at such things as paintball, a simulated war-game, in the Dorset woods.

It mattered not that they had not won. Three days later, they completed the job, winning 1–0 after extra-time – and the players' belief in their new system was total. It was all somewhat curious, given Beck's former status as a passing midfield player for Queen's Park Rangers, Fulham and Coventry. The rise thereafter was remarkable, with Beck's idiosyncratic managerial style at its heart. Before one crucial promotion match against Bolton Wanderers, he got up at the crack of dawn to stick sheets of paper to the path leading from the home dressing-room to the pitch. 'Be First. Be Bold,' each one said. He was ever full of aphorisms and inspiring quotations and would reprint them in the programme. For today's match against Plymouth, it was under the heading of 'Faith' and said: 'Just about any dream grows stronger if you hold on a little longer.'

Folklore, legend even, had grown up around Cambridge, especially since Beck was now so sick of press criticism that he was refusing to talk to journalists. Ball boys, for example, were reported to be issued with towels to dry the ball for long-throwing Cambridge players; the grass was deliberately allowed to grow on the flanks to clip opponents' wings.

To all this, on our Boxing Day, were Plymouth to be subjected. For this, they had journeyed long and far. However, they were to be appropriately rewarded for their faith and foolishness. Thank goodness for people such as these time travellers. Besides which, any team that plays in green and white stripes can't be all bad.

Plymouth looked to have weathered the Cambridge storm until twelve minutes from time, when Dublin headed home from Philpott's corner. But an equaliser came eight minutes later, when Robbie Turner converted a penalty after Andy Fensome had handled Mark Fiore's cross. Argyle did have a momentary lapse in the last minute, when a cross was turned into his own net by their full-back, Denis Salman – whose move from Millwall just before the transfer deadline the previous season had been headlined in the *Liverpool Echo* 'Salman Rush Deal' – but the referee disallowed the own-goal for an offside.

The twenty-two-hour round trip containing ninety minutes of football was therefore worthwhile for Ian Self, Robert Hellings, Noddy and the Hiltons. The journey home, to be spent savouring Plymouth's apparent edging towards safety at the foot of the table while wondering, despite their robust approach, about the frailty of Cambridge's promotion challenge, would seem just a little shorter. All round, it had been a pleasant Boxing Day – getting out of the house after a Christmas Day banged up indoors amid the traditional family tension – but not a passionate one. And passion is what Boxing Day football should produce.

Police attempts to deter people from travelling over holiday periods, especially after the Leeds débâcle and in view of the alcoholic content of Christmas, by having their team assigned long-distance away matches, are perhaps understandable. Shorter journeys might mean more people out and about for them to monitor but, if transport is properly provided by clubs who stand to make more money from increased attendances, and through a better public service, the problems could be averted. The current fixture allocation ignores the trend of the responsible fan seeking to reclaim the game. And the wishes of that responsible fan now deserve more consideration from the game's governing bodies.

III King Kenny and the Cat

For football followers as they drive up the motorway, their scarves and flags decorating the cars and charabancs, the expectations brought on by the FA Cup third round bring a welcome surge amid the post-Christmas let-down. If you and your team are in it, it can give new impetus as the season reaches its half-way point. That enthusiasm of the opening day, when promotion seemed a certainty, may have waned just a little after all, even if you never stop caring. For those who are already out, well, you can't help taking an interest in it, can you?

There are many reasons why a non-League club especially wants to make it through to round three: romance, glory, the chance to be national and not just local heroes, yes, all these. But also the opportunity to make some money for both team and club, unromantic and pragmatic as that may sound. Still, that doesn't preclude enjoying the day when the cat may look at the king – indeed, scratch his eyes out, as Wrexham of the fourth division would do to Arsenal today. We were heading for King Kenny v. Kettering.

On this gale-tossed wet January day – the Cup third round is always the first Saturday after the New Year – the GM Vauxhall Conference team were being sent to Ewood Park to face Blackburn Rovers, who were developing into one of the season's more remarkable stories. It was an example of the haves v. the have-nots, so common in football and worth investigating because so often the have-nots triumph against the odds. Blackburn were entering the competition at this point; Kettering had played eight games just to get here. Giant-killing has become the phrase.

Kettering were £250,000 in debt, a huge figure to them. There was a time when, for clubs at this level, it was not big business but a serious one. Now it was big business and more serious. Blackburn, with the benefit of being underwritten by the benefactor, Jack Walker, a steel businessman who had sold his companies for zillions, had become the new Bank of England club. Walker was to fund the ground improvements called for by the Taylor Report. He was to make available money for players to get the club into the first division or the new Premier League. Most important, he had lured out of retirement Kenny Dalglish, less than a year after he had quit Liverpool due to the pressure of it all. It was to cost £12 million. Or was it £30 million. Sums were bandied about, so astronomical that they lost their meaning. All anyone knew for certain was that, whatever was the price to join the game's élite, Blackburn were willing to pay it.

Almost a year ago to the day, I had sat in Blackburn's magnificent oak-panelled, coal-fired boardroom with their then chairman and president of the Football League, the late Bill Fox, before another FA Cup third-round tie, against Liverpool. 'The finest of the ninety-two,' he had said proudly of our surroundings, as we mused on Blackburn's future. Christmas cards from all over the country decorated the four long walls.

'The name of the game these days is sponsorship and commercial involvement,' he said. 'If the club is run in a businesslike manner backed up by commercial activity, you stand a chance of making an appearance in the first division. That should all pay for the running of the club. The gate money then feeds the team.' He had just played host to a group of sponsors, who had gathered reverentially in the boardroom for his talk about Blackburn's history. Next to him was a silver shield struck by the FA to commemorate the club's third consecutive FA Cup triumph in 1886. It was a moment symbolic of the ancient and the modern. Up above him and the splendour was the Nuttall Street stand, which has one small tea bar and one gents toilet – sited potentially dangerously in a confined corner – to serve its entire population.

'The implementation of the Taylor Report will determine the funds of many clubs,' Fox said. 'Big money will have to be found from somewhere. If we don't run it right we'll end up like all the other Lancashire clubs, in the fourth division.' And the talk got on to money men and bene-factors, of the sort that Watford had found in Elton John. 'I can't even sing in the bath,' said Fox. Yet it was an ironic conversation, given that soon he would woo Walker into parting with his money.

Fox's position was questionable, if understandable: he was the president of the Football League, desperately seek-ing to get his club into the proposed Premier League, which was to be run by the FA and which the League opposed. It was one of several things for which the man who had made his money as a potato merchant was criticised; his Vic-torian, paternalistic image was another, at a time when foot-ball seemed to need leadership of the 1990s rather than the 1890s. 'There are ninety-two Football League clubs . . .' he would, pre-Barnet, preface his answers to questions as the inquisitors sighed, having heard it all before.

But he was a genuine football lover, a man who had come via the terraces. 'A football man,' was always his proud self-description, and it was possible to forgive much of such a man. He would wax lyrical of Bryan Douglas, his favourite player, and the eyes would mist at his most vivid memory:

the 1952 FA Cup semi-final when Blackburn, as a second-division side, lost a replay to Newcastle and a controversial goal, after which he 'couldn't speak for a week.' Outside, as we spoke, the tannoy was blaring out the Righteous Brothers' song *You've Lost That Loving Feeling*. It was clear that he had not.

Eleven months later, he was dead, aged 63, of a heart attack. Now he was missing, sadly and cruelly, the fruition of what he had envisaged at that meeting, what he had worked so hard to do for so long.

Under Dalglish and his assistant, Ray Harford, Blackburn were building a first-division club and a team beginning to play elegant football. Players, such as Gordon Cowans from Aston Villa, David Speedie from Liverpool and Mike Newell from Everton, were attracted to the club, of course, by their slice of a transfer fee and a wage structure created by Walker's generosity – but also because something was happening here. Blackburn were escaping from that Catch 22 for provincial town clubs: you need good players to get first-division football but you need first-division football to get good players. In previous seasons, Blackburn had been unable to hold on to such as Colin Hendry; now he had returned from Manchester City.

All this awaited Kettering and, while their hopes of an upset were high, the portents were not good. When they arrived at their Lancashire hotel on Friday night, for example, the rain was lashing down, and the BBC's efforts to film them disembarking from the team coach came to nothing as the players dashed for the sanctuary of the hotel reception. Then the manager, Peter Morris, and another player in an adjacent room had to be moved because of a leaking roof. On the Saturday morning, the club secretary, George Ellitson, split his trousers.

I sat with Morris in the reception area that morning as he contemplated the game, having just watched a video with his team of Blackburn beating Bristol Rovers 3–0. One wondered if that was wise. It seemed inappropriate to point out to him that the next-door spires, which could be glimpsed through the leafless trees, formed a theme park called Camelot – the perfect world that never existed.

Morris's lot, compared with Dalglish's, was one of those contrasts which the FA Cup enthrallingly provides. He played more than 600 League games for Ipswich, Norwich and Mansfield in the 1960s and 1970s without ever making a fortune. The previous season, after Kettering had squandered a 15-point lead in the Conference to let Barnet into the League, he had felt like 'doing a Dalglish', walking away from football and on to the golf course, swapping the club for the clubs. However, he needed, financially, to keep working.

'Besides,' he said, 'I've got to like Kettering. We've built it up into a magic club.' At that stage of our season, Kettering were sixth in the Conference with games in hand, and an influx of new players had helped rekindle his enthusiasm. Those players had been signed on free transfers, of course. Kettering's share of today's gate receipts would go towards settling the largest of their debts, a disputed £100,000 to the Inland Revenue. The dispute had produced much boardroom accusation and reshuffling. But days such as this one made the struggle worthwhile for club officials and supporters alike. As the coach swept into Ewood Park at 1:55pm, the smiles from the 100 or so Kettering fans queuing for fish and chips, and the thumbs-up in return from the players, showed exactly that.

So did the reception from the 3000 of their 4000 travelling fans who were already in the ground when the players walked the pitch at 2pm. The club nicknamed the Poppies was blooming amid the more accustomed day-to-day trials. Even so, they have always had a healthy fund of support in Northamptonshire: at a recent crisis meeting held in a local sports centre, some 700 supporters had turned up.

By 2:15pm, the team was all kitted out. 'It'll be interesting to see who's ready by this time next week,' said Richard Hill, the former Watford and Oxford midfield player, only 28 but forced to give up League football because of injury. 'It'll be interesting to see who's playing next week,' replied Morris, trying to keep feet on ground. 'Oooh,' chorused the players in mock disgust at such a catty remark, on this day when they were the felines confronting royalty. Speaking of whom, he had apparently been spotted walking down the corridor. 'Kenny wants you to go with him to see the ref,' a Kettering official, who claimed to have seen him, informed Morris. 'Mr Kenny to you,' quipped a player. It was the first indication that the myth existed. No one was really quite sure.

Morris's nerves were 'all right until I saw their team.' Scott Sellars, the winger he feared, was fit after injury. Kettering would try to man-mark Cowans with their tough-looking midfield player, Dougie Keast, and snuff out the diminutive Alan Wright, a recent highly promising signing from Blackpool, another creative force on the left whence most of Blackburn's attacks came. Meanwhile, Kettering would seek to play their own brand of passing football; that, at least, was the theory of a team talk delivered like a firm father laying down the law. Morris, though, could not disguise his affection for his team. 'All the best to you all. Enjoy it. You'll be surprised how much time you get on the ball,' were his parting words.

But theory and hurly-burly often collide on the pitch. It is the great players who keep them separate and retain their heads while around them all are losing theirs. Such is Gordon Cowans. It was to be he who would be surprised how much time he had on the ball. Or maybe he just made it look that way.

Kettering held on for thirty-two minutes and, indeed, had

the game's first chance when a header by their defender, Trevor Slack, was cleared off the line. But then they were undone by a beautiful move involving Wright and Sellars, which ended with Speedie shooting home. From the dug-out at pitch level – still no Kenny; he remained just a legend – it could be seen just how slick and clever were the professionals as they performed their manoeuvres at high speed. Speedie's pirouettes as well as his physical resilience were especially impressive, as much so as Cowans's touch.

Kettering's half-time dressing-room was quiet. Too quiet. 'We are trying to play too many final balls,' said Morris – football-speak for not passing it around and waiting patiently for an opening to appear, rather than trying to force one. 'If we lose, it's not going to be by 4 or 5,' Morris insisted to his players. 'Let's play our football.' But, again, it was Blackburn playing their embryonic Liverpool-style football. From his position next to Morris, on a wall by the dug-out, Kettering's assistant manager, Ernie Moss, the former Chesterfield and everywhere-else-in-the-East-Midlands striker, could not help admiring it all. 'That's a great ball,' he said, as Wright crossed for Newell to head Rovers' second.

Cowans, the guileful thoroughbred now running the game, shot home the third goal from twenty-five yards. Newell's second, and Rovers' fourth, from a similar distance provoked the impetuous goal-keeper, Paul Bastock, into kicking a post and badly bruising a toe in the process. The consoling moment for Kettering, for whom their best players had been young defenders Gareth Price and Richard Huxford, came when their tiny striker, Phil Brown, volleyed home an excellent goal. But it was not to be the Poppies' day.

Dalglish emerged to shake hands with Morris, although there was still only other people's word for it. In the

Kettering dressing-room, the manager did his best to console. 'No disgrace. You learn as you go. It's the FA Trophy
next week.' And in that remark was summed up the eternal
attraction, the eternal optimism, the eternal truism of football. There's always the next game, next week or next year.

In Blackburn's crowded social club, Kettering toasted
their taste of the big time; it all prompted their magic-
sponge man, Richie Norman, to recall his 1963 Cup final
appearance with Leicester City against Manchester United,
and the goal he once scored from left-back at Old Trafford.
Back in the Blackburn offices, uniquely located in a terraced
house opposite the main entrance on the other side of the
street, there was no sign of the myth. All that was left was
a sorry-looking segment of pie. At Blackburn, they were
famed for their meat pies, but this did not testify.

A journalist was once directed into this house, where
post-match press conferences are held, and sat down on the
sofa to watch the football results on the television. 'Well, do
I get a drink then?' he enquired somewhat testily of the
other man in the room – the press steward, he supposed.
He duly received one. Except that these were not the Blackburn offices. It was only later that the journalist realised
that he had been in the wrong terraced house, the 'steward'
too frightened not to accommodate him.

Back in today, a silent deflation was in the air, the way
there is at the end of a long footballing day when tiredness
mingles with disappointment. There certainly was on the
Kettering team bus. Sense of humour prevailed, though. As
the bus was pulling away from the ground, the myth finally
appeared in front of it. The driver stopped, and Dalglish
clambered aboard. 'Would you like me to drive ahead of
you to show you the way to the M6?' he offered. 'You'll
probably be too quick for us,' said Morris.

FRY TIME: Barnet's Barry Fry
surveys his kingdom on opening day.

DOWNS AND UPS: (above) Graham Taylor contemplates England's defeat by Germany while (opposite) Kevin Keegan and his assistant, Terry McDermott, celebrate a Newcastle goal against Bristol City; (below) Bryan Robson tilts Manchester United towards the Championship windmill.

ASPECTS OF LOVE FOR THE GAME:
(opposite) football Belfast-style; (below) the women's
champions, Doncaster Belles; (above) P. Don.

LOOK OF THE DRAWN: (opposite) the United States' goal-keeper at the English Schools Festival; (above) canny aad Sunlun; (below) Ian McDonald at Aldershot.

JUST CHAMPION: Leeds's Gary Speed, Rod Wallace and Gary McAllister congratulate each other on winning the League title.

iv Goals to Newcastle

With a touch of envy, perhaps, the hard-smoking maverick talent, Duncan McKenzie, once described the less naturally gifted but more industrious Kevin Keegan as the Julie Andrews of football. It was a neat if mischievous description of such a wholesome character. He could not have envisaged the Cheviot Hills being alive with the sound of Keegan's return to Newcastle.

On a crisp, sunny February day, Keegan came back to the club he had left as a player in 1984, having helped them to promotion to the first division playing alongside Chris Waddle and Peter Beardsley. Keeganmania was not too strong a word for it. It was an extraordinary day. Indeed, it had been quite a week.

Just a few days earlier, the Newcastle chairman, Sir John Hall, had stated categorically that the current manager, Osvaldo Ardiles, would not be sacked despite Newcastle's lowly position in the second division. 'Ossie Ardiles's job is safe, even if we go down to the third division,' he had said, and there is little more categorical than that. It was said, though, before Newcastle's 2–5 defeat at Oxford, even though it appeared in print for the first time in a Sunday newspaper the following day. Hall went home, 'did some sums' and decided that a change had to be made.

Ardiles was told two days later at 7:30am, and not by Hall in person, that he was sacked. The following day, Keegan arrived on Tyneside as the new manager of Newcastle United Football Club. Thus he followed Kenny Dalglish into management in a strange twist of fate: it had been Dalglish who had followed Keegan into the sainted No. 7 shirt at Liverpool. Both had been variously cast in the role of Messiah; but they were, of course, used to Messiahs in this corner of the English footballing atlas. Indeed, it might be said that Newcastle put the mess in Messiah. This was a hotbed of football, everyone said; a hotbed of nails, more like.

It was just too tempting to bombard the situation with cynicism, for Newcastle had long deserved it. They had promised so much, delivered so little. False dawns rose with the sun in the north-east. Hall was at it again, even now: 'The second division had better stand aside, because we are coming through,' he enthused on television. It echoed a pop song of the time – which had a refrain about being bound for Mou-Mou Land.

But Tyneside wanted, perhaps needed, another new start. On this Saturday morning, the spring in the step of supporters had replaced the stooped shoulders on the way to the ground for the match against Bristol City. The station was teeming with young men in black-and-white striped shirts reading the latest on Special K, on the front pages of the local papers rather than the back. An hour before kick-off, people were hurrying up from the city centre to St James's Park, anxious to get in the queue, anxious not be locked out. Once in, in order to secure their place on the terracing they ran up the winding steps of the Gallowgate End, whose contours and greenery gave a vague impression of the Hanging Gardens of Babylon. That, like Newcastle's role in English football, was once one of the seven wonders of the world. It has been here, too, a Tower of Babel.

Here again was that triumph of hope over experience. St James's was all but filled with 29,263 souls in search of a fix. The supporters certainly deserved some gratification after all they had had to endure from a club who had not deserved them – a club some £6.5 million in debt and presiding over decline on the field. Yet this club dared to advertise to supporters, and give space to an office at the Gallowgate End, something called Newcastle United Financial Services. Would you buy a used car from this club?

Financial matters had been at the root of Keegan's second coming at the expense of the hapless Ardiles: the club's sponsors, the local brewing company, offered more money should they appoint the charismatic Julie Andrews who might, as a strict by-product of course, help them sell more beer. 'Sometimes you are not your own master,' said Hall. 'It is a gamble, but one that we had to take.' It was hardly surprising that, when Keegan arrived at the club's training ground, the first thing he had done was to clean up putrid showering and toilet facilities. 'Look at the muck,' he had exclaimed on seeing them. That might have been a sentence symbolic of the whole club.

What is it about Newcastle that when they have the most loyal, passionate and potentially voluminous support they constantly underachieve, rewarding blind faith with disillusionment? Why does the area spawn footballers who grow up so desperately wanting to play for Newcastle and who then, ambition achieved, so desperately want to get away? Yet, just as remarkably, it seems that they always want to come back. It gets under your fingernails. Like bamboo shoots. It is said that you can take the kid out of Tyneside but you can never take Tyneside out of the kid. The area has an insularity, a camaraderie and pride born of adversity, that finds its outlet in football. And while other areas glitter – significantly, London was the next port of call for its two most profitable exports of recent times, Chris Waddle and Paul Gascoigne – the city of Newcastle's concern with community prevails. It can be attractive and all-embracing – in much the same way as a boa constrictor.

Despite all this weight of expectation, ready to over-whelm him if he allowed it, Keegan duly delivered, on this day at least. As had been pointed out, St James's Park stood on the site of public executions of the past – hence Gallow-gate – but today it would not witness any more.

Keegan's playing career with Liverpool, Hamburg, South-ampton and Newcastle had always known success, which may have been why Hall wanted him. It was, though, his first job in management, at the age of 40 – the gamble the chairman had spoken of. There had, naturally, been moments of playing disappointment: a European Cup final which the German team lost 0–1 to Nottingham Forest; England's match against Spain in the World Cup of 1982, when he dragged his hitherto injured body off the substi-tutes' bench and missed a good chance as England departed the competition.

Today he entered the arena simply, with no fuss, as the electronic scoreboard proclaimed 'Welcome Back Wor Kev (T-shirts available £7.99)'. Club officials had wanted him to arrive by helicopter the way he had departed as a player those eight years previously. This was a day for the players, he insisted. It was an encouraging attitude but an unsus-tainable one. A wall of photographers barred his entry from tunnel to pitch. He sought to move through them to wave to a crowd approaching fever-pitch but could not; instead, he took his seat in the dug-out, leaving the players to their pre-match kick-about.

Newcastle began brightly enough, playing the ball neatly, quickly amongst themselves in the way that any side with which Ardiles has been involved always does. But then they had apparently done so all year. When no goal came, the self-doubt surfaced, again in keeping with the pattern of the season. It said much for their form that their goal-keeper, Tommy Wright, had been player-of-the-month for

January. Today, if anything, they were struggling even more. 'He's made a difference already,' said someone with the voice of weary, cynical Geordie experience at the end of a goalless first half. 'They're worse than usual.'

But wait, what is this? The players were catching the mood. Suddenly, the seen-it-all-befores in the crowd were dancing with delight. Kevin Scott was marshalling the defence; Kevin Brock was thriving in the midfield space he was being granted; David Kelly was buzzing again up front. And there was Gavin Peacock, preening himself and darting hither and thither almost like the Keegan of yore. 'Bill Shankly used to tell me at Liverpool to go and drop a few hand grenades out there,' Keegan was later to say. 'I told Peacock to do the same.'

Reward came after fifty-four minutes courtesy of the Bristol City goal-keeper, Andy Leaning, who was thence to have an Ancient Mariner of a game: he stoppeth one of three. Leaning could only push out Brock's corner to 17-year-old Steve Watson, who turned it back into the goal-mouth for Kelly to head home. A second followed a minute later, when Liam O'Brien tapped in. Then, after sixty-one minutes, came a splendid third; Brock sent clear Peacock, who turned and laid the ball off for Kelly to drive home his second goal. Thereafter, it was exhibition stuff against a Bristol City side feeble and accommodating, who would sack their own manager, Jimmy Lumsden, two weeks later as they lent their own voices to the relegation debate. Newcastle even upstaged the notorious referee, Jimmy Parker of Preston. He had sent off more than a dozen and booked more than seventy the previous season, and he was looking likely to surpass those figures this. Today, a model of restraint, he cautioned but three.

Keegan was cheered to the echo, 'Wor Kev's' name hanging in the breeze. So much for it being the players' day. It had been Keegan who had brought in £118,000 worth of gate receipts above the average. In the press room, we waited patiently for him. 'He's on his way,' said a steward. 'What, already? He's only had the job three days,' said someone. Fifteen minutes later, and still no sign. 'He's lost some pace over the years if he's supposed to be on his way,' offered that same someone.

When he finally arrived, an hour after the end of the match, he proved worth waiting for. 'This is the first letter of the first word of the title of the book,' he said, trying to keep the victory in perspective. He had said during the week that the snowball needed to gain momentum. Had it done so? 'Well, it's started snowing,' he said.

But he permitted himself some acknowledgement of the excitement. 'I felt elated from the word go, even if I haven't slept for three nights . . . It's nearly as good as playing. We had fifteen minutes today as good as anything they can ever have seen here.' He even revealed the secret of football management: there is no secret of football management. What was it like on the bench? 'You sit and pretend you know what you are doing,' he said, taking the mystique from the profession. Neither did he seek credit for some fortuitous circumstances. What had he said after the goalless first half to inspire his team into that purple patch of 3 goals in eight minutes? 'Not a lot. Too much has been said this week. I didn't want to fill their heads with too much.'

What was the thinking behind the substitution of Terry Wilson with David Roche, which strengthened the midfield? 'Wilson had a bit of a groin,' a bit of a groin being a groin strain, which is to the footballer as is flu to the British worker. And, added the debunking Keegan, he had left out Lee Clark, even though he was the player who had most impressed him in training. 'Don't ask me why.' What was it Napoleon said about wanting one lucky general rather than 100 good ones?

Keegan's first managerial instinct was, in fact, that youth

is not the right commodity for a relegation battle; but that experienced, wizened professionals, whose confidence and psyche are not so fragile, were the answer. 'The kids are the future,' he said, 'but you have got to look at the present some time.' He had found a better legacy left by Ardiles than he had been led to expect, and certainly better than when he had come to the club as a player, lured into carrying goals to Newcastle by Arthur Cox's promise of playing with good youngsters. 'After four days, I asked Arthur if he had given these youngsters some time off. I couldn't see them.' Promotion followed, not that season but the next.

By now, St James's was empty as the darkness closed in, and the city centre, one of the – shall we say – liveliest places in Britain on a Saturday night, was steeling itself for the impending celebrations. By now, too, the name of Ardiles was less in usage, even if there remained a well of sympathy for him, which Newcastle would have to turn into something more tangible with a sizeable compensatory cheque. He had been asked in a newspaper questionnaire shortly before his dismissal about which rules were flouted in his sport. 'There are quite a few,' he had answered.

None of this, though, was Keegan's fault; he merely inherited the cynicism. Now this still fresh, positive and honest man deserved his chance. The initial impact would wear off, and he would need someone who could demonstrate rather more expertise than the man he had temporarily brought in as his assistant. Terry McDermott, a good companion mainly, was the man at Liverpool they used to call the 'social officer'.

And he would need some of the attitude Gordon Lee had demanded at Newcastle when he said: 'Even when you're dead you shouldn't let yourself lie down and be buried.' The problem was, Lee had never seen much of that attitude. Neither had the seven other Newcastle managers of the past fifteen years. Would Keegan? Seven days later, he was following Dalglish again, when his side went to Ewood Park and lost 1−3; it would be a difficult few months.

Seven: They Also Serve

1 The Women

There are some place names that invoke sporting admiration, awe even. Kevin Keegan's home town, Doncaster, is not one of them.

The fourth-division team were bottom of the table, their manager, Billy Bremner, having left before Christmas to be replaced by his assistant, Steve Beaglehole. The club was £500,000 in debt, £200,000 of it in tax, and losing between £3000 and £4000 a week. The hope of a move to a new, council-built stadium was the incentive to keep going. That and such touching moments as when two young boys came into the ground in the week that the club was facing a winding-up order, and each offered 50p to the fund. But, in the meantime, things had got so desperate that Doncaster were considering selling the family brass – a name plate from a 1936 steam engine – and had been offered £10,000 for it. They had even roped in Paul Daniels, the magician, to help, prompting remarks about Doncaster being magic: 'Watch them disappear, then,' was the reply.

Daniels, a supporter from the distant past, was lending his name to a scheme to raise money by selling off segments of the pitch at £25 a square yard. The club had even written to that other famous native, Kevin Keegan, lightheartedly suggesting that he might reimburse them for the occasions when, by his own admission, he had sneaked into their Belle Vue ground without paying.

Dark days indeed in the People's Republic of South York-shire. But soft! What light through yonder window breaks? Enter the Juliet Bravos, ring in the Belles: the Doncaster Women's Football Club.

On this dank, dull Sunday, a few miles out of the town centre at Keegan's birthplace in the functional, unlovely colliery village of Armthorpe, Doncaster Belles could clinch the season's first trophy, the Women's National League title, if they could beat Wimbledon. Sporting pride would come to a town which was also home to a Rugby League team that once lost thirty-seven games in a row.

It was the first year of the women's league, reflecting a growth in female interest in the game not only in watching it, but suddenly now in playing it too. The Women's Football Association had reported an increase in membership of 52 per cent to 10,000 in recent years; the number of teams was up from 250 to nearly 400. Remarkably, it was a men's event that was held to have sponsored this boom when, in 1990, it was discovered that, of the 25 million people who watched on television England play West Germany in the semi-final of the World Cup, half were women. Yes, many were attracted by the colour and spectacle, by Pavarotti singing *Nessun Dorma*, by Paul Gascoigne weeping. And many were forced to sit through it because the man of the house insisted. But the WFA then reported the beginning of the upsurge in interest; Channel 4 then started televising the Women's FA Cup final; a fanzine called *Born Kicking* was even delivered. Now had come the National League.

Women's football had had an honourable history in England until men somewhat dishonoured it. It is recorded that, in the early years after the game began around 1880, women's teams were attired in leather hats, striped shirts and shorts which revealed their knees. Teams grew up mainly around the industrial areas of the north, the East

Midlands and London, and the bower of the game reached its full flowering during the First World War when the men were away fighting. The best known team, the Dick Kerr Ladies of Preston, attracted a crowd of 52,000 on Boxing Day 1920 and, during its existence, raised more than £350,000 for charity.

The following year, the women's game was banned by the FA – the men's, that is – which claimed that the money being raised by Dick Kerr's ladies was not reaching the charities. Football, it added, was not really a suitable sport for women anyway. Astonishingly, the game remained off-limits to them until 1970, another men's success finally resurrecting the demand to play it: England's World Cup victory of 1966. How far had it come?

Arriving at the Armthorpe Welfare ground, which plays host to a men's Northern Counties East League club on Saturdays, was a gloomy experience. It had a stand that seated 106 people – if they cleaned off the filthy seats, that was. The club offices looked to have been purchased from unwanted hospital stock; one of the pre-fabricated structures bore a sign saying 'Department of Mental Health Only' – which may have been appropriate for the secretary of a football club, come to think of it.

Then there was the pitch, all sand and bumps. Wasn't it Doncaster's Rugby League ground that was called Tattersfield? In the circumstances, it was a pleasant surprise that we would later witness as watchable a game as we did. It turned out that the women had thought that they had a deal with Rovers to play at Belle Vue – from which venue they had taken their name when formed in 1970 – only for it to fall through four days before the season began.

The people, of course, saved the afternoon, beginning with the man in the tea hut who offered a cup of coffee even though he was not yet open. The heart warmed to him when he addressed the customer as 'youth' (pronounced

'yoth') in that rich, almost East Midlands way of speaking.
Only when pressed did he take 25p towards club funds.
The programme, priced 40p and containing plenty of infor-
mation, put many League clubs' £1 efforts to shame.

Robert Kantecki, the club's chairman and sponsor, was
doing his best to get done all the little jobs that match-days
seem to produce for a shoestring outfit. He was also seeking
to keep happy the BBC and ITV units who were filming
snippets for their news reports. With that in mind, he had
asked his girls to display prominently the sponsor's name –
that of his company – on their shirts whenever interviewed,
especially when the cameras were pointed at the expected
victory celebrations in the dressing-room afterwards. The
BBC had thoughtfully brought some champagne with them.

Kantecki had scented a good business opportunity when
he first heard the Belles needed sponsorship. For £5000 he
got plenty of publicity, at least locally. Then he got caught
up in their enthusiasm. Now he sticks by them and sometimes even trains with a team he describes as a 'talented
bunch of athletes' – whose jobs include teaching, accounting and farming – just for the fun and friendship of it all.
The United States of America winning the World Cup in
China a few months earlier had been good for the women's
cause, he believed. The habit of throwing money at anything sportingly successful in the States might just reach
England the way that other things have done over the years,
he thought. Things like hula hoops, fast food and Madonna,
perhaps.

It may have been far-fetched, but certainly the women's
game needed some financial stimulus. The league had no
sponsors, the business community still sceptical. 'We have
said to them, "Join with us at the start, and you'll be getting
something potentially big very cheaply," ' said the secretary
of the Women's FA, Linda Whitehead, who had journeyed
across the Pennines to watch the match. It would not be to

present the trophy. So early were Doncaster winning the Championship, this being only the second week of February, that it was not yet ready.

She was aware that today's venue and circumstances were somewhat second-rate. 'Yes, they do deserve better facilities,' she said. 'But we have got to earn the right to them.' The backing of men's professional clubs was now helping, she added; following Millwall recently had come Arsenal. However, there was some debate in the women's game about the desirability of walking hand-in-hand with the men's game – and perhaps also some misgivings among the men concerning their income from sponsorship being diluted. 'We're not trying to compete with the men,' said Whitehead. 'We just want to let women play football for its own sake.'

The following year, the league would expand from twenty-four to thirty clubs, she added, with ten taking part in each division of Premier, First North and South. So the quantity was certainly there. The question concerned the quality which the league was seeking, given that teams such as Doncaster and Wimbledon had won their regional competitions with embarrassing ease in the past. Not that this year had been that different for the Belles: they had won all their ten league matches and scored 69 goals, conceding only 4, in the process.

Today would be a little different. Their own nerves and Wimbledon's keenness, not to mention competitiveness since they could still finish runners-up, would combine for a close game. After twenty minutes, the Doncaster manager, Brian Broadhurst – formerly of Chesterfield, whose daughter, Joanne, is a Belle – was mumbling that 'this isn't good enough.' 'Come on, linesman, chuffing 'ell,' was another bout of angst. By the thirtieth minute, he was shouting that 'it'll come,' although he looked none too convinced. It did, though, after thirty-eight minutes of resolute Wimbledon defending in which Marianne Searle was a tower at the back and Teresa Wiseman was fitfully excellent in goal. Then the Doncaster striker, Gail Borman, burst through the defence and slipped home the ball to break the deadlock with her 15th league goal of the season.

Relieved to be a goal ahead at half-time, Doncaster always thence looked likely winners. But it was still close and frustrating for a team accustomed to being several goals ahead by now. 'You have to get stabbed or shot to get a free-kick today,' said Broadhurst, when the TV news cameras were off him. His anxiety was eased after sixty-five minutes, when the team's top goal-scorer, Karen Walker, who had hitherto been having a quiet match, turned and shot over a flailing Wiseman from twenty yards. With her 40th league and cup goal of the season, the Department of Social Security worker had made the game safe for the Belles.

Now the tiny Gillian Coultard, England's most-capped player, was orchestrating the midfield for the Belles in her busy, bossy way, her short passing and Alan Ball-style running dominant. Wimbledon's leggy and skilful Marianne Spacey, possibly England's most talented player, was reduced to thwarted indolence. Four minutes from time, the match was sealed when the Belles' clever left winger, Jan Murray, who had been the most entertaining player on the pitch, sent in a cross-cum-shot which Wiseman allowed to drift into the far corner of the net.

The celebrations began in earnest around the Belles dug-out, where one of the contingent was clutching her tot, attired in matching shell-suit and Doncaster black and yellow scarf. Trevor Francis, who once disciplined a player, Martin Allen, for wanting paternity leave on the eve of a match to attend the birth of his child, would never have allowed it.

Oscar Wilde was not entirely correct about football being all very well for rough girls but hardly suitable for delicate boys. It was a toughish but amicable match, tense and enjoyable, even if the pace was at times laboured. Perhaps it lacked the edge of the men's game – in which it would have approximated a good standard of Sunday league football, although to compare is unfair – but it was something from which the latter could learn a few things. Like not throwing the ball away from throw-ins; like retreating ten yards from a free-kick.

The crowd of 430 were appreciative. Most of them were men, some two-thirds, which prompts the question about whether women are going to support their own. In the dressing-room, the BBC champagne had been cracked open. Spirits and voices ran high. 'I didn't think I was going to get out alive,' a photographer would later confide.

Coultard, nicknamed Sprout probably because of her five-feet-nothing stature, reflected back on it all. 'Yes, I have been quite shocked. I thought it would be better,' she said of the standards she had encountered in this first league season. 'We have set the standard, though. Others have got to catch up.'

It will get better, she said. 'The game has not changed that much, but there is a lot more skill coming into it. We try to play the ball through the midfield. It's the only way forward for the National League. We can't kick the ball from one end of the pitch to the other but we can pass it.' This must be worth persevering with.

The appeal of football for women was, quite simply, the game, she added. 'When men play they want to kill someone. Women want to enjoy a game.' Perhaps between a less violent and a more intense attitude lies true entertainment for the spectator. As for the venue, be it ever so humble it is still home. 'We like it here,' said Coultard. 'There's a good body of support in Armthorpe. Sometimes 400 people can get lost in a bigger ground.'

In some ways, the day was a disappointment, finding the

league experiencing such growing pains. But it does not do to patronise the women and tell them how well they are doing. It pays to tell it how it was. Much remained to be done if the game was to progress, for this surely could not be its peak. In the flatlands of Doncaster, though, any sporting peak would do just now. And the Belles had certainly done the most that they could: dominate their league.

What women's football does have, for all its limitations, however, is the enthusiasm of its participants, which will see it thrive. The game of football seems readily to inspire enthusiasm, after all. And it is big enough to embrace the male *and* the female, the long and the short and the tall. Bless 'em all.

II The Outpost

There was an eerie quietness to East Belfast on that Saturday lunchtime as the Royal Ulster Constabulary officers at the check-point peered into the slowing taxi before waving it through. The twenty-mile journey in from the airport, itself scarcely populated despite its status as an international travel centre, was preparation for such an atmosphere. It did not prepare, though, for a day of football-watching of such intense and draining emotion, a mixture of apprehension and sadness.

Fear in Belfast there may have been; loathing it was not to prove, however. There was too much admiration for a people determined to continue with activities that nurtured the spirit. Football being one of them. For me, this was a journey to discover how and why the game survives and prospers in the most adverse of circumstances, more adverse certainly than the mere financial troubles of the likes of Oxford United.

In this often forgotten outpost, football remains an obsession, part-diversion, part-escape route. Northern Ireland has, after all, fed off the English game for many years, following it intently. Religiously would be the wrong word. The English game has also fed off Northern Ireland, drawing across the Irish Sea wave after wave of players until all Football League clubs have or have had at least one. Once upon a time, there was one called Best . . .

Back in his home town, the eeriness was enveloping. Down the Newtonards Road and past the Glentoran Football Club Supporters' Club – where a security intercom demands identification – it persisted, continuing into the warren of streets surrounding the Oval Grounds. Among them, not so much pro-British as anti-Republican murals, painted on the side of the last terraced house at the end of the street, greet the visitor. They are magnificent in their intricacy and brushmanship, if sinister in their style. 'Welcome to Loyalist Dee Street,' announces one. 'Ulster 1914. Deserted – then I will stand alone,' proclaims another on Redcliffe Parade depicting a weeping widow. Union flags and that of St George abound. Meanwhile, 'Meeken Street supports all loyalist prisoners'.

By 1pm inside the Oval, a huge police presence was already assembled, milling in the car park. Upstairs in Glentoran's Adam Gilmore Room, which is more commonly known as the bar, a police briefing was taking place. The bar was, on police insistence, closed for the afternoon. 'My hands are tied,' said an apologetic bar manager to an early-arriving Glentoran regular. The reason for it all was not reaction to the murder the night before by the Irish Republican Army of seven building workers in County Tyrone, the worst atrocity of a recently escalated terrorist campaign, even if sensitivity in the already keener-than-usual city and province was heightened. It was this football match.

Glentoran's Irish Cup first-round-proper match against Donegal Celtic had, in theory, all the ingredients for a volatile day: Protestant v. Catholic, East v. West Belfast, League v. non-League. After all, two years before, Donegal Celtic (average crowd 150) went to Windsor Park to play Linfield (average crowd 4500) in the Cup. The crowd was almost 13,000. A riot occurred; stones were thrown, plastic bullets fired. A year on, it was all scaled down when the Irish Intermediate League team met Ards. But tension still hung in the air and, on the ground, a few skirmishes took place. This time, the RUC concluded, there was to be no repeat. Overstaffing was preferable to undermanning.

'A bit apprehensive, certainly. But that's just the way of Northern Ireland,' the Donegal Celtic manager, Raymond Bonnar, was later to say of his reaction at 1:30pm, when his team's bus passed through the green corrugated-iron gates of the Oval to be confronted by that police presence. Fear as normality. But then Bonnar was a veteran of Windsor Park those two years ago. 'It was the most frightening experience of my life,' he recalled. 'At one stage, I didn't think we were going to get out alive. The police just left us, and we had to wander some lonely side-streets in the dark.'

Celtic are from the Suffolk area of the city, where the streets are named after areas of the Republic of Ireland county of Donegal which neighbours Ulster on its western side. They were drawn at home in the tie but had, on request and advice, no hesitation in switching the match. For the Oval – watched over by the towering cranes of the old Harland and Wolff shipyard, where the Titanic was built – is relatively easily policed. Fences, some of them topped with barbed wire, surround the pitch. It might not have been going far enough for Ken Bates, the Chelsea chairman who once wanted to top the Stamford Bridge fences with devices which produced electric shocks; but it looked adequate.

Today, between the Glentoran supporters and those from the west of the city along one side of the stadium, were four fences and two lines of police, who were employing their own closed-circuit television. Unless, that is, TV cameramen in this part of the world have started wearing riot gear, helmet and all. Flags in the pattern of the Union standard but in Glentoran colours of red, black and green, confronted Donegal Celtic. Their supporters responded with just two Irish tricolours to greet their team, who play in the green and white hoops of the Celtic of Glasgow. You have to imagine that carrying them through this part of Belfast can be a health hazard.

As the game kicked off, sectarian songs and chants were exchanged and abuse hurled, along with the odd toilet roll from Glentoran supporters at a Celtic player as he took a throw-in. Thankfully, it was nothing more solid. Twenty minutes on, a crocodile of a dozen people at the Celtic end were escorted away by about twice as many police, in riot gear at that end though not the other. If they were fans being ejected, it was all remarkably peaceful. In fact, it was the turnstile operators returning to the offices with their takings, and their march was ignored.

Thirty-five minutes into the game, and a bang and a flash near the thin green line policing the Celtic contingent produced a split-second silence around the ground. 'Just a firecracker,' was the expert, blasé analysis up in the stand. At half-time surfaced the sense of humour that is a requirement for playing, but especially watching, football. It was all the more welcome in such a tense environment, a splash of colour in the greyness, a shaft of sanity. A bugler in the stand sounded a hunting charge as Glentoran, the Irish League leaders held goalless so far, reappeared. Donegal Celtic were greeted with the Last Post.

Plucky Celtic had missed an excellent chance in the first half to go ahead, when Pat Brannigan was sent clear, only to see his shot saved. One sensed that they would be made to pay for it. They were and, ironically, by a policeman; Gary Macartney, the Glentoran centre-forward and an RUC officer, scored twice after the interval. 'He's the only policeman at their end not wearing a helmet,' joked someone in the crowd. He might as well have been, so powerful was the header that put Glentoran ahead after fifty minutes.

When Macartney volleyed home his second six minutes from time, the Celtic contingent began to head for the exits.

Kick-off times in the city had been staggered today so that supporters of Linfield, at home to Loghall, and Ballymena, playing a mile away against Dundela, did not cross paths with the Celtic men. Fortunately, there was no sign of people lingering or loitering. Glentoran seem to have hit upon an excellent way of clearing the ground: a Barry Manilow record over the tannoy.

It had all passed off peacefully. 'I am more pleased with the way it has gone off the pitch than on,' said Ray Bonnar, not to disparage his team's efforts but in relief at the outcome of the occasion as opposed to the match. 'A good day,' was the conclusion of the Glentoran secretary, Derek McKeague. 'But then we don't have a history of trouble at football in Northern Ireland.' Such was the timbre of the day, though, that hard information, such as crowd figures and numbers of police on duty, was hard to come by. The attendance looked about 4000, with some 300 of them for Celtic. There appeared to be about 200 police – some 195 more than for a normal Glentoran home match, some 190 more than for a match against Linfield.

In the boardroom, that same mixture of relief and pleasure dominated the lubricated dissection of the game. Donegal Celtic officials were presented with a memento of their first visit to the Oval; they responded graciously, wishing their hosts well in the next round of the competition, hoping that they go on to win it. A similar ceremony had taken place in the Supporters' Club on the Newtonards Road before the game. Indeed, despite contrasting images, relationships between the two clubs are good, and they have exchanged players in the past.

Glentoran are, after all, proud of being a non-sectarian club, even if they exist in a loyalist heartland; several of their players and administrators are Catholic. The bonhomie of the home manager, Tommy Jackson, the former Everton, Nottingham Forest and Newcastle player, quickly disappears, however, when you bring up such matters and ask him about the circumstances surrounding the match. Bristling, he abruptly ends whatever conversation there had been. It is a reminder that, for all the external calm and amicability, talk of The Troubles – the Belfast newspapers accord them capital letters – can stir up at the very least uncomfortable feelings. Often uncomfortable is a euphemism for angry.

Jackson's opposite number, Ray Bonnar, is rather more open and forthcoming as he considers the day from the dressing-room. He wishes Donegal Celtic could become, like their hosts, a less sectarian club. He has, he says, one administrator and two players in his club who are not Catholics but dares not reveal their identities. 'A few weeks ago, the Linfield manager over here said that he could not play Catholics in his team because of the outcry it would provoke. I can understand that. If some people found out that we had non-Catholics playing, those players would be tortured.' He meant verbally rather than literally. At least, it sounded so.

Even the Under-10 team he also coaches were beginning to wonder about it all; why senior teams could not come to their Celtic Park ground for a cup tie. Try explaining it all in two simple sentences. 'We have 130 kids in our club and we are doing our bit to keep them out of trouble,' said Bonnar. 'I wish to God it could all change. Surely it's got to change one day.' There was such a touching wistfulness in his voice that you just wished you could help. The match, arrest-free, had been a miniscule step forward.

It seemed naïve even to contemplate that football had any answer of unification in a society where politics, religion and culture are tortuously, apparently inextricably, linked; where even to address the matter as an outsider is to feel inadequate and to tread on eggshells.

The game is not free from its environment, indeed, is

often a product of it. Even if not a force for good – although it surely was today – it can still be a welcome release, however. Thankfully, amid the greyness mirrored by the day and the potential for problems, Glentoran's motto had prevailed and helped to divert this outsider from the fear he ashamedly felt as he moved away from the ground back to more accustomed and comfortable haunts on his journey through the game. Says that Glentoran motto: *Le Jeu Avant Tout.* The Game Above All.

III The Referee

The receptionist at the Adelphi Hotel in Liverpool smiles when she finds the name on the computer. 'Ah yes, Mr P. Don,' she says.

Philip Don has learnt to live with plays on his initial and surname, ever since he first took up refereeing to supplement his grant when at teacher training college in West London. It goes with the territory of being that bastard in the black, as the chants from the terraces have it. For he has probably the most ridiculed and reviled job in football. If he 'plays' well, nobody notices. If he doesn't, everybody does. And somebody will lose, or feel like they have done if they have drawn, so he will not be deemed to have done well, no matter how well he has done.

Today will illustrate the conundrum. Don is taking charge of Liverpool against Aston Villa in the quarter-final of the FA Cup at Anfield. It will be an intense, oppressive match and day. And he will love every minute of it. For being a referee is a little like the circus worker whose job is to clear away the manure produced by the elephants. 'Don't you ever get tired of shovelling it night after night? Don't you ever think of giving it all up?' asks a friend. 'What, and quit show business?' comes the reply.

He has had, and still occasionally has, doubts about whether he would take up refereeing in the current, demanding climate; but, because of days such as this, being involved in the professional game at the highest level, he knows what the answer is. 'It's fun,' is the one that he usually comes out with. Twice he has considered giving up: once when he was punched by a player in the Chiswick Sunday League; once when first rejected for the Football League list.

Now, at 40 in two days' time, Don is one of the country's top officials. He has recently been recruited to the FIFA list of international referees and, later this month, he will take charge of his first match overseas, France v. Belgium in the Parc des Princes in Paris. The game's world governing body wants younger referees to help create faster matches; in 1994, the maximum age will be 45, which compares with 48 in England, after which they are assessed annually. Referees are, anyway, assessed at every match but, in the FA Cup, they do not get to meet the assessor.

At home, Don has been awarded more and more first-division matches – twelve so far this season – and he has been chosen to take part in an experiment of 'teams' of officials, a referee and two linesmen, who travel and work together on matches. There are only twelve such. His usual linesmen are Geoff Pearson from Kingston, Surrey, who is with him today; and Larry Watson from Coventry, who isn't but probably wishes he was, him being a collector of 1960s records and this being the home of the Beatles.

It is difficult for referees to get too carried away: Don is just as likely to be assigned a Middlesex Senior Cup match. And previous experiences prepare him for enjoying the big days as well as keeping the feet on the ground. He can remember, for example, in his early days taking a County Cup match in the village of Skidby, near his home city of Hull, for 7s 6d; he arrived to find cowpats still being cleared off the pitch. He can also remember the secretary at Fareham of the Southern League collecting a pound and a half of mushrooms off the pitch there before a game. Many of the 25,000 referees affiliated to English County Football Associations probably have similar stories.

Don remembers, too, refereeing Lincoln City in the days after their stand had burned down. He changed in a local sports centre and was taken by taxi to Sincil Bank. At half-time, though, he was given a kettle and tea bags and housed in the ladies toilet. A bunch of daffodils in a vase brightened it up. Then there are nights like earlier this season. To the ire of both Northampton and Aldershot, he had to call off a game late in the day due to a frozen pitch. Financially-strapped Northampton hadn't had a home game for three weeks; equally financially-strapped Aldershot had had to find the £250 that the coach driver demanded before he would drive them up the M1.

The previous Tuesday, Don had taken charge of England Under-18s v. Holland at Leicester – 'and my knees were knocking during the national anthem.' The nervousness is even more apparent today. It begins with that feeling of fear in the pit of the stomach as soon as he wakes up. Once he is up, and has managed to get down a breakfast of crois-sants, the first wave of anxiety passes. The next one will come when he enters Anfield just before midday. For the moment, at 11am – by which time he has already been to the toilet four times – he can stomach a Mars bar and a cup of coffee. It will be the last thing he eats, although he will drink as much of that substance without which football would not survive – tea – as Liverpool can supply.

At 11:30am, he considers it time to get to Anfield. He likes to be at grounds ridiculously early, 'just in case'. Just in case of what is not clear. We drive out from the city centre, getting only a little lost, past the Hillsborough Disas-ter Advice Centre, and turn right into the Anfield Road. At the Kop end, we stop and ask for directions to Stanley Park, the patch of land that separates Liverpool and Everton, where Don has been assigned a car park space. Two youths respond to the request: one utters two words, the second of which is 'off'; the other utters another two. 'Don't know.'

It is still barely noon, but already the environs of Anfield are big-match busy. Street traders are already doing brisk business. One gloating T-shirt bears a picture of the freed hostage, Terry Waite, asking: 'Manchester United still haven't won the League title?'

Don is more concerned that the parking space is several hundred yards from the ground; he might have to ask for a police escort back after the game. The week before, referee Roger Wiseman was attacked by a fan during a pitch invasion near the end of a match between Birmingham City and Stoke City. 'It was back to the bad old days,' Don worries. Two weeks later, Wiseman would ask to be relieved of his duties for the rest of the season.

Through the Shankly Gates – dedicated to the legendary former manager and inscribed 'You'll Never Walk Alone' – through the thick-pile reception, Don is shown past a little brown door marked 'Staff Only' to the referee's dressing-room. It is big enough, if not quite of the luxury of Manchester United's. There, in carpeted splendour, you can watch television while dressed in a provided dressing-gown. Here, linoleum tiles, grey ones at that, reflect a more spartan, more, well, working-class approach. There is the smell of fish and chips in the corridor outside. Inside, the bathroom, featuring a splendid tiled bath, contains a razor and a used toothbrush in an old Pot Noodle carton.

It is hot and breathless, perhaps the latter because of the apprehension that is building. Don goes in search of tea to the players' lounge, where Desmond Lynam is sitting planning BBC coverage for the afternoon with Niall Sloane, today's editor of the live *Match of the Day* broadcast; where the Liverpool players, Nicky Tanner and Ronnie Rosenthal, are signing autographs.

A plate of sandwiches is sent across. It goes untouched.

Don goes back outside, to meet up with his 14-year-old son, Tim, a Manchester United fan; he is coming up from their home in Hanworth Park, Middlesex, for the match, and to take in the atmosphere. The referee is himself, after all, a fan – of no one in particular, although Hull City's is the first result he looks for. He stands opposite the Shankly Gates, just people-watching, just observing those who pause at the Hillsborough Memorial, which contains the names and ages of the ninety-five who died, and in the middle of which a flame burns constantly.

The Aston Villa chairman, Doug Ellis, arrives in a white Rover 320 turbo, which he leaves at the gates for a Liverpool steward to park. Today is not the day to be bringing a blue Rolls Royce with the number plate AV1 through the streets of Liverpool.

As if to emphasise that he is a fan, Don buys five programmes, even though the referee's dressing-room contains several spare. He has been asked by two girls at the school in South London where he is a deputy headmaster to get them one. There are also two boys at the school where his wife teaches who want them. At 1pm, he decides to walk the pitch, that curious, privileged pastime granted to those involved. At Anfield, there is more of a thrill than at most grounds. First, you have to go under that sign which declares 'This is Anfield', thought up to intimidate the visitors. It has worked with many teams, many players, although wise judges have always believed that Anfield exposes only bad professionals, and makes the good ones. This season, however, the talismanic effect has been diminished, with teams coming and winning more often. Perhaps the beginning of the end came when Wimbledon visited, and some of their number spat at the sign as they made their way out for a match. For their part, Auxerre may have been living in the past when they succumbed to the pressure here. Even so, their home win illustrated the decline of the awe in Liverpool's name.

But can referees still be intimidated? The 'Anfield penalty' has become an established term in the game, separate from a 'real' one: it is awarded to the home team in a charged atmosphere, with the pressure on from fans and players alike. Indeed, players appear more concerned these days that the referee, rather than they, will give in to that pressure at Anfield. Don was taking Liverpool v. Manchester City last season when Adrian Heath went down in the penalty area for the visitors. 'I waved play on,' says Don, 'and a couple of Manchester City players ran up to me and said, "You are allowed to give a penalty at Anfield, you know." Later, Mark Ward went down and I did, but because it was a penalty.'

It will be a theme of the afternoon, and the Liverpool manager, Graeme Souness, has been criticising referees in the last week, first after a goalless home draw against Southampton, then in midweek after defeat in Genoa in a UEFA Cup quarter-final first leg. 'It's the last resort,' says Don. 'They're getting desperate when they're criticising the referee.'

Emerging from the players' tunnel today, the new Kemlyn Road stand under construction overlooks us. Its sheer size may do something to restore the fear in visiting players as they run out. With the sun shining, walking the pitch is an almost spiritual experience. For a football follower, a walk in the Lake District can hold no greater attraction. To think that, here, some of the most historic events in the English game have occurred. The ground is smaller than television has it, although the Kop is even more imposing than on screen, higher and deeper but, at the front, closer to the pitch than you expect.

The gates have just been opened, and the early-comers are pouring in. It is astonishing and wonderful that people will stand here for two hours just to see a ninety-minute football match. Just to see a ninety-minute football match. It is a bit like waiting to see Pavarotti and describing it as hanging around to see a fat bloke sing. The annoying thing on a football terrace can be that you spend two hours waiting for the match, guarding your little square yard of space and then, at 5 to 3, some Pavarotti comes and stands in front of you.

As Don looks now at the opposite end, where Michael Thomas scored that goal for Arsenal in injury-time to wrest the Championship from Liverpool three years earlier, a steward leans over the wall to speak to him. 'Give us a penalty in the last minute,' he says. 'We don't want a replay 'cos we're skint after Genoa.'

With Don on the field now are his linesmen, Pearson and Martin Short from Grantham, who is savouring it all 'because you don't get many like this'. There, too, are son Tim and a friend, as well as the reserve official, Mark Cowburn, and a friend of his. It is a bit like Gandhi's entourage growing as he passed on his peaceful way through India. 'You should have seen Clive Thomas's,' says Cowburn of the old Welsh ref, Thomas the Book. Cowburn is also musing on the inclusion of Paul McGrath in the Aston Villa team. 'I played against him in a reserve match when I was at Blackpool and he was with Manchester United. He called me a donkey then. I hope he doesn't remember me.'

Back in the dressing-room at 1:30pm, a man from the BBC comes in to outline the programme for the afternoon: teams to be led out at 3:03pm; a signal from him ninety seconds before kick-off to bring the captains together; then the kick-off at 3:07pm. Half-time is to be twelve minutes long. Don, as the man supposedly in charge, resents the commands, resents waiting for landlady Sharon to close the Queen Vic in *EastEnders*, the soap that shows before

Match of the Day Live. 'I'm sure it will all work out,' he tells the BBC man abruptly.

A tray of sandwiches is brought in. It goes untouched.

Until 2pm, it has been mostly time-filling. Now the real business begins. Don goes through his pre-match talk with Short and Pearson, telling them what he expects, how he needs their help with all decisions, including 'bollockings, cautions and sendings-off'. Eye-contact with him is important: 'Players are not going to get me to come and talk to you,' he concludes. The linesmen will change wings for the second half; it helps not to have the same set of fans shouting at your back. As senior linesman, Pearson will take over if Don sustains an injury.

The Merseyside police superintendent arrives. After the bomb alert at Tottenham before their League Cup semi-final second leg against Nottingham Forest the previous week, Anfield has been sniffed by trained dog. 'Do you want an escort to Stanley Park afterwards?' asks the policeman. 'Let's see how it goes,' says Don.

Now the corridor and referee's dressing-room is like Sauchiehall Street at chucking-out time. The BBC commentator, John Motson, comes in to get a glimpse of the officials, to check their Christian names. Then, at 2:30pm, arrive Graeme Souness and the Liverpool captain, Mark Wright, and the Aston Villa assistant manager, Andy Gray, and Villa captain Kevin Richardson to present the team sheets. The Villa manager, Ron Atkinson, can be seen down in the boot room, chatting away. 'No jewellery, retreat at free-kicks and enjoy it,' says Don to the gathering. The linesmen no longer go into dressing-rooms to check for dangerous studs, since the Professional Footballers' Association says that its own members will take responsibility for each other's well-being.

Don studies the team list; John Barnes, Ronnie Whelan and Michael Thomas – yes, the scorer of *that* Arsenal goal, brought to Anfield earlier in the season – back after injury for Liverpool. Something of a gamble. 'Villa are playing Dwight Yorke, Dalian Atkinson and Tony Daley up front. That'll keep me going. Cyrille Regis is playing, too. Good. He doesn't run too hard. He uses his loaf.' He has refereed Villa before this season, in a live televised match against Everton, at which the guest TV 'expert' was Howard Wilkinson, the Leeds United manager. Don had controversially reported him to the FA for remarks allegedly made to a linesman during another televised match between United and Sheffield Wednesday. Later in the season, Wilkinson was cleared.

By 2:45, Don and his officials are all changed, and he has checked that he has two watches, two whistles, two pencils. He goes through a routine of stretching excerises. 'This is the worst time,' he says. These fifteen minutes seem to last longer than the previous three hours. 'It's not too bad once you have made your first decision,' says Pearson, checking that his orange and yellow flag is unfurling properly. Finally, it is time for Don to press the bell button on the wall that tells the teams to go out. 'Enjoy it,' he says to Short and Pearson as they exchange handshakes.

In the corridor, the anxiety, the importance of it all, can be seen as Liverpool's players emerge from their dressing-room. 'Clear head, clear head, clear head,' Souness demands of each player in turn as he pats them on the back of their skulls with a force that seems detrimental to his object.

Don's first decision goes well. McGrath has pushed Barnes, and the referee stands no nonsense when the defender complains. Soon he is telling Souness to sit down. The stream of advice and abuse from the dug-outs is constant and tiresome. Les Sealey, the injured Aston Villa goalkeeper, is the worst offender. After half an hour, Don is booking Villa's Mark Blake for a foul on Dean Saunders.

None can reasonably complain. It is all fevered and oppressive. At half-time, it is that pair of spectacles, 0–0.

Ron Atkinson shoots Don a glare as they come up the tunnel. 'You're doing well, ref, don't listen to them,' says Dean Saunders. Andy Gray wonders in jest if Don can do something about sending the noisy Sealey from the dug-out. 'It's hard work. You know you are in a game,' says Don sipping his half-time tea. 'Have I missed anything? Was that a corner?' he asks his linesmen, who shake their heads. 'There is just so much going on. So many feet in. Whelan is moaning the whole time. Barry Venison just keeps asking me the time. I say, "Five minutes since you last asked me." But we'll stay cool. We'll let them lose control,' he urges his linesmen. 'You are the eyes in the back of my head. We've won the first half. Let's win the second.'

A plate of sandwiches has gone untouched.

The desperate atmosphere continues in the second half although, with tiring bodies, the game eases. The Kop seems a shadow of its former self, its silence communicating itself to players exhibiting rare self-doubt. Perhaps they sense that, 0–2 down to Genoa and lagging in the League, this might be their only chance for honours this season. And it is just not acceptable for Liverpool to go a season without honours.

Venison is booked for clipping Atkinson's heels. There is a crowd disturbance in a corner of the ground where Liverpool and Villa supporters are in proximity, but it is quickly quelled by an overwhelming police presence. There is a disturbance, too, around the Villa dug-out, where it is alleged that Sealey, in disgust at a decision, has thrown a paper cup of tea on to the pitch. Don needs those eyes in the back of his head.

Suddenly, the action is back on the pitch. Barnes turns beautifully in midfield and pierces the Villa defence with a through-ball to Thomas, who clips it past the advancing goal-keeper, Nigel Spink, and into the net. Thomas will receive the plaudits, it being only his second goal at Anfield – the first having been *that* goal – but one moment of incisive quality from Barnes has settled the issue. Now the Kop is as noisy, if not as entertaining, as it has ever been.

Don has only a couple of other controversies to deal with: Bruce Grobbelaar berates him for not allowing the trainer on to treat the split webbing of his hand – Don merely wants to know what the problem is – and a booking for McGrath, who has challenged late the Liverpool goal-keeper. He is relieved, a headache-inducing four minutes of stoppage-time added, to reach the dressing-room, although he feels sad in that familiar, curious way that it is all over. 'I have never had to blow the whistle so long and so hard,' he pants.

He was fed up with the Villa captain, Richardson, during the game telling him not to be influenced by Liverpool. '"Don't do what they tell you," he kept saying. I told him to get on with his game and I'll get on with mine.' Don makes the sensible point that players concerned with the referee's performance inevitably undermine their own. He also makes several others: concerning penalties being given when the offence seems to have taken place outside the area – often advantage is played, and the second tackle happens inside the penalty area. He adds that, by enforcing a sending-off for a professional foul, it makes defenders think twice about bringing attackers down, thus eliminating fouls and keeping the game flowing.

'It has to be right if an obvious goal-scoring opportunity is denied,' he says. 'But there is no provision for the viciousness of the challenge or the seriousness of the offence. That's where some trouble may arise. Where it becomes controversial is in the penalty area. It might look innocuous but, if it is a goal-scoring opportunity, then it has to be a sending-off. A penalty is no guarantee of a goal being scored. If it is missed, a player gets off scot-free.' Don had been criticised the previous season for dismissing the Arsenal captain, Tony Adams, in just such circumstances.

Swearing is part of the game, he accepts, and discretion and context must be uppermost in a referee's mind. 'Foul and abusive language always comes up when I talk to referees' societies,' he says. 'It's the way that it's said that is important. There is always going to be some in the heat of the moment but, in the professional game, I don't always hear it. I like to be on my bike as soon as I have made a decision.' And the criticism that some referees think they are the stars? 'Well, some are more flamboyant than others. It's human nature. I think it's a question of developing man-management skills. I like to play it low-key.' On the subject of booker extraordinaire Jimmy Parker, he says only: 'There are no grey areas with him. It's all black or white.'

Don has played it low-key today and is largely pleased with the pitch he has struck. So, too, are the police who tell him that all has gone well. They will be writing to Villa about the Sealey incident but it is literally, they say, 'a storm in a tea cup'.

'Ah, well, another experience,' he says, dressing his tired body. He will receive £130 plus expenses, which include £24 hotel allowance, as payment for his weekend – he gets £70 a day on European trips. It is not to be sniffed at, but no fortune. The unseen work is the running of up to twenty-five miles a week to keep fit. 'People talk about professional referees, but I don't see how much more professional I could be, given that it's virtually a second full-time job.' Next week he will not be 'out', his wife having 'closed' the date, as referee-speak has it. She is possibly planning something around his 40th birthday.

It has been a long, hard day, and it is time to get home for what remains of Sunday, before being back at school in the morning. Many things he has been called, but the one that does not apply is the distasteful label of 'cheat' first uttered by players then picked up by mindless sections of crowds. Thankfully, however, he does not need a police escort back to Stanley Park.

Spring

Eight: Hope Springs Eternal

1 In Reserve

The very words 'reserve-team football' can strike terror in
a seasoned professional. The 'petty' competition can make
you a 'petty little person', wrote Eamon Dunphy in his book
Only A Game? Add this, his account of playing for Millwall
Reserves at Leyton Orient: 'Back in the bloody Midweek
League again. It's an unbelievable sensation going to play
at Orient on a Wednesday afternoon in November. There is
no one there, absolutely nothing at stake, except your own
pride. You don't feel like it at all. And whereas for two
hours before a first-team game you are beginning to get
nervous, beginning to get geed up, feeling a bit of tension
and atmosphere, here you go to a ground which is empty.
It is like a graveyard. You have to walk around a bit to find
where to go in – especially at Orient.

'When you do get in there, the dressing-rooms are cold,
because they don't bother switching on the heating for the
Midweek League. They get no gate, of course, so they do it
as cheaply as they can.

'I never start getting changed until half an hour beforehand anyway, but even then you feel absolutely empty. No
tension at all. Not a glimmer of excitement.'

The Dunphy experience had been apparent to me on a
visit one weekday afternoon in April 1988 to watch Watford
Reserves. The pitch at the athletics stadium in the north of
the town was bumpy, and just a small stand confronted the

players. It housed a couple of hundred spectators and a couple of dogs. Every eff and blind could be heard as the players performed for people who were either unemployed or with nothing better to do on a Monday afternoon. Like sports writers. 'I make sure I get dosed up with football this time of year. We've got bloody cricket coming up,' said one observer.

Ernie Walley, who was once manager of Chelsea, was the Watford reserve-team manager. 'Your main function is to bring the young boys along and keep the older players happy and ready for the first team again,' he said. His aim was to make worthwhile what could indeed seem depressing. 'It is a hard job, but it can be rewarding seeing the younger players come on.' No, he didn't feel cut off from the rest of the club.

Luther Blissett did, though. He was currently transfer-listed, in his second spell with the club, after coming back from Milan and before joining Bournemouth – they both played in red and black stripes, but there the similarity ended. He would, when Elton John rejoined the Watford board in 1991, come back for a third spell.

Watford's first team were about to be relegated from the first division, and Blissett was not flavour of the month even though he was still the team's top scorer – with 4. 'Gor blimey,' he said when you reminded him. Incongruously, he had arrived in a sports car and wearing a designer silver suit *Milanese*. Entering the semi-derelict dressing-rooms, he would have read a 1958 council warning about leaving valuables around. The San Siro it was not.

'You have to create your own atmosphere,' he said. 'Every time there is a game, I want to play. You can lose a bit of sharpness but you just put your boots on and have a go.' It sounded the authentic, wholehearted 'Loofah' whom the Vicarage Road fans acclaimed in chant, the one whom Elton John was so keen to have back. That day, Watford lost 1–2 to Norwich City, and their hopes of winning the Football Combination title receded.

Even if it wasn't quite the cynical, depressing stuff Dunphy described, there was an element of gloom about it. But it needn't be like that. At Nottingham Forest in recent years, they had lifted reserve-team football almost to an art form. It had perhaps become the way Dunphy found it when he gave it a chance: 'It is amazing the pleasure you can get out of it. Even more than the first team. Because, once you start to get involved, there is no stomach-wrenching pressure. It's just your own pride, and you begin to enjoy the game.'

Archie Gemmill, a former midfield playing favourite of Brian Clough's, joined Nottingham Forest as reserve-team coach at the manager's invitation in 1987. In his first season, the team that no one wanted to play for became a must, even for the first-team regulars; all of them played at some point during the season, many of them asking to. Nigel Clough, Brian's son and centre-forward for the first team, even played at centre-half for tactical reasons. It was a measure of the camaraderie and involvement in the club from top to bottom that Brian Clough so emphasised.

They won the Central League title that first Gemmill season, all but wrapping it up on a wet Thursday night in May with a 2–0 win over Liverpool, who had won the competition six times in the previous ten years. A crowd of around 2500 turned up to witness a game that would have put many in the first division to shame, Tommy Gaynor's brace of goals bringing victory. The winger, Gary Crosby, like Nigel Clough, had volunteered to play only twenty-four hours after a first-team game against West Ham.

'Brian more or less lets you have your head but he definitely has the final say. I pick the side, but if Brian doesn't like it he changes it,' said Gemmill, who had quickly adopted the Forest management team uniform of trainers, tracksuit trousers and green sweatshirt. 'He gets involved in everything, even with the person that sweeps out the toilet,' he added. 'They have got to do that right as well. That is the basis of the success of this club. Everything has to be done properly. I am more than happy just to listen to him, because you are always picking up something new. The boss is just as pleased with the YTS boys winning on a Saturday morning as he is with the first team winning on a Saturday afternoon.'

Now, four years later on another Thursday night – always that blank and empty one for a football follower – we sat again in Forest's Jubilee Club bar and reflected on the continuing success of the reserve team. They had subsequently won another Championship and been runners-up the other twice in Gemmill's time in charge. They were again top of the table this season and tonight, on this almost balmy late February evening in whose air spring seemed to be dropping hints, they would look to consolidate their position against Manchester City.

'Oh yes, they still want to play for the reserves, but nowadays things have changed a little bit,' he says. 'Now more than any other time they really just want to be in the first team. They have still got to do it at reserve level but sometimes they think they are battering their head at a brick wall. They see for five, six, seven or eight games the first team not doing so well, and the same team playing. Sometimes they drop a little bit.

'More so than years ago there is good money to be made through so many cup competitions and a good League position. Sometimes they think they should be in there picking up the perks of it. But some will still play midweek for the reserves even if they have played for the first team at the weekend, especially during an international week. The boss believes it's better playing than training.

'Brian is still very much involved, he still runs the club.

Maybe he has dropped off slightly at youth level but he is always passing his opinion on what's happening. I have got to write out the team and give it to him. He will say "yeah, that's good enough" or "no, I don't fancy that". The lads' hearts are in it, and that's got to come from the gaffer. He is not the type of person that stands slackers at all. It's times when they are not on song and feeling sorry for themselves or depressed that he's in there handing out quite a bit of stick.'

He is still learning from Clough, he says. 'Everything about the management side and possibly dealing with directors. They are the people who keep you in a job, and you have got to be careful how you are with them, and the way you conduct yourself on such as away trips. Even on the football side I am still learning from the boss.' He will try his hand at management himself one day, he says, but it will have to be the right job. Not for him a dead-end lower-division club 'where you can be the greatest manager in the world, but where it is difficult to get success and they just get somebody else.' He is content at Forest presently because it is rewarding working with good players. He is tipped to succeed Clough when the time is right.

You sense, though, that some of his comments about players and the reserve team these days are also about his own attitude, about some frustration. The previous season, he had been suspended for a period by Clough for expressing publicly his ambition – premature and presumptuous, deemed the manager – to take over Forest's first team.

The Forest secret, if there is one, he says, may be that '90 per cent of coaching is by word of mouth. We talk rather than go out on the pitch and show them.' The Forest system, using wing-backs in a pass-and-move style, is modified only for younger players so that No. 2s and No. 3s learn first to defend; 'otherwise it can take away their learning process. We never ever kick it long unless we can help it. If we are in dire straits we will occasionally hit it up the park but we try and play otherwise.' That much will be apparent later.

It is time for him to go and prepare the team. Before you head off, Archie, what about that quotation attributed to you saying that if Graeme Souness was a chocolate drop he would eat himself? 'Och, that was nothing, just a remark in private.' He seems a bit annoyed to have been reminded of it. Then he smiles a beaming smile.

A few early-evening seekers of pints enter the Jubilee Club while, outside, the beginnings of a crowd that will reach about 1200 start to arrive at the City Ground. It is £2 to get in, £1 for juniors and pensioners, and free for club shareholders and season-ticket holders. It is a delight to have no parking problems, to park right next to the ground, indeed, one of several advantages. It is possible, for example, to get in without queuing; possible to get a cup of coffee without waiting for half an hour.

At the turnstiles, a photocopied team sheet is handed out. 'Ooh, look who's number 14,' says an excited teenaged girl, sounding lovestruck, to her friend. Up the uncrowded steps, and you arrive in a stand where you can choose your seat with an unusual freedom worth savouring. Some picnicking families have even chosen the press box, where there is a bench on which to place the food and thermos. 'Go on, you pick a seat because I always choose one next to the twat that's talking rubbish,' says one man to his mate, echoing the fear of the football fan the world over – that moment when you realise you have been seated next to the loudest, most boorish, most ill-informed bloke in the ground. It remains the most cogent argument for terracing to remain in stadia at least there you can move if you don't like the look and sound of your neighbour.

The floodlights are fully switched on only five minutes before kick-off. It is one of the many little things that tell a player he is in the reserves. His reflection in the darkened executive boxes – even though, remarkably, two or three appear occupied – is another. The reluctance of the trainer to run on the field for anything less than an amputation when, for a first-team match, he does so for a hair out of place, is the final confirmation, rudely so. And only one stand is open for spectators, while two ballboys patrol each of the other three unoccupied sides. Players have to fetch the ball for themselves sometimes, though, as if tennis players in the park.

Forest are fielding a strong side, all of whom seem to have played first-team football. It is an indication of the depth of their squad and prompts the thought that this must be the most expensive league in the country, what with the wages to pay but gate revenue inconsequential. The team includes Gary Charles and Lee Glover, who had come on as substitutes for the first team in a Zenith Data Systems Trophy semi-final victory by 2–0 over Leicester City on the ground the previous night. Glover will play for the first team the following Sunday and score Forest's first goal in a 2–1 win over Tottenham that takes them to Wembley again, for the League Cup final. Charles is back after injury, although the question occurs to you as the game gets under way: given the way he withstood a monstrous hack at his shins by Paul Gascoigne in the FA Cup final the previous season – the one that led to Gascoigne's time out of the game – just how did he get injured in the first place?

The thought occurs, too, about the least fulfilling job in the world, like being a Swiss naval commander, perhaps. At left-back is one Stuart Cash, whose lot it is to understudy the first-team captain, Stuart Pearce, also England captain-elect when Gary Lineker retires. Short of being hit by a tank, Pearce, a life-size cardboard model of whom is now available in the club's shop, is unlikely to cede his position. Cash for nothing, it seems.

A largely anonymous Manchester City team create the better chances in the goalless first half, the promising young striker, Michael Sheron, forcing Andrew Marriott into two good saves. Brian Clough is forced out of his dug-out after thirty-eight minutes to offer some words of advice. Then, after sixty-eight, Tommy Gaynor, still ploughing the reserve furrow four years on, hooks in a goal. After seventy-one, the lesser known but gifted man-of-the-match, John Moncur, bursts from midfield and curls home to secure the second and the 2–0 win. Forest would stretch their lead at the top of the table.

Even if it was all over, it was difficult to keep Brian Clough out of the action. Four years ago, he had run along the touchline to admonish the Liverpool bench during that reserve game after his right winger, Gary Crosby, had been badly fouled. Tonight he leaves the dug-out ten minutes before the end of the match in dinner-jacket and bow tie to wolf-whistles from the stand. Since none had seen him change, it confirmed what some had suspected: that the longest-serving manager in the League – appointed by Forest in January 1975 – was indeed Superman, and that the dug-out was as a telephone box to Clark Kent.

At the final whistle, it took one minute to reach the car, another to negotiate the normally chocca junction at the Radcliffe Road end of the Trent Bridge cricket ground. For the players who saw their lives summed up in a one-line result in a newspaper – which is still more than most people – it may have been a less than enticing evening. For the spectator, though, it had had its own considerable appeal.

11 Sunday Muddy Sunday

On the morning after the Saturday night before, you peer out of the window into the blackness, save for the white frost on the ground, and try without success not to disturb your partner in bed as you fish out those boots with the dried mud caked on them from somewhere at the bottom of the wardrobe. It is amazing what people will do for a game of football.

The Mecca of this branch of the game, the Sunday morning syndrome, is Hackney Marsh in East London – an enormous, bleak and barren territory which lies adjacent to the ground of Leyton Orient and between those of West Ham and Tottenham. It is the Copacabana of England, whose answer it is to that Rio beach where men supposedly play samba football compared to our heavy metal version; where 7-year-olds are fabled to juggle the ball with both feet for hour upon hour as they prepare to win the World Cup for Brazil.

Here there are no fewer than 106 football pitches – one or two in addition are devoted to some sports called hockey and Rugby Union – which are divided into four areas. Pitches 1–20 on South Marsh are not in use due to vandals having smashed up the changing-rooms and them not yet having been rebuilt. A similar fate has befallen the toilets at Mabley Green, where pitches 102–106 are situated. The rest of South Marsh, running into North Marsh and comprising pitches 21–90 is fine. On this vast expanse, before the myriad teams turn up, men practise their golf shots while others walk their dogs. The doggy deposits in penalty areas can bring an additional hazard: it is not the goal-keeper's fear of the penalty that is his main concern in Sunday football.

Today, on pitches 91–101 of East Marsh, which backs on to the new Spitalfields Market and is separated from North and South Marshes by the River Lea, the Hackney and Leyton Sunday League, founded in 1946, is in operation as usual. Here, where it is just a little more sheltered than on North Marsh – but only a little – and where it can be half a mile to your pitch from the changing-rooms, operate many of the forty-nine teams who make up the five divisions. The names are wonderfully evocative: the Stick and Weasel, Dockland Settlement, Intra-City Systems, for example. But then the place itself is wonderfully evocative.

By 10am, a mobile burger bar is up and running, though selling more black coffees than burgers, this being probably the most delicate time of the week. The car park is filling up, a number of black cabs among them. So this is where they all go on a Sunday morning, this is why you can never get one. 'South of the river? Sorry mate, not at this time of the morning. 'Ow about 'Ackney?' Perhaps that is why they are called Hackney carriages.

Team-mates greet each other above the hum of the nearby traffic – more of a roar on weekdays – on the Eastway. 'Big day today,' says one, echoing the adage that every game is a big one for someone. Girlfriends are kissed before being left to stand around in the cold for the next couple of hours.

The changing-rooms are spartan in the extreme, a collection of windowless cells arranged to have a quadrangle at their heart. The scene brings to mind a racing stables, though hardly as luxurious. In the referee's changing-room sits Peter Balding, assistant secretary of the league and its disciplinary chairman, co-ordinating the morning's events, in touch with his general secretary, Jack Walpole, by walk-ie-talkie.

'It was a shambles,' says Balding – who is a french pol-isher by trade and performs what can feel a thankless task because 'a man needs a hobby' – of the discipline within the league a few years ago. 'It needed a new committee to give it a kick up the arse.' He announces proudly that fines have gone up from £400 or £500 a year to between £1800 and £2000. These fines, levied at a meeting every Tuesday night in a social club in North-East London, are for offences such as matches taking place with no corner flags or goal-nets, teams having no first-aid boxes. Referees' reports, awarding team sportsmanship points out of 10, are heard.

The most familiar offence, natch, is the late kick-off. Matches on Sunday mornings are not delayed for the pro-fessional game's reason of crowds still getting in through the turnstiles; more for the players still arriving after going through the wringer the previous night. The more serious offences, which include sendings-off and bookings, are referred to the London Football Association. Violent con-duct can bring a five-week suspension and a £20 fine; foul and abusive language the same. Just such offences had led to a decline in the number of referees taking up the game in recent years, but it was apparently picking up again.

'We would sooner lose a team than a ref,' says Balding, who used to run a team himself out of a pub in Southgate. Peter Storey, the former Arsenal and England midfield player, turned out for him in his 40s. 'He was a different class,' says Balding. 'Every time we got a free-kick we scored. Every forward scored over 25 goals.' The league now features the Peter Storey Sportsmanship Trophy; it is something of an irony, the poacher turned gamekeeper, given Storey's reputation in his playing days as, um, uncompromising.

Today would be an opportunity to gauge the atmosphere, a chance to see if the kicking game or the unSunday language persisted. Whether the £14 which the referees received for their pains – sometimes literally, one had heard – was adequate, or if no amount of money sufficed. The first keen players, ready to hoist their own goal-nets to some leaning goal-post, emerge from the dressing-room at 10:10am, a final cigarette before kick-off between a few lips. One wondered if the condemned men had also eaten a hearty breakfast.

On pitch 95, there is indeed a big game. You can tell as much by the fact that there will be properly qualified linesmen – or at least men wearing the right black and white garb – as well as a referee. Usually, a substitute performs the task and is roundly abused, mostly by his own team-mates, for the whole ninety minutes; he rarely gets on, of course, since no else would be mug enough to take over as linesman. That is if the man, already resentful enough at not being in the team, can be prevailed upon to lift a flag in the first place.

It is in fact a semi-final in the Jack Morgan Cup, a competition for the lower-division teams, between Hackney Volunteers Social Club and Holloway and Salisbury, the latter so named because they operate out of the Holloway Tavern and were run, until he died last year, by one Ron Salisbury. There are here a few figures by McDonalds, hair by Flymo and earrings by Ratners. The new trend is also for ponytails. In the East End of London as well. There are here players who were once pretty good and players who could be if they didn't have other priorities in their life. And players who aren't, never were and never will be.

It is curious, but when you are playing in a Sunday game you can be deceived into thinking how fast and how good it is, how but for a few breaks here and there you could have been a pro. When you watch it, though, it is often

slow and scrappy. Some of the tackling would make a professional wince. London buses, which some of the
defenders resemble, are not this late.

'Every Sunday morning, I come here and watch football
and, every Sunday morning, I wonder why,' says an
onlooker gazing out at the semi-final. He hits at the paradox
of the game: Sunday football is not really a spectator sport
unless you are close to somebody involved. Then again,
any fan of the sport can hardly stop himself watching when
a game is going on. It can be dangerous, for example, driving
past public playing fields, one eye on the road, the other
on the game – 'I must just see this corner being taken.' It
can infuriate your family when you are out walking and
promise to catch them up.

Amazingly, Hackney Volunteers are a goal up at half-
time, having broken out from consistent pressure to score.
The Holloway goal-keeper has flapped at a free-kick, and
Barry has bundled the ball over the line. 'It come off me
knee,' admits the honest Barry at half-time, puffing on a
cigarette between swigs of tea. The goal knocks the stuffing
out of Holloway, who seem to have given it everything
and can't believe that they are losing. Del, that popular
abbreviated Christian name in this part of the world,
makes it 2–0 midway through the second half and adds
a third three minutes from time. It seems all up for Holloway. 'It's not worth getting me knees dirty,' says Tony,
the Volunteers' substitute, when offered the chance of a
run-out.

Then, from somewhere in the recesses of memory where
pride is hurt, Holloway conjure up 2 goals in two minutes,
setting up a frantic finale. All of a sudden, with forty
seconds left, Scully, the Volunteers' midfield dynamo, goes
down in a heap despite there being no one near him. Has
he turned an ankle, broken a leg? The game is stopped for
some five minutes while an ambulance from the London

St John's Ambulance Service (Prince of Wales's District) 342 Hackney Division is called.

As Scully is bundled into it, the Volunteers survive those final forty seconds. 'Wemberley, Wemberley,' they sing within a few moments of the final whistle. Soon, having lived to tell the tale of the cold dash across the stable-yard for a shower, they will be down the pub embellishing the morning, Scully amongst them. He has decided that the injury is not as bad as first feared. Still, he got a lift the quarter of a mile back to the dressing-rooms.

It has been a remarkably sporting contest, with players who criticise the referee being swiftly rebuked by team-mates and told to concentrate on their own game. It seems they have learned what many professionals have forgotten: that to lose discipline is to lose. It used to be that the amateur game mirrored the professional; perhaps the tables should now be turned. The language, too, save for the odd understandable remark in the heat of the moment, has been mostly moderate. It was the technical language of the game that was most prevalent, in such code that would be as Swahili to the average person: 'Big one, Bazza'; ''Oo wants it?'; ''Old up'; and 'Nuffing silly'.

It has been competitive, too, if not of outstanding quality. On pitch 91, a more skilful contest, albeit without the excitement, has been taking place, a premier-division match between Crown and Manor – winners of the sportsmanship award the previous season – and the newly-promoted Brownlow Arms. Crown and Manor, in natty red gingham shirts – indeed, a Van Goghian array of colours is on view, from orange and blue together to Aston Villa away strip – cut a dash to romp past the Brownlow 6–2. Some of the skill exhibited is surprisingly good from a young and athletic Crown and Manor team, whose members must have been close to semi- if not professional football.

Most surprising again, though, is the self-discipline. 'It

was an all-out war sometimes in the past,' says Richard Allen, the Crown and Manor manager, a youth worker at the boys club of that name in Hoxton, who describes himself, at 27, as the old man of the club. 'The behaviour of players has improved, although maybe in the lower divisions, where there isn't so much skill, there might still be problems sometimes. It did take a dip a few years ago, but the league got a grip. It was their stance as much as anything which helped. Now refs getting abused is a one-off.'

The evidence of an adjacent pitch bore him out. A black referee, in generic terms probably the bravest of all sporting officials, was conducting affairs with little trouble. A referee wearing baseball boots was more open to ribbing. But the only real haranguing going on was from a little girl watching the game. 'Daddy, I need a wee-wee,' she was saying to the home team's right-back, who had undoubtedly finished second in the debate that begins: 'Well, if you're going out to play football you can take the kids with you.' 'Hang on, love, there's only a couple of minutes to go,' said the harassed defender, who was fortunately getting less trouble from the opposing left winger. The two minutes up, it was a dash for the dressing-room – as it was for everyone, in fact, if they were to avoid the congestion in the showers, before the afternoon crowd turned up mob-handed.

Hackney Marsh today was not as crowded as it might have been in the past, with twenty-six matches taking place on the main area where sixty might have done not so long ago. That was due to teams boycotting the facilities, the cost of which had risen from £21 to £36, or £47 if a team was from a London borough other than Hackney. A planned decrease in prices for the following year would probably go some way towards remedying the situation. Players were now paying on average £3 a week each, although it was only 50p at subsidised Crown and Manor on top of their subscription of £20. It was not that the game was becoming any less popular at the grass roots. 'If anything, I notice more and more people playing,' said Richard Allen. It was more that an economic recession was affecting everyone, even if football remained a comparatively cheap form of entertainment, escapism even.

By now, the team's base – usually the pub – was beckoning. There the talk would begin with today but end with our old theme, 'There's always next week'. Clearly, with the cost merely a side issue, this English ritual would never, could never, die. While there were still people who dreamt of playing at Wembley in front of 80,000 people, then woke up to seek out those boots in the bottom of the wardrobe, Sunday football would survive – survive and prosper.

iii Old Boys

From the pie and mash of Hackney Marsh it was on to roast beef and Yorkshire pudding; just as English but a little more leisurely and refined. On another Sunday morning, on the more manicured lawns of the Lloyds Bank Sports Ground in leafy Beckenham, a suburb of South London where Kent breaks out, was to be found a group for whom football went beyond an endearing passion to an enduring one.

Veterans, or Over-35s football, like the women's game, is a growth area of the sport. That is perhaps on the basis that it is too good a game to be left to the youngsters, in the same way that some things in life are too important to be left to the experts. But more probably it is tribute to the superior fitness of older players, due partly to the advances in the treatment of sports injuries and also to the increase in leisure time of many middle-aged men. Redundancy and early retirement no doubt also play their parts and, with the children generally now grown up, the pressure to be at home at weekends is less intense.

As well as countless friendly matches being played today, there are now eleven veterans' leagues in the country. There is even a national competition, which the FA has sanctioned in line with its own recommendation in the Blueprint for the Future of Football, which noted the expansion of this branch of the game and recognised the need to respond. 'The growth is spectacular,' said the organiser of the national competition, David Shepherd, who began his mission to spread the veterans' game four years ago. 'We're catching up with the continent where it is very popular.'

Shepherd, who had enjoyed a career just below the top level in non-League football after trials with Nottingham Forest, Notts County and Chelsea, found himself playing in a junior game in Congleton, Cheshire, one day. He was changing in a shed, and was up to his knees in mud. He was getting too old, at 35, to treat himself like this, he concluded. A short while later, missing the game, he phoned a friend to see if they could get two teams out to play an Over-35s match. He asked twenty-four players, guessing that eleven would turn up. All twenty-four did. The friend had asked thirty. All those thirty turned up. They had enough for not just one but a series of friendly matches. Soon was born, in the Manchester area near Shepherd's Wilmslow home, the first veterans' competition.

Sixteen teams took part, including a team of ex-professionals from Blackpool Football Club who, not surprisingly, won it. Manchester United soon wanted to join in, and the two played a challenge match. Others followed, such as Everton, Nottingham Forest and Leeds. There were, of course, plenty of amateur teams who also became interested, from villages, pubs and companies. They are now all mixed together in local groups and then, after Christmas, the teams with the best records qualify for the knock-out tournaments, one for amateurs, one for ex-professionals. The final, contested by one amateur team and one of ex-professionals, is held at Wembley on the pre-season day of the FA Charity Shield. In 1991, John Quinn's All Stars, a team of former Sheffield Wednesday players – the competition claims the most international footballers outside the League – beat Arnold of Nottinghamshire 1–0.

There are currently 120 entries – a growth rate of 800 per cent over four years – and there will be 200 next year, said David Shepherd. The oldest player in the competition is 72-year-old Doug Ryder of Crabtree Inn Middle-Aged Spread, from Matlock in Derbyshire. 'The main reason it has become so popular is, I think, people watching marathon running on television when it was all the rage, and seeing middle-aged people doing it and thinking, "Surely I can still play football",' says Shepherd. 'Providing you play to your own physical ability you can still have a good game. Before, there was nothing available for veterans. You just clung on and became a nuisance to your team or you gave up. Now the football may not be in such a serious vein but it can still be enjoyable.'

So we came to Beckenham this Sunday morning to see why there was life in the old dogs yet. Old Bromleians, once the former pupils of Bromley Grammar School, now open to anyone wishing to join them, contained plenty of the middle-aged – people who were patently good players but who might struggle nowadays amongst younger teams. They also contained two 61-year-olds in Ronnie Burnett and Les Nelson, who just could not give the game up. Neither, judging by their performances, was the game ready yet to give them up.

The club have their own ground, at Lower Gravel Road next to Bromley bus garage, although the clubhouse was undergoing reconstruction. Oh, the pitch was playable enough, but the players were at an age where they needed their little luxuries. 'They get a bit funny if they don't get their shower after the game,' said their captain, Barry Clegg, who keeps the team's statistics on his personal computer.

In most ways, the vets' game was just the same as any other park match. Minutes before the appointed kick-off hour of 10:30am, the time-honoured cry went up from the opposition's dressing-room: 'Are they here yet?' In equally time-honoured fashion, they weren't. Old Bromleians, taking the pitch in dribs and drabs, began the game at 10:45 with ten men. They were playing a team called Red Barrel, which was neither a description of their stomachs – even if they were covered with the appropriately coloured shirt – nor a reference to the beer of that name which they had poured into them over the years. Nor was the sponsor's message on them, 'Francis Chappell – 150 years', thought to be a rude remark about their ages.

Bromleians, wearing light and dark blue and bearing the legend of 'Dave Elliott Litho', were soon under pressure, embarrassingly so since several hundred horribly fit-looking young men were throwing oval-shaped balls around in preparation for a seven-a-side tournament taking place on adjacent pitches. They stopped now and then to glance across; but such were their own shortcomings, they wisely realised, that they were in no position to criticise. The embarrassment was most acute for the Bromleians striker found in the centre circle trying very hard not to vomit, a mere twelve minutes of the game having passed. He was the one who had been talking enthusiastically beforehand about a recent aeroplane flight he had taken on which the booze was free and plentiful.

By now, Bromleians were up to eleven, their centre-back, Paul Edwards, having arrived. He immediately gave the ball away to a Red Barrel forward, who should have scored but wasted a goal open except for the goal-keeper. Edwards was left limping. 'Don't worry. It's only his pride that's hurt,' ventured a team-mate, correct if unsympathetic. By now, in fact, Bromleians had twelve men, meaning that Ronnie Burnett, who had just come to the ground to test out the recovery of his knee injury, could take his respite. He was far too modest to point it out but, soon after his departure, Red Barrel scored twice in five minutes to lead at the end of the forty-minute first half by 2–0.

It seemed that Bromleians would start slowly and then just peter out. But, in the second half, they found from somewhere a second wind and looked a different team. The departure of the rugby players for their pursuit, and with them their giggling girlfriends, surely helped. Paul Edwards showed himself a leggy defender who could pass the ball; Les Nelson an astonishing scurrier around midfield; Andy Edwards, brother of Paul, a bustling centre-forward. It was Andy who drove home, after a neat one-two, a goal that should have been the preface to an equaliser; but Red Barrel held on for the victory.

The standard had, ultimately, been surprisingly high, the stamina almost as much so. Clearly, these were men relishing still being competitive among others of the same ability and level, rather than just hanging on for dear life in a game involving younger players. They did take just a little bit longer to do things on the pitch. But not much. And, after the match, they did take just a little bit longer to get to the bar as limbs, once they had stopped, found it difficult to start up again. But not much.

There, Ronnie Burnett and Les Nelson mused on just what it was that kept them coming back to football at their ages, having both seen so many better days when they played semi-professional football. Burnett, a Bromley boy, had in fact played a few games for Charlton Athletic, although not in the first team, as a 20-year-old in the late 1940s, when Eddie Firmani was at the club. He had gone on, in 1949, to play for Bromley in their FA Amateur Cup win before a ten-year spell at Maidstone, after which he ended his senior career with Crockenhill of the Kent League.

'It's a lovely game,' he said. 'The ideal way of keeping fit except that, these days, the injuries take longer to recover from. Football is just the ideal team game, because you don't have to be a big strong bloke if you are playing in a

good side. Everybody gets a game.' He came into veterans'
football, which used to be just the odd friendly game in
those days, thirteen years ago. Now, with the leagues, they
play thirty times a season.

'Vets football has really grown over the last ten years,'
said Les Nelson. 'It's getting very popular with the youngsters,' he added, deeming anyone under 40 a youngster.
'They can't wait to get in the side. Me? Where else would
I get a game? It's given me a new lease of life.' Nelson, too,
played for Bromley and Crockenhill and, in between, with
Dulwich Hamlet, his most memorable day being an
Amateur Cup semi-final. That was in the days of genuine
amateurism, before all football was redefined as semi-
professional and players could be paid if their clubs
wished. Or was it genuinely amateur? 'There was some
money in the game in those days despite everything, but
we don't talk about that,' said Nelson, who still teaches at
a boys' school in Peckham, South London.

'Yes, it's a love of the game that keeps me going,' he
offered, 'but also because I still think I'm good enough. As
soon as I can't do the job I won't get picked. I don't think
they pick me out of sympathy.' 'It's the social side, too,'
chipped in Burnett, a retired graphic designer with the
Inner London Education Authority. 'I played with hun-
dreds of blokes who packed up too early. I come across
some of them now, they just don't have the same sort of
social life we do. Some are old men at 35. Unless they have
taken up some interest, but what else is there as good as
football?'

Has football changed? 'Oh, yes,' said Burnett. 'It's less
parochial than it used to be. The kids these days all support
Liverpool or Manchester United rather than their local
team. At Bromley, we used to get 5000 people along to
watch. Now you can knock a nought off that. At my first
game against Wycombe Wanderers, there were 8000. And

the game has got faster and faster at the expense of skill. The ball players have got to be very clever these days to survive. But it's not enough to be a good player. You've got to do some donkey work as well.'

He didn't seem to relish that prospect, although he had done his fair share over the years. Nowadays, it was time to put a foot on the ball and spray it around, enjoying it all the while, nothing to prove to anyone except yourself. It was time, too, for roast beef and Yorkshire pudding.

IV Young Boys

At the back of Morecambe on the Lancashire coast, just a couple of miles along the road from the nuclear power station at Heysham, you take a right turn in the village of Middleton down to the Pontin's holiday camp. There is no signpost and, half a mile down the winding road, you wonder if this can be the right place. But it is, and its inaccessible location is appropriate.

Here, for five days, will be billeted the English Schools Festival for Under-18 players. They call this the forgotten age-group, for most professional clubs think that they have seen and probably signed the best talent by the time it has reached the age of 16. They may be right, although there are always those who develop late or who are missed. That will certainly be the case with at least one of the 850 boys from the forty-two teams representing thirty counties, the coaches in the car park proclaiming Devon to Durham, Cumbria to Kent. There are also guest teams from the United States of America and Donegal in Ireland.

But the festival is not about discovering or grooming professional players. It is about sport and its fellowship, the thrill of playing the game. And those pleasures will be evident in abundance. As the organiser, Alan Heads, will say, 'We provide football for boys, not boys for football.'

Middleton Towers holiday village is all peeling paint and chilly chalets, newspaper stuffed in the odd window or two to keep out the wind that prevails from the Irish Sea. Money has been spent to modernise a camp – they frown upon that word these days – that was probably in its heyday in the 1950s and 1960s. But not enough money yet.

It is no matter. The accommodation is adequate, and there is plenty of stodgy English chips-with-everything food on offer in the enormous dining-room, although some of these appetites never seem satisfied. The important thing is the closeness, everyone living in each other's pockets, learning to get along, putting up with people's idiosyncrasies, making do, swapping ideas and information, respecting each other. The essence of playing in a football team, in fact.

On the Tuesday after Easter, they all gather in jackets and ties for the opening ceremony in the Berengaria Theatre, the hub of an entertainment complex in the shape of a ship, whose funnels are the landmark of the camp. Such smartness – the players, not the ship – is the first surprise about the festival. There will be many more when the games kick off the following morning. The second is the respectful audience which they provide at the hour-long opening ceremony, applauding and laughing in all the right places. Thus is challenged the timeless assumption that young people are scruffy and unable to listen to anyone older than themselves.

The chairman of the English Schools Football Association, Ron Eccles, will address them in his opening speech as 'young gentlemen'. They appear to deserve the title. 'Football is the greatest game in the world, and that is what unites us this week,' he continues. 'This is not a tournament this week. There are no cups or points to be played for. But there will be pride at stake. You will play hard but will nevertheless play fair with the correct spirit of sportsmanship. You are playing to enjoy your football and to sample the almost tangible festival spirit.' He urges them, too, not to neglect their studies. Many, soon to sit 'A' levels, will be going on to university or polytechnic.

Eccles has seen too many who give up on academic work in the certainty that they will make it as professionals, only for them and their hopes to be ditched. He points out that it is possible to complete an education and still pursue a career in the professional game. Rob Matthews, he says, played for England Schools Under-18s and is currently a student at Loughborough University; last week, he scored the winning goal for Notts County at Norwich on his first appearance.

Next up is the guest of honour, Gordon McKeag, successor to Blackburn's Bill Fox as the president of the Football League, a former chairman of Newcastle United and still on the board of the club; no doubt he is glad of the temporary respite from the Keegan-led struggle against relegation. 'Professional football is in a sorry state, dominated by unashamed self-interest,' he laments. It is refreshing, though, for a jaded football club director to see young men so keen and eager for the game, he adds.

The Premier League, he believes, could do severe damage to the game. 'We are told that skills will improve,' he says. 'I see no evidence of that. It is a risk we must all guard against. It is important for every one of you who may be looking for employment that the clubs lower down the League should not only survive but flourish.' It is in the schools, he says, that young players must learn dedication and discipline. 'Football is not just about winning games, particularly at this level. It is about winning friends. Football is like a drawing by Matisse. The great art is to make it seem simple, and the best players do just that,' he says, before finishing with a candid piece of advice: 'If you can't enjoy it then give it up and take up fishing.'

It is all largely appreciated by the players. They even suppress well their jealousy when the England Schools team is introduced to them. You hope that their applause is an expression of the knowledge of how lucky they are to be part of all this, to have been selected, to be experiencing it, because you know yourself that warm memories later come from nights, from weeks, such as this. But they probably know no such thing, as you never did because, of course, youth is wasted on the young. They are, quite rightly, so busy experiencing it that it will have passed them by before they know it.

After the formalities, the young gentlemen are free to fraternise, to exchange gossip and opinion, to wonder forlornly how to get into Morecambe for the evening – strictly forbidden unless accompanied by a master – and to chat up the young girls who work at the holiday camp. The teachers, meanwhile, gather in the Wheelhouse, the bar at the stern of the ship-shaped entertainment edifice. There they will swap stories of their season, talk of the diamond of a player they are nurturing for next year. Oh, and the problems with government cutbacks and the national curriculum.

Being a PE teacher or football master is a two-headed monster. The extra wages for doing the job are miniscule, the prestige often negligible. But the real reward lies in the pride and pleasure of seeing a player develop, if not into a professional, then into the best that the boundaries of his talent will allow. At the very least, there is the satisfaction of having developed a boy's relationship with the game, be he participant or spectator. And, of course, they get five days at Pontin's during the Easter holidays.

The main topic of conversation this year concerns the demands being placed on young players to play too many competitive games, for school and club. It follows the revelation that the Football Association's School of Excellence at Lilleshall in Staffordshire, set up to bring on the most talented of the country's young players from 13- and

14-years-old onwards, had made alarming discoveries about injuries to young players.

A month earlier, thirty-four young players, the top of the crop identified by the FA's scouts, had gathered at a hotel in Telford for the final interview before the selection of sixteen to attend the school. It transpired that eight were told after being tested by doctors at Lilleshall that, for medical reasons, they could not be accepted on to the course. One was even advised not to play any sport again in his life. The injuries were often spinal and all were stress-related, caused by too much football too young. Over-playing is the word teachers use.

The issue had been identified in the FA's Blueprint for the Future of Football, published in 1991, the supposedly definitive document on the state of the game. It said that, as far back as 1984, the average number of matches being played per season by the élite players in the country was 101. Twenty top-class players in the last ten years, it estimated, had been lost due to stress-related injuries. The statistics seem bland, but then you realise that each number refers to a young life.

'The age of the greatest pressure on players is getting younger,' says Alan Heads who, as well as organising the week, is an ESFA councillor and a teacher in the north-east. 'It used to be Under-15 because of the proliferation of competitions, and that being the time when professional clubs were most interested in young players. Now it's Under-13s. We know Under-15 players who are playing four times a weekend,' he adds. He cites the example of an England triallist who was due to play for his school on a Saturday morning but reported injured. In the afternoon, he went to watch his club side and was press-ganged into playing.

John Morton, chairman of the England Under-18 selectors and deputy director of the upper school at North Westminster School in London, blames the county FAs, who make money from the clubs and, ultimately, the FA. The state of schools football, he says, varies from area to area. 'What is happening is that kids are not playing as many games due to lack of teachers and facilities. So clubs have grown up to provide football for kids, and the best players are playing district, county and Sunday football. In the spring, the Sunday teams have often got behind with their matches so, to finish them, they are playing three or four games a week.' It leaves no time for coaching and training, Morton says. He used to divide his pitches into grids of ten yards by ten yards to get boys playing within them; but he has not done so for a while.

'I don't know how many games my best young players are playing. The pro clubs also cheat because they run teams at Under-12 and 13 level in the guise of supporters' clubs teams. There are too many vested interests.' He is encouraged by more players staying on at school to do 'A' levels in these days of the Youth Training Scheme, the government's attempt to reduce youth unemployment, which rewards the employer who takes on a school-leaver. Under it, clubs can flatter a youngster by taking him on, not because he is outstandingly gifted but because he offers cheap labour. Staying on at school, however, can be another problem, since some young players are already playing semi-professional football at 17.

Over-playing has always been with us, Morton concedes. After all, any boy with an aptitude for a game he loves wants simply to play it as often as possible. For many people, the memories are fond of arriving half an hour early at school for a kick-about; having another in every spare minute of every break; maybe practice after school; maybe two matches a week. Then the odd pick-up game on the local park. Yet, as in the senior game, the real worry has arisen through not only the increasing number of competitive matches, but also their intensity, with proud and pushy parents bellowing unqualified instructions from the touchline in language they have picked up on television. No, not from Channel 4 films, but from interviews with coaches or 'expert' commentators.

It is why, Morton believes, the schools are best qualified to oversee youth football. Most football masters, he says, have a good grounding with the FA's preliminary coaching badge, unlike some Football League managers. They are also interested in the boy who is not outstandingly talented, for whom the alternative can be only cubs football. He still thinks, though, that parents can and should be involved in assisting teachers. 'It is a pity but, in the leafy suburbs, there is not enough football played in schools, although parental support is high. The teachers don't seem to be as committed as they are in the cities.'

He identifies another problem: the lack of backing from local authorities. 'They are now wanting money for pitches,' he says. 'I can see a real crisis in the inner city. The kids who have the talent there will be hardest hit.' Support for ideas to reduce the strain on the youngest players, such as smaller pitches with smaller goals, is unlikely to come from those local authorities, he says, since there would be no revenue from them. That and the cost of converting the facilities.

Peter Amos, manager of the England Under-18 team and a teacher in Weston-Super-Mare, cites the case of Hung Dang to emphasise the over-playing problem. Dang, a much-publicised Vietnamese boat-boy, joined Tottenham from the FA's school but developed a back problem. A spell with Exeter City did not work out. Now he was with Chard in Western League football. Amos raises a further point. In Plymouth, he says, he came across a team of 10- and 11-year-olds being paid £10 a game. The exploitation of young players was taking a more sinister turn. 'The FA are the only people who can solve the problem, but I think there's a lack of understanding of what is going on.'

John Morton finds hope in a meeting he has had with Charles Hughes, the FA's director of coaching and education, the previous week. Hughes was currently considering a study into the exploitation of young footballers. But there appears to be no easy answer. It is time to sleep on it all, making one's way back to the drafty chalets, past the Snack-A-Tack fast-food joint where growing young gentlemen, who have eaten their evening meal just a few hours earlier, are queuing for all manner of things stuck between bread rolls and flirting with the waitresses.

It is tempting to conclude that the English Schools Festival – this is the twenty-eighth, the third at Morecambe, five having taken place at Bognor Regis and twenty at Skegness – does not do its bit to reduce the over-playing problem, since the teams play five times in five days. In all, there are 105 matches around Lancaster, Blackpool, Lytham St Anne's, Preston and Blackburn. It is a worry, too, to see teams training early in the morning on the first day on the training pitch at the camp, and to hear Peter Amos say: 'They won't be so keen by the end of the week. They'll be like the walking dead.' Except that here the physical and moral welfare of the players is paramount, overseen by people qualified to do so.

There is another concern, a phenomenon even, currently standing to increase the physical demands on young players: the direct-play, or long-ball, style. Amos, having demolished a good solid breakfast, stands and watches Essex 'A' – semi-finalists in the National Schools Championship – on a pitch in Lancaster that morning and shakes his head a few times.

Essex are playing a guest representative team from the Midwest area of the United States of America. The visitors are regimented, technically sound but tactically naïve: midfield players play in midfield, wingers stay on their wings. There is little initiative or invention. For their part, Essex are all hump and bump, urged on from his shooting-stick by an adviser named Vince Craven, who had reacquainted them with the direct methods in a one-hour team meeting the previous night. Craven had also been recruited in the past by such as Dave Bassett, when with Wimbledon, and Charles Hughes, guru of route-one football at the FA, to provide statistics.

'Knock it long,' and 'give it a good long hit,' Craven advises. 'What does it prove?' Amos wonders. 'That youngsters can be athletes rather than footballers? I think it can take some of the enjoyment out of the game for them.' He had, he says, to alter the approach of the Essex captain, Ian McIntyre, when he came to the England set-up, getting him to attempt to distribute the ball less hurriedly; at international level, the ball can be lost for long periods in which it can be tiring trying to retrieve it. 'He was a clever enough lad to adapt, to learn not to dive in but to be patient,' says Amos. 'Some players aren't and, at a young age, they can only play one way.'

Amos is quite taken by a talented, leggy striker called Danny Imray and enquires about his background. 'Brains in his bollocks,' says Craven. By this time, the USA team have surprised Essex by taking a lead against the run of play. Then Imray takes over, scoring twice. Although he has looked wayward he has continued to want the ball and to want to do something different with it. He has been rewarded, having refused to be suppressed. Essex eventually run out 3–1 winners.

Amos is left, over a solid lunch, slightly depressed. His spirits are lifted slightly by watching a video being shown outside the dining-room which illustrates the remarkable coaching methods, and the skills of his protégés which result, of the Dutch coach, Wiel Coerver. Amos has resolved in the afternoon to take in Cumbria v. Inner London. It is on a synthetic surface, which should get us back down to earth – or rather plastic. Indeed it does, and it deserves a somewhat sweeter-smelling setting than the backdrop of a refuse site between the adjoining boroughs of Morecambe and Lancaster. London, all exotic haircuts and names to match, are full of tricksy skills. Many of these boys will be YTS with League clubs in the capital next season.

One who has so far, astoundingly, missed out is a defensive flyer called Jason Walker, an England international the previous year, who is attending his third ESFA festival. He will go to Bromley College to take an HND course in leisure management, and try to find himself something better than Penhill Standard, a junior club for whom he has been playing. 'Yes, I am surprised when I see some of the people getting League clubs,' he says. 'It's a question of being in the right place at the right time.' Hope springs eternal here, too. Sadly, however, there is no scout at the match. In days gone by, there might have been one Eddie Edwards – not the Eagle of ski-jumping, but a talent spotter from South Yorkshire – who died in his 80s recently. He covered the festival for many years, finding a number of boys who had been missed at the Under-15 level or who had developed unexpectedly.

Cumbria are more physical but with a good grasp of skills, notably in the shape of a promising midfield player called Paul Cadwell, who shoots frequent glances towards the sidelines to check if Amos is watching him. 'They also say a few daft things loudly when they know you are there,' says Amos's assistant, Paul Brackwell. It finishes an enjoyable 3–3, faith restored. Even in the Essex match, though, behaviour had been impeccable. There was only one comment overheard in the two matches being directed at a referee, and then not in foul language. The referee may indeed have been having a bad game, but the Cumbria master nevertheless made a note into his tape recorder to speak with the offender later. It must pay off, insisting on jackets and ties being worn for evening meals.

It was the end of a thoroughly fascinating, rewarding and enjoyable stay. There were problems, issues and controversy at this level of the game, probably healthily so for it seemed in a good condition despite everything. The biggest problem would have been if no one noticed. But many clearly cared.

'Time for tea,' said Amos. 'All you do is eat and watch football,' I replied. 'I know. Lovely, isn't it?' he said.

Nine: Almost There

1 Home

Just as with your parents and relatives, you can't choose the football team you support. It is assigned to you. It is either handed down through the family, like some character defect or skin blemish; or you start watching it as a youngster, because it is the nearest one to you.

Then you are hooked. Try as you might to forget about it, ignore it or exchange it for something better, it will not go away. It remains with you for the rest of your life. You can try switching allegiance to bigger clubs, more successful clubs but, annoyingly, irritatingly, it has you in its hold.

No matter where you are in the world, you have to find out how it has done, probably as secretively as possible since you are semi-ashamed to admit to supporting it. The problem becomes more acute when you support a non-League team. For League supporters, it is quite easy to find out how your team has done. For us, there is frequently the problem of phone calls to grounds trying to get some sense out of somebody who is probably pulling a pint or counting the takings.

Sometimes, too, you have to explain to people where exactly the team you support is located. Nobody ever had that problem with Liverpool or Manchester United. You try to identify with those teams, just to keep up with the kids at school or not to appear to be some sort of train-spotter later in life, but it's no good. Dalliances in the formative years of the 1960s with, say, Burnley, Nottingham Forest and Manchester City just because you liked their shirts and they had seasons of fleeting success – and you could tease your friends that your team was doing better than theirs – never really satisfied.

So the road led back this season, as it ever did, to the home-town club of Weymouth. Quite a big seaside resort on the south coast. In Dorset. About twenty-five miles west of Bournemouth. Southern League. Southern Division of it, actually, although Once Upon A Time they were among the top non-League clubs in the country. Runners-up in the first season of the Alliance Premier League, now the GM Vauxhall Conference. Their nickname is the Terras. It's a pun, because the club colours are terracotta – which is more claret, really – and blue. Geddit? Oh, never mind. How are Spurs getting on?

You just can't help apologising for them and for your own sense of inferiority. Sorry about that. But I love them. And I hate them. The memories have been rich and poor, magnificent and ludicrous, stored and erased. Sounds familiar?

I came to them as a small boy, taken by Dad as it should be law that everyone is, in the early '60s, brought up on the folklore of an FA Cup third-round appearance at Manchester United in 1950. Weymouth lost 0–4. I later paid £25 for the programme. From there, my passion developed to the point where I even apply for the manager's job whenever it crops up, the last time in January 1991. 'The chairman thanks you for your application for the vacant position of manager of Weymouth FC but regrets to inform you that the position has now been filled. Wishing you every success for the future,' came the polite but humourless reply.

Our Recreation Ground – the Rec for short, not the Wreck as some nearby Dorchester Town fans wittily dubbed it – was next to the harbour and seemed huge then, our own little repertory theatre of dreams. The floodlights, bought from Portsmouth, which promptly failed after twenty minutes of a grand switching-on match against that club, seemed to give it a professional aspect.

The earliest personal memory there was of Frank O'Farrell's team winning the Southern League Championship in 1965; of O'Farrell, who went on the next season to manage Torquay United, then that biggest United in Manchester, wearing the No. 6 shirt and dashingly heading a shot off the line. We all seem to have those little cameos that somehow appeal and stick in the mind. Weymouth needed to score 4 in their last match that season to make it 100 League goals for the season, but they won only 3–1. Playing alongside O'Farrell was the stalwart, Tony Hobson, who went on to play almost 1000 games, and probably almost that many, too, for Weymouth Cricket Club.

The next season, Weymouth retained the Championship under Stan Charlton, these days the club secretary. Another cameo came that year in a match against Hereford United, in which the Gentle Giant, the former Leeds and Juventus colossus, John Charles, kicked the ball out of play so that an injured Weymouth player could receive treatment. The ground responded loudly to such sportsmanship. That was the thing about non-League football, and it still is although, in the media age, some of the mystique has inevitably left it. You could always glimpse players on the way down, still with the speed of thought even if the speed of foot had gone. Then there were players on the way up, young and enthusiastic, seeking to catch eyes, whose careers it was enjoyable to watch knowingly in later years. It has been described as football's mezzanine floor.

League clubs were just huge professional organisations that we were sometimes drawn against in the Cup and hosted with respect, or visited in awe. Bournemouth were a world away. They were in Hampshire in those days, after all. Now how strange it seems that these are considered the small clubs. Strange, too, that this season in the cold would later lead me to speak to Vic Halom, whose 2 late goals for Leyton Orient at Weymouth in 1967 so saddened me as a 12-year-old. And John Morton, that England Schools selector encountered at Morecambe: in 1975, he had kept goal for Dartford at Weymouth in an FA Trophy quarter-final that the Kent side won 2−1. It was the year that we were going to Wembley. Football may be a national game, but there is something about it that makes it ever villagey.

That 1974−75 season also saw an astonishing FA Cup tie against Peterborough, then near the top of the third division. The first-round match was drawn 0−0 at London Road before a replay was drawn 3−3 after extra-time, the Posh twice equalising with a minute of the game to go. We lost 0−3 in the second replay at Peterborough, and the gloom of the familiar long night trip home after defeat remains vivid.

That team contained one of the best strikers ever in non-League football, Alan Beer, who went on to the Cities of Exeter and Leicester, where a knee injury sadly ended his career prematurely. He it was who scored the only goal on that special night, my fiancée's 18th birthday, when she stood with me by the half-way line on the Sidney Hall side − to which I had graduated from the Gasworks End − and cheered Weymouth into the first round of the FA Cup at the expense of hated rivals Yeovil Town.

The most bizarre memory was in 1976. In a Southern League match at Hillingdon Borough, Weymouth were 1−4 down with eight minutes left. They won 5−4. It was a bit like reflecting on an escape from a punch-up. What an exciting relief, but how did I get there in the first place?

The tie with Peterborough ranks, in the long run, second in Cup memories. It was beaten in 1982 at Cardiff, against whom Weymouth were 0−2 down at half-time. Then

Anniello Iannone, one of the club's longest-serving and best-loved, a man-of-the-people sort, a window-cleaner of Italian extraction, headed home a goal. Ten minutes from time, Trevor Finnegan slid home an equaliser and, amazingly with minutes to go, Gerry Pearson knocked in a winner. The *Guardian*, for whom I was then working, had kindly indulged me and allowed me to cover the match. 'I should declare an interest. I have followed this maddening shower for twenty years through terrible Cup disappointments. On Saturday, it all seemed worth it,' I wrote in my match report.

It went on: 'It must all have seemed worth it, too, for people like Peter Ebrill, who has covered thousands of miles to watch them (he used to play in our cricket team, and him with a wooden leg), and Bob Lucas, the team physiotherapist who played in that third-round match against Manchester United in front of nearly 40,000 in 1950 (he worked on the buses with my Dad). And there is Mark Baber, who supplied the cross for the winning goal (I played against him at primary school). For all of them you were just pleased as punch.'

In the mid-1980s, I began to notice the same dozen or so people at all the London games that Weymouth played, exiles like myself. There were Zill and Blin, who were actually from Watford but had been to Weymouth on holiday, liked it and decided to follow the football team; there was Andrew at college; Dave from Harrow; Paul the train-driver from High Wycombe. We formed ourselves into the London Supporters' Club and drove to places such as Nuneaton and Kidderminster, on whose terraces you would suffer that embarrassment of starting up a chant in which no one joined. You would arrive at these towns and, seeking the way to the ground, you would find someone dressed in the home club's colours – usually the non-League loony that every club has, whose scarf is twelve-feet long and was knitted by his mother in the 1950s and who tucks his jumper inside his trousers. He then gives you complicated directions, ending with 'You can't miss it.' All the while we were dreaming of being promoted and driving to more glamorous places. Like Rochdale and Halifax.

It seemed that we would make it, too. For far too long we had been plagued by the envy with which football fans struggle. When Cambridge United were elected to the Football League in 1970, we had done the double over them, 2–1 away, 4–1 at home. We provided the opposition in Scarborough's last match before they became a fourth-division side, the first to receive automatic promotion from the GM Vauxhall Conference, in 1987. Then, in 1988, we were top of the table, having won our first five games, having beaten newly-relegated Lincoln City, 3–0 no less, at home in front of more than 3500. Finally, we were going to be a League club.

We had a League ground, after all. We had moved from what now seemed to me, as a grown-up who had been to a lot of League grounds, the dinky little Rec to a purpose-built, 10,000-capacity concrete bowl on the edge of town, on the site of the old speedway track at Wessex Stadium, just past the bird sanctuary of Radipole Lake. It may not have had the charm of the past but it had the hope of the future. Its official opening was marked by Weymouth beating a strong Manchester United team 1–0.

But it all turned sour. The club lived beyond its means, paying wages it could afford only in the short term, and subsided into mid-table. The following season, in its 100th year, it was relegated for the first time, finishing bottom after the one worse team, Newport County, newly down from the fourth division, went out of business in mid-season. Worse followed. The club then went down again to the Southern Division of the Southern League. Now the questions began to be posed.

What had happened to all the money, not just from the £3 million sale to a supermarket of the Recreation Ground – after all, it could be accepted that much of it had been spent on the new stadium – but from gates averaging more than 1000 and the sale of virtually a first-division team? There was Graham Roberts who went to Tottenham, as did a few years later the goal-keeper, Peter Guthrie. There was Andy Townsend to Southampton; Tommy Jones to Aberdeen; Tony Agana to Watford; Shaun Teale, now with Aston Villa; and Steve Claridge, now with Cambridge United.

Everything was wrong. At the new ground, anyone with a waist of more than 28 inches could barely squeeze through the turnstiles. The home supporters had to walk past the queues for the away end, on the rare occasions when there were any. So much for segregation. The ground seated only 1000. It was bad luck but also bad judgement – those twin characteristics – as the Taylor Report was about to happen. Weymouth were thus forced to rely on youngsters – or actually boys, it looked like – who wanted only the shop window to strut their stuff without wearing high price labels. They came on loan from Bristol and the locality. It was hopeful and depressing – those twin characteristics.

But wait. In the August of our season, they looked a lively little bunch under a manager, Len Drake, who believed in knocking the ball about; so they beat Dunstable 3–0, with a small midfield player called Chris Shaw looking a diamond. I got back to see them in November, when an unpleasant Baldock Town team – what were we doing playing Baldock Town? – full of weary, slow old pros just managed to keep up with a few trailing legs and drew 0–0. The adolescents grew a little that day.

The title slipped away with two defeats by the eventual champions, Hastings United. But the second promotion place was all but theirs. Still, it wouldn't be Weymouth if they didn't make the traditional crisis out of a drama. In March, they lost four league matches in a row, and Havant Town were at their heels. The money problems resurfaced, and the club was revealed to be £250,000 in debt. A share issue was the answer. It raised £13,000. Still, an old friend was helping out on the field: Anniello Iannone, now somewhere in his late 30s, dredged up a goal for his latest club, Fareham Town, last but one in the table, to beat Havant on the Friday night. On this, the following day in April, if Weymouth could beat bottom-of-the-table Gosport Borough they would be back in second place.

It was cold and windy as it always is at Wessex Stadium – even though the sun was shining – as we squeezed through the turnstiles having bought our copy of the new fanzine, *Terrarising*. Geddit? Finally, the turmoil at the club had produced a voice of discontent. It had taken a while. And something else had changed. The mascot, who supported Liverpool, he said, was from St John's School, local cup-winners. In my days there, we did not win a game for two seasons nor did we even score a goal until my final year. Then we astonished ourselves by finding 3 goals from somewhere in the second half of a match we had been losing 0–2 at half-time.

Weymouth, resplendent in terracotta and blue with white bits and 'David Hanger Windows' on their chests, should have scored in the first thirty seconds against a jittery debutant goal-keeper. But, having negotiated the first ten minutes, Gosport, good and angry at being on their way to relegation to the Wessex League, began to fancy it.

Things looked up at half-time when I won the third prize of £7 in the raffle. Something told me it would have been wrong to keep it, however; the share issue fund was now £13,007.

You just knew Weymouth were not going to score in the

second half, during which they naturally missed chance after chance through the two talented young touch-players up front, Steve Clifford and Tony Cook. It is at times like this that basic instincts take over. No matter how much pretty football they play, how ethical a team they are – or how much you yourself believe in those things – in the heat of this moment you just want your side to thump the ball in the opponent's net (or actually just crossing the line will do), by whatever means they can. And for the referee then to blow his whistle for full-time.

Classy young defender Gary Fullbrook was carried off. As the St John's Ambulance man ran on with his medical kit, there came the shouted comment: 'You'll never get him in there.' It finished goalless. As someone once noticed with wonderful insight: you never get a good game when there are crisp packets blowing across the pitch.

When Weymouth drew again, 2–2 at Salisbury, two days later and Havant won 1–0 at home to Newport (Isle of Wight, no less), it seemed all over. We were now 2 points behind with two games to play. But the parcel landed back in Weymouth's hands the following week; Buckingham – no limericks about them ever again, please – beat Havant 3–0 as Weymouth were beating Canterbury, who had attracted seventy-six spectators for the first meeting between the clubs, 2–0 at home. If they could beat lowly Erith and Belvedere on the final day Weymouth would be up. Simple.

Not quite. Weymouth were a goal behind at half-time, while Havant were winning at Hythe. In the second half, with the help of 2176 fans, Weymouth turned it all around and won 4–1. Havant's 3–3 draw was now an irrelevance. Happy days were here again. We were on the march. We're going up the league. The Southern one, that is. But it would surely not be long before we were back in the Conference and, from there, in the fourth division. Money? Don't worry about it.

The appeal of non-League football can be great: few parking problems; an absence of malice; being a part of something quite exclusive in a downbeat sort of way; no queues for pie and pees. But, even if they do regret it a little when they get there and they pine for the good old days, non-League clubs and their supporters desperately want that experience of the promised land that is League football.

Then you don't have to explain what league your team plays in, or where the place is. You don't have to apologise for it. Sorry to have taken up so much of your time. Still, the meek shall inherit the earth, they say. If that's all right with you, that is.

ⅠⅠ Away

All walks to football grounds are beautiful in their own way. But the one to Fulham Football Club along the north bank of the Thames from Putney Bridge underground station is probably the most beautiful of them all.

Or was. Fulham were planning to move from their highly desirable riverside property of Craven Cottage and join Chelsea at Stamford Bridge just a couple of miles towards Central London. It was precisely because Fulham was a highly desirable riverside property that a property development company called Cabra Estates, who owned the Cottage and wished to develop it, were proposing to pay Fulham to quit the ground. Fulham would then use much of the money to pay Chelsea to share the Bridge, money which Chelsea would in turn use to help secure their independence from Cabra, who also owned the Bridge.

It was one of those tortuous and protracted sagas in which football clubs have indulged in recent years, especially since the Taylor Report and the consequent scramble to find the money to improve grounds. Whatever the rights and wrongs of the situation, it seemed certain that Fulham would quit their home. The will-they, won't-they phase had passed. Now it was a question of when; it would probably be at the end of this season. The time was ripe for one last visit, one last walk down by the riverside.

Fulham was a love affair that began on the rebound.

Studies took me from Weymouth to London in the early 1970s, and when I could no longer get home every weekend I needed a team to follow to give football-watching the edge of partisanship. No, you can't choose your team, but you can live with the illusion for a while. The big clubs of the capital did not really appeal. That was too simple. Fulham fitted the bill since they were unusual, underdogs, unfashionable and virtually every other un-. There was a purpose to supporting them: they needed you more than the big clubs. And they rewarded you with a more colourful, if frustrating experience. The sort you don't get gazing out from a Thames-side penthouse.

It was a case of What Kind of Fulham I? No wonder the fanzine these days was called *There's Only One F in Fulham* (one 'effin' Fulham? It took me a little while, too). The play-offs were invented for them, or rather the fringe of them – as in the phrase that seemed to appear in the Sunday papers every week: 'Fulham, on the fringe of the play-offs, . . .'

There was, of course, the humour attached to a club of whom it was said that they had a great future behind them. For years, they held on to the first £100-a-week footballer in the pass-master, Johnny Haynes. But equally revered now in nostalgia, if not at that time of the 1960s, was Tosh Chamberlain, a left winger of comparatively little ability, but large charm. There was the story of him kicking the flag when attempting a corner-kick. And there was the even better one of him failing to reach a wonderful through-pass by Haynes, who berated him from the half-way line: 'You 'effin' idiot, Chamberlain.' The referee was in the process of booking Haynes for bad language when a breathless Chamberlain arrived on the scene. 'Don't book him, ref. He's right. I am an 'effin' idiot.'

When last heard of, Tosh was working as a park-keeper in Kingston, Surrey. In the same county, at Woking, was to be found Les Barrett, working as a telephone engineer. Barrett was a successor to Chamberlain on the wing and a personal favourite. He was small and thin and drifted in and out of games. The poor lad would often freeze as he hugged that lonely left touchline. But when he did decide to honour the game with his presence – to borrow the expression your sarcastic schoolmaster used to use of you – the whole place lit up. He was a scurrier with legs that ran at thirteen paces to the dozen, a crosser and shooter of hit-or-miss tendencies. He was why you went to watch Fulham.

Strangely, and as though fed up with the old script, Fulham reached the FA Cup final in 1975. It was an astonishing one-off run by an astonishing team, mid-table in the second division but featuring class acts such as Alan Mullery and Bobby Moore at the end of their careers; the twilight of the gods. After they had beaten Hull City and Nottingham Forest – taking seven games about it – in the third and fourth rounds, they went to the first-division leaders, Everton, in the fifth and won 2–1. In the sixth, Barrett scored the only goal at Carlisle. Then came a semi-final against Birmingham City at Hillsborough.

It was notable for John Mitchell's beautiful volleyed goal at the Leppings Lane end, in which stood your correspondent. Such was my appreciation for the achievement that my denture flew out and had to be retrieved from a shoulder in front. Birmingham, then first-division and featuring Trevor Francis and Gordon Taylor, fought back to equalise, and a replay at Maine Road was necessary. Mitchell astoundingly bumbled home a goal with the last kick of the match – except for the one which restarted it before the final whistle. If Hillsborough had seen his finest goal, Maine Road saw probably his worst but certainly most important.

The black and white colours had to be concealed as we made our way back to the coach. The journey up the M6 had seen Birmingham supporters invade it at a service station and make off with scarves, singing: 'We'll be running round the Bullring with the Cup.' We had also passed the Birmingham team bus in a traffic jam coming into Manchester and held up a headline declaring: 'It Must Be Fulham.' Kenny Burns's reply, in gesture form, was short and sharp.

Once on the coach for the return journey, a voice behind seemed to sum it up. 'Every year you watch all these teams going to Wembley, and now it's going to be us,' he said. Of course, the final was lost, 0–2 to West Ham, but no matter. We had a day at Wembley. It could never have been easier to get a ticket; they even went to Portsmouth fans, who swelled the Cottage crowd from the usual 8000 to 17,000 two weeks before the final in the expectation of getting one.

I dabbled with Fulham for a few more seasons after that – in those days, it was the edge of the promotion race they were always on – watching Rodney Marsh and George Best mostly delight, occasionally annoy, as they wound down their careers with some style. Ever since, I have always looked out for their results in the way that you do with a team that has touched your life in some way. It was in deference to the memories that, on this March evening, I now found myself outside Putney Bridge station.

On a night for stepping backwards, the clocks had just gone forward so that every step could be savoured in the light with a lightness of spirit. On the corner of the Fulham Palace Road, the King's Arms, where we used to gather for our pre-match, um, team talk, was now closed down. Still, the King's Head down the road seemed to be doing all right with the bands playing there. It was Funk My Old Boots tonight.

From Putney Bridge, though, earth had not anything more fair, the office tower block apart. Upriver to the left stood the boat-houses of the rowing clubs and the huge riverside pubs; to the right, the floodlights of the Cottage

could be seen. The very sight put a spring into the stride.
Down the steps past All Saints' Church and through Pryor's
Park, where the nude statues provoked a silent titter or
twain, then into Bishop's Park. It was not quite as
remembered, but then nothing is. Through the trees and
the children's adventure playground could still be spotted
Fulham Palace. Past the euphemism called the Dog Exercise
Area to the bandstand, now scarred by graffiti, none of it
informative. The boating lake was now empty, no doubt
due to the water shortage in the south-east. From here could
be glimpsed the floodlights again, having slipped out of
view in the leafy walk.

It was all a little faded, a little run down. So, indeed, was
Craven Cottage, but that at least had more excuse. After all,
what point was there spending money on a ground on its
deathbed?

Emerging from Bishop's Park pointed up the reason for
not wearing the Fulham scarf. Here, at the Putney End, the
visitors' territory, where I once had to run from Bristol City
fans who had spied the colours, were parked the away
coaches. Tonight, Fulham were at home to well-supported
Stoke City who, being third-division leaders, were accompanied by nine coachloads. As a boy I had always thought
that the Stoics came from there, in the way that I thought
Queen's Park Reindeers were a Scandinavian club and
Hydrangeas a northern non-League team. Stoke were now
managed by Lou Macari, who had left Swindon at the time
of the financial shenanigans there to be succeeded by Ossie
Ardiles, who was replaced by Hoddle when he went to Newcastle, where he was replaced by Keegan. Got it? What was
that about villagey old football and its managerial merry-
go-round?

Once through the coaches, the celebrated Cottage could
be seen inside the gates. It was a sort of old-fashioned pavilion that housed offices and dressing-rooms and had a

balcony of seats for directors and guests overlooking the pitch. There was talk of dismantling it then re-erecting it at Stamford Bridge.

Along Stevenage Road, little had changed. There even remained some seventeen-year-old graffiti: 'Mullery is God' and 'Six-Feet-Two, Eyes of Blue, Ernie Howe is After You.' Supporters were also urged to join the Thames Bank Travellers, which conjured up images of charming little outings, perhaps by bicycle on a summer's afternoon, but which added up to something rather less genteel. The unintentional sense of humour was also still intact: a sign pointed people to the Age Concern Sports and Social Club. Whether this was for the team was not clear.

The place to be, really, was the Hammersmith End, which was standing room only for home fans. There was always plenty of standing room, though. 'Don't throw it away,' said the gateman, as the £5 note slipped out of my grasp at the turnstile. 'I'm doing that coming in here,' I replied. He smiled the smile of a Fulham devotee before saying: 'No, they're not playing bad now.' It was good to be back.

The back third of the Hammersmith End was closed off these days for safety reasons, as was that at the Putney End; grass was now growing on the terracing. Hammersmith was covered, Putney not, which is as it should be: away fans expect to be cold and wet. It is part of the traditional torture of which Lord Justice Taylor did not approve, and who, joking apart, could blame him? Home fans, particularly the Epsom Boys who were so fond of inscribing their identity on the corrugated iron, were entitled to a bit of cover, the old-time directors had finally conceded.

The ground in general was not what it was. The Sir Eric Miller Stand, named after a benefactor whose tangled business dealings led to him committing suicide, was once state-of-the-art and looked down splendidly from the length of the Thames side. Now it was all flaky paint. One by one, the letters spelling 'Fulham Football Club' on its overhang had come off, until just 'Fulham' was left.

No other football ground seems to attract the single fan as much as Craven Cottage. Perhaps it is a sad loneliness that drives people to seek out kindred spirits here; perhaps an unwillingness to admit to friends and relatives that you support Fulham. For that would be to subject yourself to inevitable social stigma; thus are visits here rendered necessarily clandestine. Kindred spirits, though, these supporters certainly are. Only here could someone shout, 'What a howler,' at some player's mistake and not be laughed out. Here, too, could you hear an exchange about Fulham's corpulent keeper, Jim Stannard, who was urged as the opposition prepared to take a free-kick just outside the penalty area: 'Keep it covered.' 'He only has to stand there to do that,' came the reply.

As usual, Fulham were a nice team. They even played in unjazzy, simple black and white still, with no sponsor's name on the front. The first half drifted somnolently on until the tannoy man, who had hitherto been outstanding by playing excerpts from Bruce Springsteen's two new LPs released this week, left on his microphone, and a loud feedback noise filled the air. Didn't he know people were trying to sleep?

The chants of 'Come on you Whites' hardly disturbed the peace, petering out after only two refrains. Then Fulham scored. Martin Pike's free-kick was knocked down by Gavin Nebbeling, and the heir to Les Barrett's No. 11 shirt, Kelly Haag, who sounds more like a brand of Dutch coffee, slammed home. Les might have been proud. Stoke were stunned and, when their tiny forward, Mark Stein, headed against the bar a minute from half-time, you knew it was not going to be their night. Besides which, Fulham would be attacking their favourite Hammersmith End in the second half.

Fulham will surely move up from the fringe of the play-offs to being actually in the play-offs; Stoke, a competent but uninspiring third-division team, will surely slip off the top. This is it. The promotion run starts here.

Stein scores. It finishes 1–1.

The walk back, in the darkness, is never quite the same. With the park gates closed, you are siphoned off past the town houses and groups of flats called mansions, and the floodlit tennis courts that are better patronised than they should be with a football match going on nearby. It is all a bit of an anticlimax; but then that's Fulham, that's football. It was sad to think that this could be the last time. We would worship Craven images no more.

iii Neutral

Leppings Lane is an innocuous enough thoroughfare. The short and winding road, at the back of Sheffield Wednesday's Hillsborough ground, wends its way quietly over the River Don about half a mile up to the Penistone Road, towards Manchester and, this being Sheffield, a steelworks.

It is lined mostly by terraced and just about semi-detached housing, bisected by alleys known hereabouts as ginnels and punctuated by small businesses, several of which have closed down, this being Sheffield in a national economic recession. The Hillsborough Tyre Company survives, though, as does Mitchell's Fish and Chips – especially on match-days – Scott's News, and Eric's Men's Hairdressers. Off it run streets of more terraced housing, the 'For Sale' signs considerably outnumbering the 'Sold' signs. There are plenty of 'Vote Labour' posters at this general election time.

It all seems very ordinary. Leppings Lane, however, is the most notorious street-name associated with English football. For on the terraces at this end of Hillsborough perished ninety-five people on 15 April 1989 at the FA Cup semi-final between Liverpool and Nottingham Forest. It was the English game's worst tragedy.

Now, the Taylor Enquiry and Report later, the FA were bringing back a semi-final, between Norwich City and Sunderland, to the ground. Sheffield Wednesday were keen to demonstrate how the ground had improved. The much-criticised South Yorkshire police were keen to show that they could handle such an occasion. All insisted that Hillsborough had changed, that its facilities had been updated and upgraded. This was a chance to rehabilitate themselves. Yet there were many who believed it to be indecently hasty, and not only those directly involved that day, who had been there as witnesses or who had watched horrified on television as loved ones became embroiled. Some litigation, too, was still being pursued.

The FA had first approached Sheffield Wednesday the previous autumn about the feasibility of the event, meeting informally also with the police and Sheffield City Council. Six months later, the Wednesday secretary, Graham Mackrell, sat in his office five days before the match and considered the work that had been done and was yet to be done. Outside, builders hammered away, preparing the ground for a new stand that was to be built in the coming summer.

They would be out of the way by Sunday, match-day. Indeed, most of the work to be done towards putting on the semi-final had been completed. On the following day, Wednesday, they would have a meeting for the 300 or so stewards who would be on duty. Such briefings were routine and regular, said Mackrell, but this was 'an extra one, making sure everyone is right up to date.'

It was especially noticeable in our conversation that he did not use the phrase that had sadly slipped into common usage, the Hillsborough Disaster. Nor did he refer to the Leppings Lane end; that was the West End of the ground. 'What happened here in 1989 was a blow to the people of the city, who are very proud of Hillsborough and particularly in relation to the work that has been done,' he said. 'The club have got on and done it and not just sat around and done nothing.' The 'new' Hillsborough was ready to be shown off to the world, he added. 'Very much so. My board would not have put me and my staff through unnecessary pressure if they weren't happy to stage a semi-final.'

Money was scarcely a factor. Wednesday would receive about £75,000 from their 10 per cent share, after VAT, of the gross gate, programme and catering revenue. In bygone times, the host club used to have a large allocation of tickets. Now they receive a token amount. The atmosphere in the city was very supportive, Mackrell said, even if local residents were largely against the return of a semi-final. As with some Liverpool families, the immediacy remained with many, and the scars in many cases had not yet healed.

Being the club and ground which spawned the Taylor Report, with the recommendation of all-seater stadia at its core, Wednesday had been under more pressure than most clubs. 'Yes, without any doubt,' said Mackrell, an accountant by training who had started in the game with Bournemouth, then moved to Luton before coming to Hillsborough five years previously. He was considered one of the brighter young things of football administration. 'The Taylor Report contained criticisms of the club, the police and the local authority, so all three parties have had to be very proactive in relation to how they dealt with it,' he continued. 'Things were possibly demanded of us and have been done that maybe weren't demanded elsewhere.' A gangway being widened here, a staircase altered there, for example.

At first, other clubs turned to Wednesday to find out how they were implementing Taylor, but now, said Mackrell, the best ones were ahead of the 1994 deadline for all-seating. Many, too, he conceded, were dragging their heels, hoping that attitudes in government might change and that the report might be modified.

How exactly had Hillsborough changed since the fateful day? First, the Leppings Lane end so horribly exposed had

had to be completely rethought and changed. Outside, just off the street, a holding area for supporters had been created by knocking down the exit gates – the opening of one of which just before the kick-off three years ago had led to the surge and the consequent crushing – and turnstiles. They had then been rebuilt some fifteen yards closer to the ground.

Inside, the terracing had had to be redeveloped, the terrible tunnel feeding it being reconstructed to be wider and more airy, in theory at least. All was closed while the work was carried out. Now, the angle of viewing having been altered appropriately by the regrading of the concrete, seats had been fixed, and the roof had been extended over them. It was now known as the West Stand Lower, its capacity reduced from the standing 8700 of 1989 to a seated 2600. Together with the upper section of 4200 seats and the remaining elevated terracing in one corner set aside for 1100, it would accommodate the Norwich support.

There would be a system of colour-coded tickets corresponding to turnstiles marked with the relevant colour for the visitors from East Anglia. With ninety-three turnstiles, Wednesday claimed still to have the largest number serving any Football League ground. Including the installation of an electricity substation, it had cost around £1 million, said Mackrell. There had also been other work demanded by the Taylor Report of all clubs, such as new evacuation areas, landline telephones and a police observation box.

A further £4 million would go on redeveloping the South Stand, which housed the club offices. When it was finished, with its new restaurants, suites and 3000 more seats, the 16,300-place Kop, assigned this Sunday to Sunderland, would be seated at a further cost of £1.3 million. That would, Wednesday planned, be ready for that Taylor deadline for first- and second-division clubs. Against a current capacity of 41,200, Hillsborough would then have an all-seat capacity of 38,000; that could rise to 40,000 should the club seat the expensive elevated terraced section. Half the cost would come from the Football Trust organisation; the rest would be met by the club or, more specifically initially, their bankers.

Those were the facts and figures of the changing Hillsborough. But what was the feeling of it? Walking through the Leppings Lane end that chilly and slightly chilling Tuesday afternoon, it did feel less claustrophobic than the memory of standing on it in 1975 for the semi-final between Fulham and Birmingham. Hindsight now recalls the crush of that day, though mercifully without the fenced-in feeling that produced panic fourteen years later. The tunnel, however, still prompted misgivings; they had similarly been provoked at Wembley for the Everton v. Liverpool final but a month after the Hillsborough Disaster, when I saw police trying to coax a woman Everton supporter to follow the herd down a subway towards the stadium. Through fear she would not budge, tears overcoming her.

On the Sunday of the semi-final six minutes before the kick-off, the time when three years ago the mayhem was unfolding, Leppings Lane was calm and peaceful as I passed through its turnstiles to take up a place in the North Stand. The colour-coding system was working, and the police were evident but restrained, even if an understandable tension could still be sensed. It helped that these were Norwich people filing in, dignified and restrained themselves. The FA might well have reconsidered had big-city supporters been involved. They had already decided that Liverpool would not, of course, be sent to Hillsborough.

Liverpool were involved, in fact, 170 miles south in the other semi-final, at Highbury against Portsmouth. Pompey's presence at this stage of the competition, like Sunderland's, illustrated in this final season of the Football League in its present form that the second division, which would become the first, had much to interest and offer. Indeed, a groan went up at Hillsborough a few minutes before kick-off: Liverpool, their match having kicked off at midday – this one starting in mid-afternoon so that the BBC could cover them both in succession – had equalised minutes from the end of extra-time. Ronnie Whelan, fortunate still to be on the pitch after perpetrating some reckless early tackles, had touched home after John Barnes's free-kick had hit the post. This in response to one of the game's new young prodigies, Darren Anderton, whom Liverpool coveted and who had given Portsmouth the lead minutes after the start of extra-time.

That Hillsborough groan demonstrated that, while there may well have been a warmth and a sympathy for the people of Liverpool, there was not for its team. Their enduring success, even with an average team playing averagely, was still a source of bitter envy for rivals and opponents. Instead, the warmth was shown in moving gestures from Norwich and Sunderland supporters, even if the FA had discouraged formal ceremonies at Hillsborough that day. Norwich supporters, many undoubtedly uncomfortable with the eeriness of their location, laid daffodils, to represent both their team's colours of green and yellow and the message of hope and regeneration of flowers, before the Leppings Lane end. And then, a few minutes before the start, both sets of supporters joined in a stirring rendition of *You'll Never Walk Alone*. It was an inspired and inspiring moment, one that showed football's bonding process – even if it often seems a fragmented sport – and indomitable spirit. Tears were shed, and more would be before the end of the day.

Indeed, the fans were almost the real protagonists of the day. Sunderland's, throaty and irrepressible, unfurled huge red and white flags on the Kop; those from Norwich, colour-

ful and charming, waved inflatable canaries. The fashion
for these air-filled mascots had largely passed, but Norwich
retained them. In some ways, that symbolised the tardy
time-frame in which their city existed. So, too, did the old
club song they sang noisily: *On The Ball City*. If only they
and Portsmouth, with their Pompey chimes of 'Play Up
Pompey, Pompey Play Up', could make it to Wembley, we
would be in for a throwback final.

One hoped that Norwich could make it for another
reason. In 1989, they had been the beaten team in the other
semi-final, against Everton at Villa Park. Their passing
game, even if it had taken into account the longer ball at
times this season, had deserved a final for a few years.
They were in danger of being more forgotten than most
semi-finalists.

For few, apart from a team's own supporters, remember
the semi-finalists. Players believe it is the worst stage at
which to lose. After all, with a final you get the day, the
experience. People at least remember you. If you are
involved in promotion, it can slip after Cup defeat at this
point, such is the sense of deflation. If in mid-table, you
can be sucked into the relegation process. If you are already
in relegation trouble . . . The pain is no less acute for supporters. The sense of anticipation, of the day out, of basking
in the reflected glory, of the self-worth which a final appearance can bring, is so high that its piercing is cruel. On
final-four day, the fan works himself to a pitch of emotion,
and an emotional hangover can be far more debilitating
than any alcoholic one.

Sadly, it was to be for Norwich again today. Their lean
young striker, Chris Sutton, had good early chances but
was not yet sharp. It might have been different had they
fallen to someone more experienced. Then, before half-
time, Sunderland produced what was to prove the best
passage of the match, a neat passing movement down their

right flank. It was rounded off by John Byrne, a skilful striker born in Manchester but an international for the Republic of Ireland – whose governing body's initials of FAI are believed to stand for Find An Irishman. His header home maintained his record of having scored in every round.

Sunderland held on to that lead to clinch a date with destiny. The Wearside fans interrupted their celebrations only to jeer a group profiting on the pitch from the absence of fences; soon they were again singing *You'll Never Walk Alone*. Their team had not played especially well, but then few do in semi-finals. The fans were experiencing through football the old saying about sex: that when it was good it was very good; that even when it was bad it was good. This was sex and the single goal.

Norwich, by contrast, clinched a date with obscurity; their play in the second half seemed to confirm it. For them, the final whistle signalled the end of an era, the break-up of a team. It also foreshadowed the poignant sight of a small boy in Norwich favours sat in the North Stand crying a river of tears. It was a Sunderland supporter who turned to him to offer comfort. Together, they slowly made their way out of the ground, into Leppings Lane, where quiet flowed the Don.

Ten: Endgame

1 Leeds and Chokers

It was the Choker's Championship. But, even coughing as they had done in the last weeks of the season, we all thought that Manchester United would still splutter their way to the League title. Instead, Leeds United got a hold of themselves and the prize. Thus, the Labour Party having lost the election, it proved to be the year of the Reds being unelectable.

The damage was self-inflicted. By Manchester United as well, come to think of it. When Leeds lost 0–4 at Manchester City on Grand National day, it looked as if the race was won, United receiving some guidance over the fences by the nag in the stable next door. It seemed fitting. After that two-horse race of 1985, in which they finished fourth, United were to win the two-donkey derby. A 1–0 victory over Southampton – the goal scored by the Ukrainian, Andrei Kanchelskis, who was described by the United manager, Alex Ferguson, as 'a match-winner' – served to confirm that they were a shoo-in.

But Leeds saddled up again, and Sheffield Wednesday came late on the rails, and United cracked under the whip. They lost 1–2 at home to Nottingham Forest, then 0–1 at West Ham, who would be relegated as the first division's bottom club. Kanchelskis was dropped, along with the gifted midfield player, Neil Webb, as Ferguson resorted to packing the side with competent but dull journeymen. It was safety last. The title that should have been secured by then was finally lost on the penultimate weekend of the League season. On the Saturday, Sheffield Wednesday, needing to win their last two matches, could only draw at Crystal Palace. That, to their delight, gave them a place in the following season's UEFA Cup; but it narrowed the field again to two.

The next day, Leeds kicked off at midday against Sheffield United at Bramall Lane. Later in the afternoon, Manchester United were at Liverpool. 'I'd rather Everton won the Championship,' said the home goal-keeper, Bruce Grobbelaar, adumbrating the nature of United's task against a club unusually uninvolved in the title denouement, even should Leeds lose.

But they didn't. They fell behind to a goal by Alan Cork but equalised on the stroke of half-time, through Rodney Wallace, due to a mix-up in the Sheffield defence. An injury to the Sheffield goal-keeper, Mel Rees, left him hobbling about for the second half, and he missed a cross to allow the Leeds full-back, John Newsome, to head his team 2–1 ahead. An own-goal by the Leeds striker, Lee Chapman, when a cross by John Pemberton cannoned off him, restored parity. Then, eleven minutes from time, Leeds's substitute striker, Frenchman Eric Cantona, took the ball forward. It was taken from him by the Sheffield defender, Brian Gayle, but, as Rees came apparently to collect, Gayle headed it over him. Leeds had won 3–2.

Now Manchester United, in the dressing-room at Anfield, knew that they were 4 points behind and would need to win both today and next week at home to Tottenham. By the same token, Leeds, streets ahead on goal difference, must fail to win their last match, against depressed Norwich – seemingly a gimme. One sensed that United sensed that the chance had gone; that they were fated to be runners-up.

The game reflected it. They played well, hitting post and

bar three times, but were beaten 0–2. Ian Rush scored the first, his first goal ever against Manchester United. Liverpool's fans taunted United's by singing the song that had sustained their visitors for much of the season: *Always Look On The Bright Side Of Life*. A UEFA Cup place, and the League Cup they had won a month earlier by beating Nottingham Forest 1–0 at Wembley, was now not the bright side; it was merely an indication of how good the season might have been. The early boast of The World's Greatest Club gaining a march on England's Greatest was now reversed with a vengeance.

It was in the League Cup, in its fifth round, that United had beaten Leeds emphatically 3–1 in January, to great jubilation. As the hymnist wrote: 'Before the great Three-One, they all exulting stand.' It came in the middle of a remarkable three-game series between the two teams at Elland Road in the space of eighteen days. United also won the third contest, in the third round of the FA Cup, by 1–0, to encourage the theory that they were the better team. The first meeting, a League match, had ended 1–1.

It all ended, however, not with the bang of those confrontations but with a whimper. Leeds's own-goal, mistake-riddled triumph against a one-legged goal-keeper somehow seemed symbolic of the season. It was perhaps apposite, too, that the movement for the winning goal had been launched by Cantona, perhaps freshest of the Leeds players having joined from Nimes on loan only in January. But, while all that was true, it had remained a compulsive competition. 'Cynical ex-pros may say the League is not as good as it was, but you cannot doubt its competitive edge,' said the Crystal Palace manager, Steve Coppell. 'It's why it is revered around the world.'

No cynic one Gary Lineker, even if almost an ex-pro; but he summed up well the demands of the season, the end of which was witnessing the end of him as a Football League player before he went to Japan to join the Nagoya club, Grampus Eight, in a new National League competition. During his farewell tour, he gave an audience to football writers at Groucho's, a club in London's Soho frequented mainly by media figures, notably actors and writers. 'We've always played a lot of games in this country, but football has not always been played the way it is now, which is far more physical than it has ever been,' said one of the biggest and best media figures of them all. 'Far more teams are playing in that direct style, which is very tough, physically, to play against. It is getting more demanding on the older legs.

'Because of the number of games, it's not unusual for nine of your eleven to be carrying some injury or other. They'll give everything, but there's no zip, no sharpness. We're over-played. And, on the continent, they think we're crazy.' The problem had been identified in that FA Blueprint for the Future of Football which outlined the concept of the Premier League. It recommended an eighteen-team competition. Then the League chairmen got to work. They wanted twenty-two, and a compromise of twenty, not until 1994–95, was agreed. The FA council acquiesced.

'At the moment, it's a struggle to play in some matches, and that did influence me when I made up my mind to go,' Lineker continued. 'Changing back to a twenty-two-club first division was an odd decision at the time and remains an odd decision now. The problem is that we play too often, and the character of the English player is such that he will give everything each time. The quality won't be there, though. If players aren't feeling 100 per cent, which is impossible if you're playing that frequently, the standard will drop, and you'll get more people just whacking it forward and looking for rebounds.

'I watch the Italian football on television and think: "Bloody hell, they're quicker than us and sharper than us," but they're not. It's just that they're fresher. That's the difference. Our Championship is now just a case of who is least tired – who can last the longest.'

He spoke, too, of his own career, an exemplary one that had brought him an OBE and in which he had never been booked. He would remain England's captain, until the summer's European Championship finals, after which he would retire from the international game. Not that he always enjoyed being Captain Courteous – or Golden Bollocks, as some less reverent, probably envious, fellow professionals had it. Or the Queen Mother of football, as he was described by a play then running in London's West End called *An Evening With Gary Lineker*.

'All that goody-goody stuff gets a bit sickly at times. It can be embarrassing,' he said. 'Nobody is that nice. I know what I'm like, and my family know. I suppose that's all that matters.' Family was central to him: Grampus Eight had put at his disposal in Japan a medical team to monitor the treatment of his and wife Michelle's baby son, George, who had contracted leukaemia.

Naturally, he said that day at Groucho's, he remembered his first goal: for Leicester City against Notts County in 1979, five minutes from the end. They needed to win to stay in the second division, and the goal won the match 1–0. At club level, his favourite goal had been a shot from twenty-five yards against Manchester United in the League Cup the previous season, the unusual distance making it memorable for the penalty-box predator. At international level, a lob against Northern Ireland five years previously, even if Pat Jennings had not been in goal, had been his favourite. A World Cup game against Poland in 1986 in the Mexico finals also stuck out. England needed to win to qualify from their group; they did, Lineker scoring a hat-trick in the 3–0 win. His greatest achievements at club level were the FA Cup victory with Tottenham the previous season; also a European Cup-Winners' Cup triumph with

Barcelona in 1989, when he was assigned the unfamiliar right wing by Johan Cruyff, the manager who was preparing to sell him.

The choice for me on the last day of the League season was to go to Old Trafford to take in Lineker's last match in English football, to witness for one last time the sharpness around the goal, the speed of thought and sleight of foot and head; or to take in Leeds, to see the champions crowned. Leeds won, appropriately. The sight of a United disappointed yet again might just be too gloomy, as would it be to have confirmed the belief that Lineker was going too soon, even if, at 31, he wanted to bow out at the top. United duly won 3–1 to underline what might have been; and Lineker duly scored to maintain his astonishing League record of a goal every 167 minutes. Before this Three-One, however, there was precious little exulting.

Lineker was beaten to the first division's leading goal-scorer's title by Ian Wright of Arsenal, who scored a hat-trick on the final day as his team beat Southampton 5–1; that in itself also served to confirm what might have been for the London side, but for the falterings of winter, and what might be the next season. Wright's 29 surpassed Lineker by one.

Earlier that May day, King's Cross was its usual, bustling, Saturday-morning self with football fans of various hues and persuasions heading for all points north, brushing past a virtually unnoticed Maidstone United team preparing to exploit a cheap British Rail deal that would get them to Doncaster. Peaceful optimism was in the air; it was on Saturday nights here that things could get difficult, when the aggrieved pessimism of the losers could surface.

There seemed more Leeds United followers than any others – exiled Yorkshiremen and the cross-bred Home Counties fans who grew up wanting to be associated with the success of the Don Revie era of the late 1960s and early

1970s and still retained a rapport. One such was Simon Bucknell, although he scarcely conformed to any stereotype, certainly not those who had dragged Leeds's name through the mud of many foreign battlefields. The 26-year-old owner of a computer company from Chelmsford in Essex sat in first-class with his father, Peter, who was not as passionate in his attachment to Leeds but more 'a supporter of good football'. They contemplated the day ahead, along with a nearby group of fans flourishing the video camera with which they planned to capture it.

Simon had converted his primary school in Cambridge to supporting Leeds, he said, and he himself had never since wavered. 'There is something unique about the supporters. They will always outsing everyone else, especially the London teams when you watch them in London. They are very friendly. But we still get treated like cattle a lot of the time,' he added. Was that not inevitable, given the rioting at the European Cup final of 1975, the ripped-out seats being hurled as Leeds lost 0–2 to Bayern Munich; and then the riots at Bournemouth two years ago this very weekend, when fans without tickets could not get in to see Leeds promoted to the first division?

'That is history, but I suppose we are always going to be reminded of it,' said Simon. 'I have hardly seen any trouble. I have learned not to make any trouble but, when you wear your Leeds colours, people look at you as if you are a hooligan. I suppose people are going to be intimidated by the reputation when we play in the European Cup next season.'

'The game has improved, and the players have a greater sense of their responsibility,' said Peter. 'At every game, they come and thank the crowd for their support at the end of the match.' 'Yes, and at the beginning Leeds kick a ball into the crowd for them to play with. It releases the tension and all helps,' added Simon.

Leeds station was also abuzz, the fans debouching in blue

and yellow – the club colours which Revie had changed to white in admiration of Real Madrid – from all parts of the country. The taxi queue outside was longer than normal, and there was only one destination. The driver could deposit us only a few hundred yards from the ground, though, such was the throng. 'People have been hanging around here since 10 o'clock,' he said. 'A lot of them haven't got tickets. They're just here.'

Much of the celebration seemed ungracious and unsubtle. 'Boll**cks to Manchester United,' read one T-shirt. 'Are you watching, Manchester?' chanted the Kop, more taunt than query. 'Who's got the bottle now, Mr Fergie?' wondered a message on the closed-circuit television pictures inside Elland Road. And the banner in what used to be the Scratching Shed and was now the family enclosure, reading 'Bats breaks ya balls' with reference to the Leeds midfield player, David Batty, did not quite have the ring of the 'Norman bites yer legs' of the Hunter of yore.

Still, much had been made of Manchester United's twenty-five years without the title; it had been eighteen of decline and frustration for Leeds. The jokers who came dressed as jesters, and those with faces and hair painted in blue and yellow and wearing hastily printed 'Champions' T-shirts, caught more the carnival mood.

The scramble for tickets outside was sadly encapsulated by a young Irishman begging a commissionaire to tell anyone in the guest suites that if they would only come down and get him in, he would give them the cut-glass Leeds memento tray he was holding. Meanwhile, newspapermen were being directed for their tickets to a window marked 'Press, Blind'. Perhaps it was Leeds's little joke. Forgive us our press passes. Inside, when Leeds emerged on to the pitch at 2:25pm, to an Elland Road already full and to music from *Chariots of Fire* and the *Rocky* films, torn-up newspaper was used as confetti by some in the crowd. A pointed statement, no doubt.

Fifty-two photographers confronted Leeds as they passed the Championship trophy amongst themselves. The biggest cheer, to rival the noise from a couple of frightening fireworks, was accorded Howard Wilkinson. When he had come to second-division Leeds as manager in October 1988, Wilkinson had had removed from corridors and offices all the pictures extolling the Revie era – the period when the club dominated the English game without claiming as many prizes as it should have, when its professionalism and use of questionable tactics in its all-embracing desire to win led to jealousy and resentment within the game. It was, Wilkinson discerned after he had succeeded several ex-Revie players, time to move out of the past in which the club had been living. It was time for the faded old actress to stop clinging longingly to the publicity stills shot in her youth.

One of the most respected figures within the game – he had served his time in non-League and in regional coaching jobs – Wilkinson took on the task because he could see through the tarnished glamour to a new future. And the money was available to create one. Having turned them away from relegation to the third division in his first season in charge, he took them up on that sweltering May day in Bournemouth in 1990, the promotion based on a pragmatic, power-football approach. Then came phase two. Vinnie Jones, symbol of that Leeds, was released to Sheffield United. In came Gary McAllister from Leicester to pass the ball; Tony Dorigo from Chelsea to deliver more quality; Rod Wallace from Southampton to score more ground-based goals.

Elements of Wilkinson's promotion side still remained: Lee Chapman's heading and scoring ability from within twelve yards of goal; Gordon Strachan's talent for bonding the team together, even if his slowing skills had been somewhat overstated in these days of dearth for the creative player. Batty, if limited in vision, provided some grit in midfield, on the left of which Gary Speed was developing into a clever crosser and header. Mel Sterland provided an experienced eye at right-back, John Newsome replacing him well latterly when he was injured. The central defence of Chris Fairclough and Chris Whyte proved less porous than had been imagined. When it did part, John Lukic in goal proved sturdy, keeping twenty clean sheets during the campaign as he added to the Championship medal he had won with Arsenal three years previously.

It was thought of them that they did not have the strength in depth to sustain a challenge, but injuries did not trouble them as seriously as some. They had seasoned professionals, too, to fill breaches, notably Steve Hodge – whose career and temperament had taken disappointing turns – and John McClelland. And then came Eric Cantona, entertainer extraordinaire who struck an immediate rapport with fans who chanted 'Ooh, aah, Cantona' in response. The boost he had provided in the second half of the season had been perhaps the decisive element in the title race.

They were probably not great champions but they were champions. Anyone who has known, say, what it takes simply to get up on a stage and perform, let alone perform better than others, would appreciate their virtues. 'I am not saying they are the best team Leeds have produced or the best team that Leeds are going to produce but they are champions, and let us enjoy that,' said Wilkinson in his manager's message relayed over the tannoys before the kick-off. Elland Road hushed itself to hear.

The match against Norwich in the spring sunshine was inevitably something of a let-down. By now, Elland Road was *en fête* but no longer on fire. With the title having been won six days earlier, it seemed that all passion was spent, and the match demonstrated how flat English football can fall when nothing is at stake. How much it relies on its conversation with the crowd. 'Sometimes, anticipation is better than realisation,' Wilkinson would say later. 'The players have had a good week. They certainly played like it.'

The game was enlivened by the ever eye-catching Cantona and a splendid goal by Wallace, who gambolled past two defenders on the half-way line, outran two more and angled home cutely and acutely a left-footed shot to give Leeds a 1–0 victory. When Strachan came on as a substitute he gave Leeds a more inventive impetus, but they could not dominate nor stroke the ball about in the way that Revie's class of '74 might have done. Norwich, for their part, were clearly still suffering from post-semi-final depression. They passed the ball nicely enough, but the game should be about a bit more than nice.

At the final whistle, Leeds, the only team unbeaten at home in the League all season, embarked on a lap of honour as seventy-four cannon shots, representing the number of their League goals, were simulated on the tannoys. The parade, however, had to be aborted as some 150 sought to accompany them. Their being jeered by 32,500 offered hope for improvement in Leeds's behaviour the following season in the European Cup.

Surrounded by journalists in the press room, Wilkinson was not yet ready to think about that competition. 'Can we just enjoy it for a couple of days before the acid starts flowing again?' he inquired. One suspected, though, that he knew exactly what he needed to do – as he had on that day in Bournemouth – to continue the team's progress and perhaps reach the lucrative last-eight league stage of the European Cup. The securing of Cantona on a three-year contract for a transfer fee of £900,000 from Nimes was a first step.

Any new players in mind? he was asked. 'Yes. Maradona, van Basten. I don't know about Gullit.' Then the pragmatist in him took over. 'The key is always performances,' said Wilkinson, ever the coach, ever distrustful of mere results and fleeting success. 'If I think their performance has been capable then I will be happy. There has got to be a winner and a loser, that is sport; but it is the performance that is important to me. Sometimes, that's not good enough for supporters, though.

'They have stood the test, they have nerved it out well,' he said of his team. 'I thought at the start of the season that we had the fourth strongest squad. They have nearly got more than 10 out of 10. It is an opportunity for the club and the city to go forward.'

The new era was the important thing. A new East Stand was being built at Elland Road, financed by a better conceived bond scheme than Arsenal and West Ham had attempted to implement earlier in the season. No outrage and protest here. The £500 being sought guaranteed £100 off the season-ticket price each year for seven years – during which prices would be held – plus benefits in buying Wembley tickets. In the new stand would be a new museum. 'When they open it for the new season, it will be full of replicas and cups from the Revie era, and in one corner will be something from this year. Perhaps then everyone will be happy,' said Wilkinson.

As we made our way back to the station, under the banner draped from a road-bridge saying 'Simplement Le Meilleur', past the celebrating crowds – and 250,000 of them would come out the following day for the players' traditional open-top coach tour of the city and civic reception – into the square outside the Queen's Hotel, there was a rare sight over the city. It was a double rainbow.

II Parting Shots

And then there were ninety-two. Again. On 25 March 1992, Aldershot died as a Football League club. They were the first to go to the wall during a season since Accrington Stanley thirty years previously. 'Accrington Stanley? Who are they?' the conversation went between two young boys in a television commercial.

After several months of brinkmanship, with players and creditors not getting paid, the 66-year-old club that was bottom of the fourth division folded with debts of around £1.2 million. 'There were no last-minute proposals, and no one walked in with a bag of money,' said a statement from the liquidators, simply and sadly, as the League's deadline passed for the club to show that they could be viable.

Passing near the ground that day I felt drawn to it, to express perhaps some silent sympathy, or regret at not having seen them in their hour of need and chipped in a few pounds. I was planning to see the last match, but then there had been so many last matches. The joke had changed from Aldershot's strikers having hit more photographers than Frank Sinatra to the club saying more farewells than him. It had been like reading about Italian politics, the balance of power constantly changing. They would survive, then they wouldn't. The difference was that there were no pornography queens running Aldershot. Maybe if they had thought of that . . .

The wind was whistling down Aldershot High Street, in which the club was situated. The board carrying forthcoming fixtures was empty and tilted; the listing listed, as had the club all season. Only one banner was hung from the green railings that run the width of the ground. 'Aldershot – The Shots – RIP,' it said. A red and white scarf – although Aldershot played in red and blue – was tied alongside. Perhaps the paucity of *mementos mori* was a sign of the apathy that seemed to accompany Aldershot's demise. Ironically, attendances had been up 2 per cent, but 2 per cent of not very much is not very much.

The neat little club office block – past the locked-up Portakabin that housed the promotions department – which Aldershot had built on their council-owned Recreation Ground was covered in graffiti. 'Please directors don't let the Shots die,' went one line; 'Aldershot FC must live,' declared another. They were both overtaken. Now the plaintive was replaced by the angry. 'You the directors let this club die. You didn't care. The blood of Aldershot will always be on your hands.' Some twenty signatures supported it.

The playing surface looked immaculate; perhaps Rushmoor Borough Council, owed £225,000 in rent, could sell it to Manchester United or Aston Villa. 'No unauthorised ball games allowed on this pitch,' said a notice.

'Who are you?' came the voice of one of two men approaching. 'I'm just looking around,' I said. 'We are security put in by the council. There's nothing for you here,' he replied gruffly. 'Would you mind leaving?' 'I'm not going to steal anything, am I?' I said rhetorically. 'You should be getting people in here, not throwing them out.' The feeble joke cut no ice. It was time to go; too cold to stay, as Aldershot had found out.

The fear was that the club were not alone, that, but for the grace of bank managers, several more could and would follow. For financial reports were indicating that Football League clubs were in crisis, collectively in debt to the tune of £130 million. The situation was serious, even if not critical. Or was it critical, but not serious? Football, after all, had been in financial crisis for as long as anyone could remember and probably would be for as long as anyone kicked a ball around. Aldershot, however, was a shock to those who believed that football clubs would survive no matter what, that someone would always come to the rescue.

A report by one Dr Simon Pitt, once of the London Business School, did reveal some superficially worrying facts. He had canvassed the ninety-three clubs and received sixty-one replies to a confidential questionnaire. 'Very few English football clubs are solvent, and many operate with considerable losses and make substantial losses each season,' it concluded. What was new? Twelve were in danger of going under, it also revealed. Only twelve?

Pitt's prognosis was that most clubs were 'not capable of either managerially or financially facing that challenge' of dealing with a debt of £130 million. The game was facing 'one of the biggest challenges in its history.' But then it did so every year.

His report did reveal the cost of League football, for which revenue through the turnstiles had dropped 28 per cent in the 1980s. Transfer fees had risen in the first division by 323 per cent in eleven years; players' wages had risen 210 per cent in a seven-year period in the 1980s. Policing costs had doubled to £6.1 million in the last year. Football had, in addition, failed to invest in good marketing talent, the report remarked; had failed to raise money by successful share issues or debenture schemes; and had not fully realised the implications of the Taylor Report.

Pitt acknowledged that a football club was like no ordinary business, since the majority of its overheads were fixed. It could not just cut its work-force; it needed to maintain a certain quota of players. Indeed, the average playing staff for a League club was thirty-two, with wages and signing-on fees accounting for 90 per cent of costs. The statistics went on: from 1979 to 1990, transfers had risen from £17 million for the season to £55 million; £307 million was spent during the 1980s, of which the first division forked out £183.5 million. The knock-on effect meant that the second division spent £2.8 million in 1986 and £19 million in 1990, an increase of 785 per cent. The third division rose 414 per cent in that period, the fourth 825 per cent.

The game, said Pitt, was 'undercapitalised and overborrowed', and he continued: 'In any other business circumstances, small companies such as these with high fixed overheads and declining marginal revenues would have gone bankrupt a long time ago. Most clubs only survive because of the deep pockets of wealthy individuals.'

The League could not argue with the report, although they again pointed out that no member club had gone out of business during a season due to bankruptcy since Accrington Stanley. Newport County had died after relegation, to rise from the ashes as a non-League club, as had now Accrington. But Aldershot changed the view, besides which the League did not see so many benefactors coming into the game now. They worried more about the creation of the Premier League and what it would do to the financial position of the smaller clubs, some of whom made it through some months due to the odd payment towards players' wages from the Professional Footballers' Association.

Brian Talbot was aware of most of this: he had been managing director of Aldershot earlier in the season. But, once bitten, he was not twice shy. We had met in midwinter to discuss why he was still seeking to buy a football club, despite daily discovering more potential Aldershots.

Once a midfield beaver with Ipswich, Arsenal and England, Talbot was just trying to stay in the game he so loved. That he loved it was apparent as he clung on to his playing days by turning out for Sudbury Town of the Southern Division of the Southern League at the age of 38. He had been *in situ* as a player with West Bromwich Albion in 1988 when Ron Atkinson left the club for the second time, and he got the job of player-manager. Two years later, it turned sour when Albion lost at home to non-League Woking in the FA Cup, and Talbot was sacked. He took the manager's job at Aldershot, then became managing director, but left when money became too tight to mention.

Now, away from that, Talbot was working to put himself through it all again. He and a business partner, a 27-year-old property developer named Mark English, wanted to secure control of a football club. They were based in an office in Harley Street, which seemed appropriate given the inflated fees paid for healing in that part of Central London. The large block, which housed small businesses such as dentists – as revealed by the fear-inducing smell in the corridors – was owned by English, who intended to use it as collateral on any deal he did for a club.

Talbot had looked at six lower-division clubs in detail so far and commissioned reports and company searches on twenty of the thirty-two League clubs which a survey by a company of brokers had suggested would welcome investment. In other words, which were skint and on the edge. As we talked, a telephone call came in from a desperate-sounding director of a fourth-division club, who were losing £7000 a week. For Talbot, it was almost a typical call. He sounded considerably more relaxed than the man on the other end.

He had, he said, recently met with the chairman of another fourth-division club. 'Mr Chairman,' said Talbot.

'Your debts are more than £700,000 and rising by £5000 a
week. But you want £350,000 to sell up? Why?' The chairman sat and thought for a moment. 'Because I love it so
much,' he replied. It showed up the attitude of some running the game: a naïve delight in doing so for the love of a
game they discovered in boyhood; the local kudos it brings;
but an unrealistic desire to get back the money they have
brought to it. 'They can't love it that much if they would
see it die rather than step aside and take the loss,' said
Talbot. Nevertheless, they were working out ways of holding on to something that is at the least onerous, but more
likely ulcerous.

And what was it, too, that made someone like Mark English, who undoubtedly worked with his head in his business dealings, let his heart take over when it came to
football? It seemed a little like the businessman who blus-
tered and cursed all day at the office then billed and cooed
when he got home at night and put his child to bed. But
then, which football fan, after all, has not dreamt of winning
the pools, taking over his local club, first getting rid of
the chairman, closely followed by the manager, and then
running it all himself, or even herself?

The answers gradually came from Talbot. 'Yes, I have
been surprised at some of the things I have found,' he said
of his dealings with clubs, although he wondered why anything any more should surprise him in the game. 'Quite a
few are in trouble, although no one really likes to admit it.'
It may explain why up-to-date accounts of clubs were so
hard to come by. 'Most clubs in the third and fourth divisions are in trouble. We're not looking at first- and second-
division clubs, because they are either not for sale or, if
they are, their debts are horrendous,' he continued.

'A lot of clubs want you to put in cash as a gift, perhaps
for a seat in the stand, when you ask them what they are
offering in return. When you say you want 60 per cent of

the shares, they suddenly say they are not willing to give away their control. But some of them are not in a good bargaining position. Still, if they want to struggle on, good luck to them.' Talbot added that many of the directors he met were fearful only for their own position within the club. He insisted that they would not be swept away with his new broom, that he and English would need them for their knowledge and goodwill.

Talbot and English would seek to become managing director – or chief executive – and a director respectively. They would seek to emulate what Terry Venables and his backer, Alan Sugar, creator of the Amstrad computer company, had done at Tottenham Hotspur, a club seemingly coming round, financially at least, after being administered the smelling salts. Talbot insisted that English, who was a Tottenham supporter with his own box at White Hart Lane, was no Sugar daddy; but that he did differ from most wealthy people willing to put money into football, in that he was prepared to put up the collateral of bricks and mortar. Banks, Talbot added, responded to that. Most were tired of being presented with intangible assets, such as players. Buildings didn't break legs.

Talbot had found it much more difficult than he thought it would be. Clubs were not – surprisingly, it might have been thought – biting off his hand. 'You start by thinking, "Yes, this should be easy", but as you find out more you think, "I'm not having that." And people are a bit wary of you. They wonder what is your ulterior motive. But there is no ulterior motive.' He could hardly blame them, once they have discovered that English is a property developer. The recent history of football has been scarred by examples of people seeking to get for redevelopment the prime sites that many football grounds occupied.

So, accepting that it was all above board, what was it then – given the evidence – that kept alive football people's passion for the game and even, Aldershot notwithstanding, its lame ducks? What kept them drawing at its well? Talbot believed it might just be, or should be, akin to buying a racehorse; not expecting it to win any money but to enjoy watching it run. 'Mark just wants some fun,' said Talbot. 'Being involved with a club gets the adrenalin flowing more than just watching them. Me? Well, it's my game, my life. I suppose it's something to do with eternal youth,' he said with a smile.

'You talk to a lot of people, and all you hear about are all the problems, the police problems, the player problems, the hooligan element, the seating problems. Yes, it's a business but it's also a sport. People have got away from that, unfortunately. If you go into a football club you have to be prepared to lose money. It's a bonus if you don't. But I believe a club can be run on an even keel, with Mark's business sense, my footballing brain and the support of the local community – and that means the council as well as the fans. They have got to decide if they want a football club representing them around the country. Of course, you hope you are going to turn a club round and make it successful. After six months, you might think, "What have I taken on here," mind.'

Football may have been complacent in always banking on such figures as English. Indeed, Aldershot had been for a while when a teenaged property developer called Spencer Trethewy stepped forward to save them, only to turn out to have less backing than he claimed and to slip into business obscurity again. But the supply did seem to endure to some extent. The new element was now the manager/managing director working in league with the money-man. Perhaps in that alliance was the future well-being of some clubs. Perhaps, though, football would remain in many cases merely magnificent folly.

The poor will always be with us, the saying went. In

football, at least we thought that they would always be with us. Sadly, Aldershot weren't.

Actually, the Shots regrouped one mo' time this season. On a mild May evening, the Recreation Ground, permission of the council, opened its gates for a testimonial match for Ian McDonald, the left-back and coach who had taken over from Talbot as player-manager and manfully sought to keep the club going. The warmth in the air matched the feeling going through those delightful turnstiles which, with their frosted, coloured glass, resembled those huts on seaside promenades where families spend wet afternoons on holiday until it is time to go back to the bed-and-breakfast.

Once inside, it was a short walk through the little pleasure garden of shrubs and neat flower beds of red poppies and bluebells up to the High Street End – probably the only end in the country with no seating or terracing, merely a walkway. It would, after all, have been barbaric to have paved paradise and put up a parking lot. The adjacent railway track brought home commuters from London to a town of some 80,000 civilians on the Surrey-Hampshire border although, with it being such a big military centre, the real population was considerably more. The graffiti had been washed away from the club offices. No security men threw you out.

This idyllic scene, though, hid few of the problems of the ground: the Kop end, with its ten ugly posts restricting view and its perimeter fence offending, needed work; the floodlights could not be used because expensive bulbs needed to be replaced.

Southampton Football Club and 1810 spectators, a section of whom sang 'There's only one Ian McDonald', came to pay their respects and £5 admission to the beneficiary, who had been with the club for ten years, and to Aldershot. The game, with Southampton fielding up front the England striker, Alan Shearer, whom they valued at £3 million, was a mirror of Aldershot's season. They fell behind in the first half but, with McDonald's excellent left foot offering them hope, they kept going and equalised midway through the second half. A goal ten minutes from time consigned them, however, to a 1–2 defeat.

The result, of course, mattered not. It was a night to lament the past – £3 bought you the programme of the last home match, against Lincoln City – and to find hope for the future. Some was offered by a half-time announcement that a group of supporters had formed Aldershot Town FC, secured the Recreation Ground on a three-year licence, and applied for the Isthmian, now Diadora, League. 'We could be back in the Football League in six to ten years,' it added, to a few groans.

The dressing-rooms, offices and bars buzzed again afterwards, as once they did and as they should do weekly. The club chaplain, the Rev. John Marshall, buzzed, too, in his Brummie way, telling all about the fifteen-minute appearance he had made for McDonald in a testimonial match at Camberley earlier in the week. 'I just have a love of the game,' he said. 'I can help here, just by being on hand, in a more pastoral way. I think the players feel they can talk to me. I'll be here next season, if they are still going. I'll buy a season ticket. I know all of the supporters. There aren't many of them.'

McDonald sat in the dressing-room for possibly the last time, sipping from a can of beer. He had been offered the job as manager of the new club by its organisers but was hoping for a post in the full-time game. Seeing that he was drawing the dole, and had been doing so since the week before Christmas, one could hardly blame him. 'It's been a very emotional night, just seeing everybody back. It's been nice to see them again,' he said, pondering the past – he had played for Barrow and Workington, both of whom had also gone out of the League – and considering the future.

'We had about ten last games, but I think we have laid Aldershot to rest tonight.'

There was the odd swipe at the local council; he believed that they could have done more, in the way that Calderdale had in order to keep Halifax alive, by realising the value of a professional football team to the town. But he preferred to look forward. 'We've cried our tears. Let's hope people support the new club.'

He was planning, he said, in partnership with the former physio, Steve Wignall, to set up a coaching school in the area for children between 5 and 14. He believed that he could help in the area of kids getting the right coaching and not over-playing. He was seeing the bank manager in the morning. As he spoke, a fan poked her head around the dressing-room door. 'If you want any typing done, give me a ring,' she said.

It was a night heavy with poignancy and contrast. The match was taking place just two days before the FA Cup final, at which would appear Malcolm Crosby as Sunderland's manager. Crosby had been a player at Aldershot and, ten years previously, had gone to York City in a swap deal for McDonald. Such are the ironies of the game. Crosby's success suggested that, just as a training ground, Aldershot was probably worth saving. As a football club, providing entertainment and interest for the town, it certainly was.

In the home of the British Army, McDonald would soldier on. Aldershot would soldier on. 'I don't have many other talents,' he explained in a by-now empty dressing-room. 'I am just a football person. You get these people, and I am one of them.'

III Final Fling

In the club shop at Roker Park, they had deliberately not imported any merchandise to mark their appearance in the 1992 FA Cup final; they preferred instead to sell off the old stock. Now you saw why the the local dialect described the place as 'Canny Aad Sunlun'.

Still, on the Wednesday morning before the match against Liverpool, the stuff was going, and the cupboard was looking bare. It had been going at the rate of £60,000 worth a week since the win over Norwich, compared to the £10,000 usually at this time of year. Left were items such as the book on Sunderland Greats – they might have tittered on Tyneside, but it stretched to ninety-two pages – and T-shirts depicting two of them, Charlie Hurley and Raich Carter, who had been a member of Sunderland's 1937 Cup-winning team. That seemed to be taking old stock a bit too far.

The Hurley T-shirt, dedicated to the centre-half who was once named as Sunderland's player-of-the-century, was priceless. 'Constructed entirely from pre-cast concrete, Charlie Hurley is without doubt the greatest human being to have ever lived,' it said. Whole families were named after him, and he often played when fatally injured with his head missing, it added.

In its small way, it was an example of how Sunderland revered its past and was almost reluctant to move on, of how myth and reality became confused. I met Hurley a few years ago, when he was living in Hertfordshire. He was then more interested in playing tennis than watching football, having little feeling for the modern game. The very fact that the 1973 FA Cup final – when Sunderland, then as now a second-division team, gloriously overcame the odds to defeat the titanic Leeds United 1–0 – was being talked about as much, if not more, in this year's build-up illustrated it too.

Close by the ground, the Wolseley pub overlooking the docks was showing a video of the 1973 final on the Thursday night. The following night, it was back to *karaoke*. Everywhere, the *Sunderland Echo* was selling reprints of their splendid 1973 'They've Done It' sports edition, in the original pink, which also informed that Bobby Charlton was taking up a managerial appointment with Preston North End.

A visit to the place during Cup final week revealed a mass of contrasts, mainly of old and new, in both culture and values. The landscape, with its idle docks, bore witness to decline and recession; yet everyone talked of commercial and sporting optimism. Modern structures were springing up, even if many were in the fashion for neo-classical architecture; yet there were examples everywhere of things falling apart. Roker Park was an obvious example. In keeping, the sign pointing to the club shop that should have read 'Shop on the Park' said 'Sho on th Park.'

With the Taylor Report ever occupying thinking, the talk was of moving to a new stadium on a green-field site. It was thus hardly worth spending much on the current ground, in front of which a large poster on behalf of the Tyne and Wear Development Corporation welcomed you to the New North-East. In shipbuilding, mining and heavy engineering, some 30,000 jobs had been lost since 1973; unemployment stood at 12.4 per cent compared to 6 per cent then. And yet.

People pointed to encouraging signs of upturn: the town being awarded the status of a city; the local polytechnic being upgraded to a university. Then there was the granting of first-class status to Durham County Cricket Club, with £2 million worth of sponsorship behind them; and Sunderland South having declared the first result of the general election a month earlier – efficiency rather than publicity stunt, it was insisted. And, of course, there was Nissan, the Japanese car manufacturers who had set up shop out on the Washington Road, bringing 4000 jobs to Wearside. They had decided – almost unheard-of – to close the factory on the Saturday afternoon. They had also painted in to the grass outside the plant a large Sunderland crest, underneath which was written, 'Simply the Best'.

The rebirth was inevitable, insisted Derek Horsfield of the Tyne and Wear Development Company, a private agency, as we spoke in his office in Washington, County Durham. He was surrounded on the business park – what used to be called an industrial estate – by half-built structures that recalled the city itself: it would be nice when it was finished. 'I am not a football fan,' he dared to admit, 'but sport does have an impact industrially and commercially. They said that, after 1973, everyone worked their socks off, and production went up because there was a sense of well-being about the place. This is an enthusiastic and loyal work-force up here.

'This area has not been as badly hit as it was in 1979, '80 and '81, and it is very resilient. A lot of the problem has been the banks tightening up because of their property problems in the south-east.' Investment was improving, exports were up, and management had learned from a decade ago, he said. 'There is an air of success about the place, but I don't think it's surprising any more.'

There were less enthused voices elsewhere, possibly more in tune with the working, or unemployed, person rather than the entrepreneur. 'As players, we were very much in touch with local people,' said Vic Halom, centre-forward in the 1973 team who had stood in Sunderland North as a Liberal Democrat in the general election, having chosen to move back to the area eighteen months pre-viously. 'I can remember ships being launched. We used to go down to the Boilermakers' Club for a couple of pints on a Sunday lunchtime. It's that type of place. Sunderland was that type of club. You are not separated from the people, stuck up on a hill behind a fortress.

'I am glad the business community is optimistic because, without them, we have had it. But we need more invest-ment and not only in leisure and tourism. Marinas are no good. They may be nice to walk around on a Sunday morn-ing, but we need real jobs. I believe the old skills on Wear-side can be redirected, and a small shipyard could be opened. From that acorn, it could grow.'

Between it all – the reverence for the past, the coming to terms with the future – was the teak-tough spirit of the present. Sunderland folk were optimistic but realistic too.

'The area is like an island, surrounded by sea and rivers, and one and a half hours before you get to another big city,' said Alec King, the Sunderland commercial manager, ignoring Newcastle. 'People will turn out for things, but you have to attract them.' There was pandemonium sur-rounding him as he spoke in his office at Roker Park, with telephones ringing continuously, people flitting from office to office. And this was with the 17,800 tickets they had been allocated already distributed.

He had become involved with the tickets because it was all hands to the pump. 'I had a call from someone in Aus-tralia asking for a ticket,' he added. 'I said, "I have enough trouble getting one for somebody in Roker Avenue." We've gone back to the Sermon on the Mount to read how He did it with five loaves and two fishes.'

As do all good football clubs, Sunderland reflect their locality. The present is omnipresent in these days when not even the one-time Bank of England club, in such a football-daft location, can bank on support; where the commercial manager has assumed more importance than the secretary. King, a former bookmaker and sailor, was one of Lawrie McMenemy's more successful signings – from Grimsby, 'another drafty place' – in his expensive spell as manager of the club from 1985–87. He has since been instrumental in Sunderland winning awards for their community and family work. They have a double-decker bus which they send around the district as a promotional vehicle. At Roker Park, they employ a full-time school-teacher, and they bring in 6000 schoolchildren a year to have lessons at the club for a day.

'It's a place where you have just got to get involved with them. If you were a take-it-or-leave-it club, they would dump you. We call ourselves the Caring Club, which can be a rod for our back when we don't live up to it, but that's as it should be. They are very gentle, very nice people who just want you to be honest with them. They are not into fancy Dans.' That would, he agreed, make for some interesting conversation around the Wembley concourse, where the ticket-touting imagineers ply their trade.

King estimated that Sunderland would make around £1 million out of a final which generated between £8 and £10 million in revenue; that would be some compensation for a poor League season. Sunderland had been too involved for comfort in relegation issues, sacking the manager, Denis Smith, and only awarding the caretaker-manager, Malcolm Crosby, the job full-time after the threat had receded. But the windfall would not stop the drive to recruit more sponsors, more businesses linking up with the club. King was

Kent. An undignified exchange took place on the pitch. 'I think we should have kept them,' joked Malcolm Crosby as he put a brave face on his disappointment before the press. 'There was just too big a distance between our back and front men,' he said of the way Liverpool had stretched them.

'He's always had a lot of potential and he proved it today,' said the Liverpool assistant manager, Ronnie Moran, sub-bing for Souness, of McManaman, a player who offered the club genuine hope as they continued their transition period from one era of success to another. 'But it's not a triumph for any one person. We all muck in together. That's the Liverpool way.' It was, though, a personal triumph for Rob Jones, a young man with the future of English football at his feet, who had threaded his way through our season. He might be remembered beginning the season being throttled by his goal-keeper when playing for Crewe at Barnet. His progress had continued with a first cap and a display of remarkable maturity in England's 2–0 win over France at Wembley in February. Now it had ended with him eclipsing his grandfather, Bill, who had played for Liverpool in the 1950 final, which was lost 0–2 to Arsenal.

Phil Don had also enjoyed his day, he said as he stood in Wembley's banqueting hall savouring it all. 'McMana-man was looking for the penalty. Besides which, he fell a pace after the challenge,' he explained of the one moment that troubled him. It was now 7:30pm, and the last of Wem-bley's 2500 part-time staff employed for the day – there are 250 full-time – were ending their twelve-hour stint, leaving the stadium to the twenty-four-hour security. The compe-tition that had begun in front of 173 spectators at Wembley Football Club eight months earlier had ended before 79,544 at Wembley Stadium.

Suddenly, a sense of emptiness, a feeling of loss descended, as it always does at the end of the Cup final.

The domestic season, our season in the cold, was over. There was, though, some comfort in Ronnie Moran's words: 'We'll be back in training on 9 July . . .' There was also another season to which to look forward, as sure as the light of morning follows the darkness of the night. Maybe there are three certainties in life.

Postscript

It all ended in tears for BARNET, despite their regrouping after the defeat by Crewe and by Christmas looking as if they would be champions of the fourth division, particularly when topping the table in November. Yet a slump in the second half of the season saw them make the play-offs only in seventh place. In keeping with Barry Fry's ambitions, they were joint top goal-scorers in the Football League with 81, the same as Arsenal and Brentford, the third-division champions having played forty-six games to Barnet's forty-two.

Barnet then beat Blackpool 1–0 at home in the first leg of their semi-final play-off; but it should have been more, leading to an acrimonious scene in the dressing-room between Fry and Stan Flashman. Fry claimed that he had been sacked, as he had done earlier in the season when he refused Flashman's instruction to sell Gary Bull to Notts County. He was fed up, he said, with the constant criticism from Flashman and could work with him no longer. He remained in charge of the team for the second leg, but Barnet lost 0–2 and were eliminated. The row cooled down after a couple of weeks, as a cease-fire was called with the players backing Fry, even paying for him to join them on a holiday in Greece.

Crewe also made the play-offs, in sixth place, but lost over two legs to Scunthorpe. They in turn were beaten by

Blackpool on penalties in the final at Wembley. Burnley were the fourth-division champions.

In March, Fry had a testimonial against Arsenal, but the club as a whole encountered financial difficulties, even facing at one point a winding-up order that was eventually overcome. Despite that, they entertained splendidly an Aldershot side in its death-throes when it visited Underhill, and Barnet supporters raised £600 in a whip-round for them. Barnet beat Aldershot 5–0, a result that was expunged when Aldershot went out of business.

Kirstine Fry went into labour four days after the Crewe Alexandra match, as Barnet were drawing 5–5 with Brentford in a League Cup tie. Son Adam phoned Barry at Underhill at the end of the match, and he dashed back to Bedford to help deliver Anna-Marie, who weighed in at 7lb exactly.

The absence for much of the season of Glenn Hoddle with a calf injury undermined SWINDON TOWN's attempts to win promotion from the second division, which was won by the team they beat 4–1 at Portman Road, Ipswich Town – an equally attractive outfit if not more so. Swindon could only flirt with the play-offs, eventually finishing eighth. Hoddle's style and achievement were noted especially by Tottenham Hotspur supporters, however, and at the end of the season his name was being linked with the club when they dismissed the coach, Peter Shreeves. It was believed, though, that Hoddle was not keen to work in the shadow of the managing director, Terry Venables.

Whereas optimism turned to realism for Barnet and Swindon, realism became optimism for Sheffield United and Wembley. Such are the swinging fortunes of football in the space of nine months. SHEFFIELD UNITED recovered astonishingly from their poor start to finish ninth in the first division. Dave Bassett then signed a three-year extension to his contract at the end of the season, by which point he had allowed Brian Marwood to go on a free transfer. During it, Tony Agana was sold to Notts County for £750,000.

By the beginning of our season, Bassett had sold Vinnie Jones to Chelsea for £575,000. The two sides were drawn together in the fifth round of the FA Cup, a match which Chelsea won 1–0. Jones was booked after five seconds. It should be pointed out that, in the description of United's session with the expert in team dynamics, Simon Meyerson, all expletives were deleted. Readers would still be ploughing through it had they been left in.

WEMBLEY, too, turned around remarkably after Christmas and, of their last thirteen league games, they won nine and drew four, finishing fifth and missing promotion by only 2 points. They enjoyed a good run in the FA Trophy, too, beating Stevenage, Harlow and Chalfont St Peter, before losing 2–4 to Woking, who were to be promoted to the GM Vauxhall Conference, in the first round proper. Wembley also reached the final of the Middlesex Senior Cup, in which they were unfortunate to lose 1–2 to Yeading at Hendon.

Sadly, in early June, Wembley's main stand burned down, leaving them to face a summer of trying to get the ground ready for the new season. They even doubted whether they would be able to stay in the Diadora League.

•

The country-club debate rumbled on. The defeat by Germany proved to be ENGLAND's only one of the season, before they went to the European Championship finals in Sweden in June. They beat France 2–0 at Wembley in February; they drew 2–2 with Czechoslovakia in Prague in March, and by the same score with the Commonwealth of Independent States in Moscow in April; then, in May, they beat

Hungary 1–0 in Budapest and drew 1–1 with Brazil at Wembley.

The defeat of France, who came to London unbeaten in nineteen games over almost three years, was especially impressive. It featured excellent debuts at right-back by Rob Jones – though a shin injury diagnosed after the FA Cup final prevented him from going to the European Championships – and up front by Southampton's Alan Shearer, who scored the first goal, against the run of play it should be said. The second was scored by Gary Lineker, who had come on as a substitute at half-time. He had been upset by his omission, and the captain's relationship with Graham Taylor became even more difficult when the manager criticised his attitude after the match against Brazil. Lineker had missed an early penalty, which would have equalled Bobby Charlton's record of 49 goals for England, and took little further part in the game.

It was an example of another teething problem in the transition from the Bobby Robson era to that of Taylor. Between that and the jumping of Bryan Robson before he was pushed had come the Chris Waddle issue; Waddle was not chosen again after the Turkey match. Yet, apart from personality clashes, more significant in the longer term for England was the way in which the Brazilians highlighted a gap in technical ability between the two countries, their control and passing being considerably sharper.

By this time, England had puzzlingly reverted to playing a 4–4–2 formation, which Taylor said was more suited to the English way. He had used against France the 5–3–2 which he had said he intended to employ when he took over from Robson in 1990 and which had taken England to the semi-finals of the World Cup. However, the last warm-up match before the European Championships, which England won 2–1 against Finland in Helsinki in early June, saw the old 5–3–2 wheeled out once again.

The treatment of Lineker and the unsettled formation and personnel – in his first twenty matches, Taylor called up seventy-three players to England squads – led to criticism of confusion. Taylor insisted, however, that he was clear in his own mind.

The gulf in technique which was revealed by Brazil was emphasised on the club front four days later, when Wembley hosted an enjoyable European Cup final between Barcelona and Sampdoria. The game was won 1–0 by the Spanish team with a fiercely driven free-kick by the Dutchman, Ronald Koeman, in the depths of extra-time, and both teams looked considerably fresher than any of their English counterparts might have done in May. English club football was the length of a pitch behind, it was said, due to too much of the power-game. While there was undoubtedly some truth in that, it ignored several other factors, not least that Manchester United had beaten Barcelona in the Cup-Winners' Cup final a year earlier.

The watching Leeds manager, Howard Wilkinson, made the point that, while the finalists' technique may have been good in two-thirds of the pitch, it was lacking compared to English strikers in attack. And an Italian journalist in the press box remarked that no wonder Italian football was so desperate to get Paul Gascoigne. It all added up to the age-old conclusion: that while English football may lack a little in polish – on which it could improve and was doing so – it still got results, even if it had been a poor season in Europe. As Brian Glanville once wrote, pen in cheek: 'Football, like live theatre and the English novel, is permanently in decline.'

Bobby Moore suffered a heart scare but proved yet again that he has plenty of it. England's Rugby Union team lost to Australia in the World Cup final.

The season ended with the sense that Manchester United, Liverpool and Arsenal were reclining in the short term rather than declining in the long term. There were silver linings to MANCHESTER UNITED's cloudy season of European disappointment and domestic despair, in which Alex Ferguson's words of 'we are the danger' proved prophetic. With hindsight, their mistake was in not buying a striker – such as Lineker – who would have converted their all-round talent into goals. The League Cup, in which they beat Nottingham Forest 1–0 in the final, and the FA Youth Cup, in which Ryan Giggs inspired them to victory over Crystal Palace, were two such compensations. Giggs's season suffered its nadir when he missed a penalty in the ludicrous shoot-out against Southampton in a fourth-round FA Cup replay.

LIVERPOOL were beaten – 2–0 away, 2–1 at home – by Genoa in the next round of the UEFA Cup, which was eventually won by Ajax of Amsterdam. Fortified by Michael Thomas from Arsenal, they ended the season on a stronger note than had looked possible by winning the FA Cup. Their League position of sixth, however, one ahead of Aston Villa, was their worst for twenty-seven years.

A few days after the FA Cup final, it was revealed that Graeme Souness had come close to resigning after being censured by the Liverpool board of directors for agreeing to give the story of his heart surgery, in return for a donation to charity, exclusively to the *Sun* newspaper; the paper was reviled on Merseyside for its coverage of the Hillsborough Disaster and was seeking to restore its image and sales in the city. The directors had decided that it was insensitive of Souness to do so at the time of the third anniversary of Hillsborough.

When he heard of Souness's heart trouble, Barry Fry commented: 'He should try managing Barnet.'

ARSENAL, too, finished the season strongly after a winter of discontent which saw them lose to Coventry in the League Cup before the defeats by Benfica, then Wrexham of the fourth division in the FA Cup third round. They eventually finished fourth in the first division, a position which had seemed well beyond them.

In May, the club knocked down their North Bank terracing in order to replace it with seating in line with the Taylor Report, a fate which also befell Manchester United's Stretford End. The funding of the new North Bank, by a bond scheme in which supporters were asked to pay £1500 for the right to purchase a seat in the edifice, had caused controversy all season.

The Benfica manager, Sven-Goran Eriksson, left for Sampdoria to be replaced by Bobby Robson, who had coached PSV Eindhoven to their second successive Dutch Championship. At least Europe saw something in the English that they wanted.

●

TELEVISION'S importance to modern English football was never more graphically illustrated than in 1992. Within a week of the end of the season, club chairmen from the embryonic Premier League met to discuss a deal. A joint proposal from the BBC and BSkyB was approved; it would bring in £304 million over five years, making the previous ITV deal of £44 million over four – which at the time had seemed huge – look paltry.

ITV, who had bid £262 million, immediately cried foul. They pointed to the Tottenham chairman, Alan Sugar, alerting BSkyB to the size of their bid moments before the meeting started. Sugar, who admitted making the call but claimed that BSkyB already knew of the ITV bid, stood to benefit personally, since his Amstrad company were the market leaders in the sales of satellite dishes. He declared his interest to the meeting but was still allowed to vote.

ITV would be left with just the Football League and the

League Cup – BBC and BSkyB having renegotiated their contract for the FA Cup and England games – for which they had agreed to pay around £25 million over four years. They even took out an injunction in the High Court, seeking to get another auction at which they would increase their bid. The injunction failed, but it emerged in court that it had been the Premier League's chief executive, Rick Parry, who had told BSkyB the amount of the ITV bid. 'I thought it might get us more money,' said Parry, of what Brian Glanville described as the Greed-Is-Good League. Parry was right: BSkyB's original tender had been £280 million.

Not unusually, football was torn. The Premier League had voted 14–6 for the BBC/BSkyB bid on Parry's recommendation because they would be getting highlights on the terrestrial channel and live matches and magazine programmes on the satellite. But there was immediate criticism: few people would get the service, and those who did invest in a dish would be required within two years to pay-per-view – insert a card in their decoder which registered their choice of a game and charged their account accordingly. This would, of course, mean more revenue for the Premier League, which felt that the armchair fan had had it too good for too long and would now have to pay.

Three leading managers – Howard Wilkinson, Alex Ferguson and George Graham – condemned the deal in that it would mean live football on a Monday night, and so increase the strain on certain clubs. There would be sixty live games a season. Over-exposure to a smaller audience would be the result. However, the chief executive of the FA, Graham Kelly, claimed that it would enhance the Premier League: clubs would no longer need the revenue from as many games and would be able to vote for an eighteen-club league, as envisaged in the Blueprint for the Future of Football. The club chairmen were not immediately sympathetic to that argument.

Among the most distasteful elements of the whole affair was Parry's statement to the meeting of chairmen which suggested that the backing of the five national newspapers owned by Rupert Murdoch, who also owned Sky TV, would be forthcoming. The newspapers naturally announced their editorial independence. It was a tangled web, characterised by greed and bad management. Football undoubtedly had a valuable 'product' to offer, television a valuable service to provide; but both had gone about securing a deal to their mutual benefit with – not for the first time – no input from and little real interest in the consumer, be he either attending spectator or TV viewer. Not for the first time either, football had failed to observe the rules of business in its dealings.

OXFORD UNITED became part of Robert Maxwell's estate, and his 89.5 per cent stake in them was sold by the administrators to, a little curiously, a company called Biomass Recycling Ltd. Pat McGeough became the chairman. Remarkably, the club escaped relegation by 2 points and one place, thanks to a 2–1 win at Tranmere on the final day of the season.

It was at the expense of PLYMOUTH ARGYLE, who sacked David Kemp in February and replaced him, for his first managerial appointment, with the former England goal-keeper, Peter Shilton. He could not, however, bring them the impetus they needed, and they finished third from bottom. Said superfan Ian Self of Camborne: 'Don't tell the others, but I wasn't too disappointed we were relegated. It gives us a chance to do fourteen new grounds.'

CAMBRIDGE UNITED made the play-offs but were thrashed 1–6 on aggregate by Leicester City. They, in turn, were beaten 1–0 in the final at Wembley by BLACKBURN ROVERS, who looked champions for three-quarters of the season – Kenny Dalglish taking his total on signings to £5.5 million with the purchase of Chris Price from Aston Villa,

Duncan Shearer from Swindon, and Roy Wegerle from Queen's Park Rangers – before they lost six matches in a row as part of a thirteen-match sequence with only one win. They slipped into the play-offs, in which they first beat Derby County, who were only in sixth position thanks to a 3–1 win at Plymouth on the final day of the season. And was Juventus built here, wondered John Roberts in the *Independent* of Ewood Park.

KETTERING TOWN finished third in the GM Vauxhall Conference behind Colchester United, who were promoted back to the Football League, and Wycombe Wanderers. The week after the defeat at Blackburn, they won 3–2 at Bashley in the FA Trophy, and then 1–0 at VS Rugby, before losing to Marine in the third round.

They were taken over in March – by Mark English and Brian Talbot; English became a director, Talbot chairman. Peter Morris resigned as manager at the end of the season, after four years in charge; he felt unable to work in the new regime, according to a club insider. Talbot resigned as chairman a day later; he felt unable to work any longer with English, according to the club insider. English then became chairman.

Dave Cusack, who had left Boston United, became manager. Morris became manager of Boston United. English also bought Maidstone United and became managing director, but left after a week saying that he had discovered debts larger than he had been led to believe. For their part, Maidstone counterclaimed that his dealings with them were, at best, contorted.

NEWCASTLE UNITED avoided relegation by winning their last two games, in which their winning goals came five minutes and one minute from time respectively. As David Lacey wrote in the *Guardian*, though, Keegan's reign became more manic than messianic. In March, he was ready to resign because he could not buy a centre-half. He was then reassured by Sir John Hall, who put up the money himself to buy Brian Kilcline from Notts County. Hall's £13 million rescue package did not immediately materialise but, at the end of the season, Keegan eventually signed a three-year contract, along with Terry McDermott. By that time, Sir John had acquired 64 per cent of Newcastle's shares, despite saying that he wanted to quit the club.

Osvaldo Ardiles became, in May, manager of West Bromwich Albion, who sacked Bobby Gould, who returned to Coventry City as joint manager.

GLENTORAN enjoyed a hugely successful season, except in the Irish Cup, in which they lost to Glenavon 0–4 in a quarter-final replay. Otherwise, they won the League title and the Gold Cup, sponsored by TNT – the delivery company, not the explosive. Tommy Jackson was named manager-of-the-year in Northern Ireland.

DONCASTER BELLES completed a league and cup double when they won the Women's FA Cup by beating Red Star Southampton 4–0 at Prenton Park, home of Tranmere Rovers. Karen Walker scored a hat-trick, finishing with 58 goals for the season, 22 of them in the cup. Wimbledon finished third in the league.

As well as being awarded the FA Cup final, PHILIP DON was chosen to represent Great Britain's referees at the Olympic Games football tournament in Barcelona. It was announced that, for the first season of the Premier League, referees would wear coloured clothing. Other than black and white, that was. Jimmy Parker ended the season having issued seventy-three yellow cards and ten red.

●

NOTTINGHAM FOREST won the Central League Championship with more than a month of the season left. In their final match, they beat Liverpool 4–1. The first team's only trophy of the season was the Zenith Data Systems Cup, which they won by beating Southampton 3–2 at Wembley. Archie Gemmill's son, Scot, scored 2 of the goals. Stuart Cash, Stuart Pearce's deputy, was given a free transfer.

HACKNEY VOLUNTEERS SOCIAL CLUB were beaten 1–3 in the final of the Hackney and Leyton Sunday League's Jack Morgan Cup by Lithuania Victoria 'A'. Crown and Manor, although only finishing seventh in the Premier League, won the league's sportsmanship award for the second year in succession. After hearing of a planned boycott of the Marsh, the London Borough of Hackney reduced the price of a pitch to £25 for the 1992–93 season. Fines in the league, reported Peter Balding, just topped the £2000 mark.

OLD BROMLEIANS were caught on a bad day but otherwise had an excellent season, winning sixteen and drawing four of their twenty-three matches. Ronnie Burnett was persuaded by the younger members of the squad to accompany them on the end-of-season tour of the bright lights of Holland. Les Nelson was forced to make his excuses.

There were no teams who won all five matches at the ENGLISH SCHOOLS FESTIVAL, but Middlesex, Warwickshire, the Isle of Man and Merseyside were unbeaten. Essex 'A' won two, drew two and lost one. Merseyside went on to win the County final, beating Cornwall 2–0. Under Peter Amos, England Under-18s enjoyed an undefeated season, beating Holland, Wales and the Republic of Ireland all by 2–1, then drawing 2–2 in Switzerland after being 0–2 down.

WEYMOUTH spent the early summer seeking to sign all the promising young players they had had on loan. They announced their first friendly, against Portsmouth, for 25 July. It confirmed what Paddy Barclay said of the game: 'Most sports matter for two or three weeks a year. Football only doesn't matter for two or three weeks a year.'

FULHAM finished on the fringe of the play-offs, ninth in the third division. As a public enquiry began on whether Cabra Estates should be allowed to knock down the listed buildings at the ground, the club decided to stay at Craven Cottage for one more season – but Chelsea had other ideas. Come next season or not at all, the Chelsea chairman, Ken Bates, told his counterpart, Jimmy Hill.

STOKE CITY missed automatic promotion but made the play-offs, in which they lost to Stockport County, who were in turn beaten by Peterborough United in the final. Stoke extracted some revenge by winning the Autoglass Trophy at Wembley, beating Stockport 1–0 with a Mark Stein goal.

England were awarded the 1996 European Championships but, strangely, HILLSBOROUGH was not among the venues which the FA announced they were planning to use – even though they had hinted during the arrangements for the Cup semi-final that it might be. The new Conservative Government, elected in April, relaxed the recommendations of Taylor that lower-division stadia should be all-seater.

Dave Stringer announced his resignation as manager of NORWICH CITY, accepting instead an administrative post with the club and a seat on the board. He was succeeded by Mike Walker, a former Colchester United manager. ALDERSHOT TOWN appointed Steve Wignall, the old club's physiotherapist and coach, as manager as they prepared for non-League football. Ian McDonald joined Millwall as a coach.

LIVERPOOL poured salt on ITV's wounds by signing a deal for the BBC to screen their European Cup-Winners' Cup matches; but there was no small compensation for the independent camp in securing the rights to the European campaigns of Leeds and Manchester United.

That great hope for the future of the English game, Paul Gascoigne, who played no part in the season except for some indifferent footwork in a Newcastle night-club, which led to further surgery on his knee, finally proved his fitness to sign for Lazio of Rome for £5.5 million. 'It's like seeing your mother-in-law drive over a cliff in your new car,' lamented Terry Venables at his departure. 'It has been like waiting for a baby – a very big baby,' said a Lazio official.

For Gazza, it had truly been a season in the cold – though scarcely as enjoyable as ours.